The shape of Larry Niven's worlds is unique. As a writer, he is one of the few who is said to follow in Arthur C. Clarke's footsteps. But this is not quite accurate. For although both men are indubitably hardcore s.f., Clarke extrapolates brilliantly and realistically from what is known, while Niven postulates a hypothesis—creating a whole new world or set of worlds, and then extrapolates brilliantly the reality that would fill the hypothesis. Or at least he writes well enough to give that illusion. Perhaps it can be honestly said that both writers create an imaginary something, and then proceed to make it possible. And in either case, the world of science fiction is enriched.

This collection contains stories about creatures now familiar to s.f. cognoscenti—like puppeteers and kzinti and a human belter—but beyond that there is evidence of new aspects of Niven, namely as a straight short story writer, a mystery writer, and an occult writer. There's no telling where he'll come out next, and in the meantime, you can't go wrong with this gem of a volume.

Other titles by Larry Niven

WORLD OF PTAVVS
NEUTRON STAR
A GIFT FROM EARTH

Also available from Ballantine Books.

This is an original publication—not a reprint.

THE SHAPE OF SPACE
LARRY NIVEN

BALLANTINE BOOKS • NEW YORK

To Fred Pohl
Who gave me my start,
and a lot of free advice.

Contents

The Warriors

——— ◄◆► ———

"I'm sure they saw us coming," the Alien Technologies Officer persisted. "Do you see that ring, sir?"

The silvery image of the enemy ship almost filled the viewer. It showed as a broad, wide ring encircling a cylindrical axis, like a mechanical pencil floating inside a platinum bracelet. A finned craft projected from the pointed end of the axial section. Angular letters ran down the axis, totally unlike the dots-and-commas of kzinti script.

"Of course I see it," said the Captain.

"It was rotating when we first picked them up. It stopped when we got within two hundred thousand miles, and it hasn't moved since."

The Captain flicked his tail back and forth, gently, thoughtfully, like a pink lash. "You worry me," he commented. "If they know we're here, why haven't they tried to get away? Are they so sure they can beat us?" He whirled to face the A-T Officer. "Should *we* be running?"

"No, sir! I don't know why they're still here, but they can't have anything to be confident about. That's one of the most primitive spacecraft I've ever seen." He moved his claw about on the screen, pointing as he talked.

"The outer shell is an iron alloy. The rotating ring is a method of imitating gravity by using centripetal force. So

1

they don't have the gravity planer. In fact they're probably using a reaction drive."

The Captain's catlike ears went up. "But we're light-years from the nearest star!"

"They must have a better reaction drive than we ever developed. We had the gravity planer before we needed one that good."

There was a buzzing sound from the big control board. "Enter," said the Captain.

The Weapons Officer fell up through the entrance hatch and came to attention. "Sir, we have all weapons trained on the enemy."

"Good." The Captain swung around. "A-T, how sure are you that they aren't a threat to us?"

The A-T Officer bared sharply pointed teeth. "I don't see how they could be, sir."

"Good. Weapons, keep all your guns ready to fire, but don't use them unless I give the order. I'll have the ears of the man who destroys that ship without orders. I want to take it intact."

"Yes, sir."

"Where's the Telepath?"

"He's on his way, sir. He was asleep."

"He's always asleep. Tell him to get his tail up here."

The Weapons Officer saluted, turned, and dropped through the exit hole.

"Captain?"

The A-T Officer was standing by the viewer, which now showed the ringed end of the alien ship. He pointed to the mirror-bright end of the axial cylinder. "It looks like that end was designed to project light. That would make it a photon drive, sir."

The Captain considered. "Could it be a signal device?"

"Urrrrr . . . Yes, sir."

"Then don't jump to conclusions."

Like a piece of toast, the Telepath popped up through the entrance hatch. He came to exaggerated attention. "Reporting as ordered, sir."

"You omitted to buzz for entrance."

"Sorry, sir." The lighted viewscreen caught the Telepath's eye and he padded over for a better look, forgetting that he was at attention. The A-T Officer winced, wishing he were somewhere else.

The Telepath's eyes were violet around the edges. His pink tail hung limp. As usual, he looked as if he were dying for lack of sleep. His fur was flattened along the side he slept on; he hadn't even bothered to brush it. The effect was as far from the ideal of a Conquest Warrior as one can get and still be a member of the kzinti species. The wonder was that the Captain had not yet murdered him.

He never would, of course. Telepaths were too rare, too valuable, and—understandably—too emotionally unstable. The Captain always kept his temper with the Telepath. At times like this it was the innocent bystander who stood to lose his rank or his ears at the clank of a falling molecule.

"That's an enemy ship we've tracked down," the Captain was saying. "We'd like to get some information from them. Would you read their minds for us?"

"Yes, sir." The Telepath's voice showed his instant misery, but he knew better than to protest. He left the screen and sank into a chair. Slowly his ears folded into tight knots, his pupils contracted, and his ratlike tail went limp as flannel.

The world of the eleventh sense pushed in on him.

He caught the Captain's thought: ". . . sloppy civilian get of a sthondat . . ." and frantically tuned it out. He hated the Captain's mind. He found other minds aboard ship, isolated and blanked them out one by one. Now there were none left. There was only unconsciousness and chaos.

Chaos was not empty. Something was thinking strange and disturbing thoughts.

The Telepath forced himself to listen.

Steve Weaver floated bonelessly near a wall of the radio room. He was blond, blue-eyed, and big, and he could often be seen as he was now, relaxed but completely motionless, as if there were some very good reason why he shouldn't even blink. A streamer of smoke drifted from his left hand and crossed the room to bury itself in the air vent.

"That's that," Ann Harrison said wearily. She flicked four switches in the bank of radio controls. At each click a small light went out.

"You can't get them?"

"Right. I'll bet they don't even have a radio." Ann released her chair net and stretched out into a five-pointed star. "I've left the receiver on, with the volume up, in case they try to get us later. Man, that feels good!" Abruptly she curled into a tight ball. She had been crouched at the communications bank for more than an hour. Ann might have been Steve's twin; she was almost as tall as he was, had the same color hair and eyes, and the flat muscles of conscientious exercise showed beneath her blue falling jumper as she flexed.

Steve snapped his cigarette butt at the air conditioner, moving only his fingers. "Okay. What have they got?"

Ann looked startled. "*I* don't know."

"Think of it as a puzzle. They don't have radio. How might they talk to each other? How can we check on our guesses? We assume they're trying to reach us, of course."

"Yes, of course."

"Think about it, Ann. Get Jim thinking about it, too." Jim Davis was her husband that year, and the ship's doctor full time. "You're the girl most likely to succeed. Have a smog stick?"

"Please."

Steve pushed his cigarette ration across the room. "Take a few. I've got to go."

The depleted package came whizzing back. "Thanx," said Ann.

"Let me know if anything happens, will you? Or if you think of anything."

"I will. And fear not, Steve, something's bound to turn up. They must be trying just as hard as we are."

Every compartment in the personnel ring opened into the narrow doughnut-shaped hall which ran round the ring's forward rim. Steve pushed himself into the hall, jockeyed to contact the floor, and pushed. From there it was easy going.

The floor curved up to meet him, and he proceeded down the hall like a swimming frog. Of the twelve men and women on the *Angel's Pencil*, Steve was best at this; for Steve was a Belter, and the others were all flatlanders, Earthborn.

Ann probably wouldn't think of anything, he guessed. It wasn't that she wasn't intelligent. She didn't have the curiosity, the sheer love of solving puzzles. Only he and Jim Davis—

He was going too fast, and not concentrating. He almost crashed into Sue Bhang as she appeared below the curve of the ceiling.

They managed to stop themselves against the walls. "Hi, jaywalker," said Sue.

"Hi, Sue. Where you headed?"

"Radio room. You?"

"I thought I'd check the drive systems again. Not that we're likely to need the drive, but it can't hurt to be certain."

"You'd go twitchy without something to do, wouldn't you?" She cocked her head to one side, as always when she had questions. "Steve, when are you going to rotate us again? I can't seem to get used to falling."

But she looked like she'd been born falling, he thought. Her small, slender form was meant for flying; gravity should never have touched her. "When I'm sure we won't need the drive. We might as well stay ready 'til then. Besides, I'm hoping you'll change back to a skirt."

She laughed, pleased. "Then you can turn it off. I'm not changing, and we won't be moving. Abel says the other ship did two hundred gee when it matched courses with us. How many can the *Angel's Pencil* do?"

Steve looked awed. "Just point zero five. And I was thinking of chasing them! Well, maybe we can be the ones to open communications. I just came from the radio room, by the way. Ann can't get anything."

"Too bad."

"We'll just have to wait."

"Steve, you're always so impatient. Do Belters always move at a run? Come here." She took a handhold and pulled him over to one of the thick windows which lined the forward side of the corridor. "There they are," she said, pointing out.

The star was both duller and larger than those around it. Among points which glowed arc-lamp blue-white with the Doppler shift, the alien ship showed as a dull red disk.

"I looked at it through the telescope," said Steve. "There are lumps and ridges all over it. And there's a circle of green dots and commas painted on one side. Looked like writing."

"How long have we been waiting to meet them? Five hundred thousand years? Well, there they are. Relax. They won't go away." Sue gazed out the window, her whole attention on the dull red circle, her gleaming jet hair floating out around her head. "The first aliens. I wonder what they'll be like."

"It's anyone's guess. They must be pretty strong to take punishment like that, unless they have some kind of acceleration shield, but free fall doesn't bother them either. That ship isn't designed to spin." He was staring intently out at the stars, his big form characteristically motionless, his expression somber. Abruptly he said, "Sue, I'm worried."

"About what?"

"Suppose they're hostile?"

"Hostile?" She tasted the unfamiliar word, decided she didn't like it.

"After all, we know nothing about them. Suppose they want to fight? We'd—"

She gasped. Steve flinched before the horror in her face. "What—what put that idea in your head?"

"I'm sorry I shocked you, Sue."

"Oh, don't worry about that, but *why?* Did—shh."

Jim Davis had come into view. The *Angel's Pencil* had left Earth when he was twenty-seven; now he was a slightly paunchy thirty-eight, the oldest man on board, an amiable man with abnormally long, delicate fingers. His grandfather, with the same hands, had been a world-famous surgeon. Nowadays surgery was normally done by autodocs, and the arachnodactils were to Davis merely an affliction. He bounced by, walking on magnetic sandals, looking like a comedian as he bobbed about the magnetic plates. "Hi, group," he called as he went by.

"Hello, Jim." Sue's voice was strained. She waited until he was out of sight before she spoke again.

Hoarsely she whispered, "Did you fight in the Belt?" She didn't really believe it; it was merely the worst thing she could think of.

Vehemently Steve snapped, "No!" Then, reluctantly, he added, "But it did happen occasionally." Quickly he tried to explain. "The trouble was that all the doctors, including the psychists, were at the big bases, like Ceres. It was the only way they could help the people who needed them—be where the miners could find them. But all the danger was out in the rocks.

"You noticed a habit of mine once. I never make gestures. All Belters have that trait. It's because on a small mining ship you could hit something waving your arms around. Something like the airlock button."

"Sometimes it's almost eerie. You don't move for minutes at a time."

"There's always tension out in the rocks. Sometimes a miner would see too much danger and boredom and frustration, too much cramping inside and too much room outside, and he wouldn't get to a psychist in time. He'd pick a fight in a bar. I saw it happen once. The guy was using his hands like mallets."

Steve had been looking far into the past. Now he turned back to Sue. She looked white and sick, like a novice nurse standing up to her first really bad case. His ears began to turn red. "Sorry," he said miserably.

She felt like running; she was as embarrassed as he was. Instead she said, and tried to mean it. "It doesn't matter. So you think the people in the other ship might want to, uh, make war?"

He nodded.

"Did you have history-of-Earth courses?"

He smiled ruefully. "No, I couldn't qualify. Sometimes I wonder how many people do."

"About one in twelve."

"That's not many."

"People in general have trouble assimilating the facts of life about their ancestors. You probably know that there used to be wars before—hmmm—three hundred years ago, but do you know what a war is? Can you visualize one? Can you see a fusion electric plant deliberately built to explode in the middle of a city? Do you know what a concentration camp is? A limited action? You probably think murder ended with war. Well, it didn't. The last murder occurred in twenty-one something, just a hundred and sixty years ago.

"Anyone who says human nature can't be changed is out of his head. To make it stick, he's got to define human nature—and he can't. Three things gave us our present peaceful civilization, and each one was a technological change." Sue's voice had taken on a dry, remote lecture-hall tone, like the voice on a teacher tape. "One was the development of psychistry beyond the alchemist stage. Another was the full development of land for food production. The third was the Fertility Restriction Laws and the annual contraceptive shots. They gave us room to breathe. Maybe Belt mining and the stellar colonies had something to do with it too; they gave us an inanimate enemy. Even the historians argue about that one.

"Here's the delicate point I'm trying to nail down." She rapped on the window. "Look at that spacecraft. It has enough power to move it around like a mail missile and enough fuel to move it up to our point eight light—right?"

"Right."

"—with plenty of power left for maneuvering. It's a better ship than ours. If they've had time to learn how to build a ship like that, they've had time to build up their own versions of psychistry, modern food production, contraception, economic theory, everything they need to abolish war. See?"

Steve had to smile at her earnestness. "Sure, Sue, it makes sense. But that guy in the bar came from our culture, and he was hostile enough. If we can't understand how he thinks, how can we guess about the mind of something whose very chemical makeup we can't guess at yet?"

"It's sentient. It builds tools."

"Right."

"And if Jim hears you talking like this, you'll be in psychistry treatment."

"That's the best argument you've given me," Steve grinned, and stroked her under the ear with two fingertips. He felt her go suddenly stiff, saw the pain in her face; and at the same time his own pain struck, a real tiger of a headache, as if his brain were trying to swell beyond his skull.

"I've got them, sir," the Telepath said blurrily. "Ask me anything."

The Captain hurried, knowing that the Telepath couldn't stand this for long. "How do they power their ship?"

"It's a light pressure drive powered by incomplete hydrogen fusion. They use an electromagnetic ramscoop to get their own hydrogen from space."

"Clever . . . Can they get away from us?"

"No. Their drive is on idle, ready to go, but it won't help them. It's pitifully weak."

"What kind of weapons do they have?"

The Telepath remained silent for a long time. The others waited patiently for his answer. There was sound in the control dome, but it was the kind of sound one learns not to hear: the whine of heavy current, the muted purr of voices from below, the strange sound like continuously ripping cloth which came from the gravity motors.

"None at all, sir." The kzinti's voice became clearer; his hypnotic relaxation was broken by muscle twitches. He twisted as if in a nightmare. "Nothing aboard ship, not even a knife or a club. Wait, they've got cooking knives. But that's all they use them for. They don't fight."

"They don't fight?"

"No, sir. They don't expect us to fight, either. The idea has occurred to three of them, and each has dismissed it from his mind."

"But why?" the Captain asked, knowing the question was irrelevant, unable to hold it back.

"I don't know, sir. It's a science they use, or a religion. I

don't understand," the Telepath whimpered. "I don't understand at all."

Which must be tough on him, the Captain thought. Completely alien thoughts ... "What are they doing now?"

"Waiting for us to talk to them. They tried to talk to us,
and they think we must be trying just as hard."

"But why?—never mind, it's not important. Can they be
killed by heat?"

"Yes, sir."

"Break contact."

The Telepath shook his head violently. He looked like he'd
been in a washing machine. The Captain touched a sensitized
surface and bellowed, "Weapons Officer!"

"Here."

"Use the inductors on the enemy ship."

"But, sir! They're so slow! What if the alien attacks?"

"Don't argue with me, you—" Snarling, the Captain delivered an impassioned monologue on the virtues of unquestion-
ing obedience. When he switched off, the Alien Technologies
Officer was back at the viewer and the Telepath had gone to
sleep.

The Captain purred happily, wishing that they were all this
easy.

When the occupants had been killed by heat he would take
the ship. He could tell everything he needed to know about
their planet by examining their life-support system. He could
locate it by tracing the ship's trajectory. Probably they hadn't
even taken evasive action!

If they came from a Kzin-like world it would become a
Kzin world. And he, as Conquest Leader, would command 1
percent of its wealth for the rest of his life! Truly, the future
looked rich. No longer would he be called by his profession.
He would bear a *name* ...

"Incidental information," said the A-T Officer. "The ship
was generating one and twelve sixty-fourths gee before it
stopped rotating."

"Little heavy," the Captain mused. "Might be too much
air, but it should be easy to kzinform it. A-T, we find the
strangest life forms. Remember the Chunquen?"

"Both sexes were sentient. They fought constantly."

"And that funny religion on Altair One. They thought they could travel in time."

"Yes sir. When we landed the infantry they were all gone."

"They must have all committed suicide with disintegrators. But why? They knew we only wanted slaves. And I'm still trying to figure out how they got rid of the disintegrators afterward."

"Some beings," said the A-T Officer, "will do anything to keep their beliefs."

Eleven years beyond Pluto, eight years from her destination, the fourth colony ship to We Made It fell between the stars. Before her the stars were green-white and blue-white, blazing points against nascent black. Behind they were sparse, dying red embers. To the sides the constellations were strangely flattened. The universe was shorter than it had been.

For awhile Jim Davis was very busy. Everyone, including himself, had a throbbing blinding headache. To each patient Dr. Davis handed a tiny pink pill from the dispenser slot of the huge autodoc which covered the back wall of the infirmary. They milled outside the door waiting for the pills to take effect, looking like a full-fledged mob in the narrow corridor; and then someone thought it would be a good idea to go to the lounge, and everyone followed him. It was an unusually silent mob. Nobody felt like talking while the pain was with them. Even the sound of magnetic sandals was lost in the plastic pile rug.

Steve saw Jim Davis behind him. "Hey, Doc," he called softly. "How long before the pain stops?"

"Mine's going away. You got your pills a little after I did, right?"

"Right. Thanks, Doc."

They didn't take pain well, these people. They were too unused to it.

In single file they walked or floated into the lounge. Low-pitched conversations started. People took couches, using the sticky plastic strips on their falling jumpers. Others stood or floated near walls. The lounge was big enough to hold them all in comfort.

Steve wriggled near the ceiling, trying to pull on his sandals.

"I hope they don't try that again," he heard Sue say. "It hurt."

"Try what?" Someone Steve didn't recognize, half-listening as he was.

"Whatever they tried. Telepathy, perhaps."

"No. I don't believe in telepathy. Could they have set up ultrasonic vibrations in the walls?"

Steve had his sandals on. He left the magnets turned off.

". . . a cold beer. Do you realize we'll never taste beer again?" Jim Davis' voice.

"I miss waterskiing." Ann Harrison sounded wistful. "The feel of a pusher unit shoving into the small of your back, the water beating against your feet, the sun . . ."

Steve pushed himself toward them. "Taboo subject," he called.

"We're on it anyway," Jim boomed cheerfully. "Unless you'd rather talk about the alien, which everyone else is doing. I'd rather drop it for the moment. What's your greatest regret at leaving Earth?"

"Only that I didn't stay long enough to really see it."

"Oh, of course." Jim suddenly remembered the drinking bulb in his hand. He drank from it, hospitably passed it to Steve.

"This waiting makes me restless," said Steve. "What are they likely to try next? Shake the ship in Morse code?"

Jim smiled. "Maybe they won't try anything next. They may give up and leave."

"Oh, I hope not!" said Ann.

"Would that be so bad?"

Steve hid a start. What was Jim thinking?

"Of course!" Ann protested. "We've got to find out what they're like! And think of what they can teach us, Jim!"

When conversation got controversial it was good manners to change the subject. "Say," said Steve, "I happened to notice the wall was warm when I pushed off. Is that good or bad?"

"That's funny. It should be cold, if anything," said Jim. "There's nothing out there but starlight. Except—" A most peculiar expression flitted across his face. He drew his feet up and touched the magnetic soles with his fingertips.

"Eeeee! Jim! Jim!"

Steve tried to whirl around and got nowhere. That was Sue! He switched on his shoes, thumped to the floor, and went to help.

Sue was surrounded by bewildered people. They split to let Jim Davis through, and he tried to lead her out of the lounge. He looked frightened. Sue was moaning and thrashing, paying no attention to his efforts.

Steve pushed through to her. "All the metal is heating up," Davis shouted. "We've got to get her hearing aid out."

"Infirmary," Steve shouted.

Four of them took Sue down the hall to the infirmary. She was still crying and struggling feebly when they got her in, but Jim was there ahead of them with a spray hypo. He used it and she went to sleep.

The four watched anxiously as Jim went to work. The autodoc would have taken precious time for diagnosis. Jim operated by hand. He was able to do a fast job, for the tiny instrument was buried just below the skin behind her ear. Still, the scalpel must have burned his fingers before he was done. Steve could feel the growing warmth against the soles of his feet.

Did the aliens know what they were doing?

Did it matter? The ship was being attacked. His ship.

Steve slipped into the corridor and ran for the control room. Running on magnetic soles, he looked like a terrified penguin, but he moved fast. He knew he might be making a terrible mistake; the aliens might be trying desperately to reach the *Angel's Pencil;* he would never know. They had to be stopped before everyone was roasted.

The shoes burned his feet. He whimpered with the pain, but otherwise ignored it. The air burned in his mouth and throat. Even his teeth were hot.

He had to wrap his shirt around his hands to open the control-room door. The pain in his feet was unbearable; he tore off his sandals and swam to the control board. He kept his shirt over his hands to work the controls. A twist of a large white knob turned the drive on full, and he slipped into the pilot seat before the gentle light pressure could build up.

He turned to the rear-view telescope. It was aimed at the solar system, for the drive could be used for messages at this distance. He set it for short range and began to turn the ship.

The enemy ship glowed in the high infrared.

"It will take longer to heat the crew-carrying section," reported the Alien Technologies Officer. "They'll have temperature control there."

"That's all right. When you think they should all be dead, wake up the Telepath and have him check." The Captain continued to brush his fur, killing time. "You know, if they hadn't been so completely helpless I wouldn't have tried this slow method. I'd have cut the ring free of the motor section first. Maybe I should have done that anyway. Safer."

The A-T Officer wanted all the credit he could get. "Sir, they couldn't have any big weapons. There isn't room. With a reaction drive, the motor and the fuel tanks take up most of the available space."

The other ship began to turn away from its tormentor. Its drive end glowed red.

"They're trying to get away," the Captain said, as the glowing end swung toward them. "Are you sure they can't?"

"Yes sir. That light drive won't take them anywhere."

The Captain purred thoughtfully. "What would happen if the light hit our ship?"

"Just a bright light, I think. The lens is flat, so it must be emitting a very wide beam. They'd need a parabolic reflector to be dangerous. Unless—" His ears went straight up.

"Unless what?" The Captain spoke softly, demandingly.

"A laser. But that's all right, sir. They don't have any weapons."

The Captain sprang at the control board. "Stupid!" he

spat. "They don't know weapons from sthondat blood. Weapons Officer! How could a telepath find out what they don't know? WEAPONS OFFICER!"

"Here, sir."

"Burn—"

An awful light shone in the control dome. The Captain burst into flame, then blew out as the air left through a glowing split in the dome.

Steve was lying on his back. The ship was spinning again, pressing him into what felt like his own bunk.

He opened his eyes.

Jim Davis crossed the room and stood over him. "You awake?"

Steve sat bolt upright, his eyes wide.

"Easy." Jim's gray eyes were concerned.

Steve blinked up at him. "What happened?" he asked, and discovered how hoarse he was.

Jim sat down in one of the chairs. "You tell me. We tried to get to the control room when the ship started moving. Why didn't you ring the strap-down? You turned off the drive just as Ann came through the door. Then you fainted."

"How about the other ship?" Steve tried to repress the urgency in his voice, and couldn't.

"Some of the others are over there now, examining the wreckage." Steve felt his heart stop. "I guess I was afraid from the start that alien ship was dangerous. I'm more psychist than emdee, and I qualified for history class, so maybe I know more than is good for me about human nature. Too much to think that beings with space travel will automatically be peaceful. I tried to think so, but they aren't. They've got things any self-respecting human being would be ashamed to have nightmares about. Bomb missiles, fusion bombs, lasers, that induction projector they used on us. And antimissiles. You know what that means? They've got enemies like themselves, Steve. Maybe nearby."

"So I killed them." The room seemed to swoop around him, but his voice came out miraculously steady.

"You saved the ship."

"It was an accident. I was trying to get us away."

"No, you weren't." Davis' accusation was as casual as if he were describing the chemical makeup of urea. "That ship was four hundred miles away. You would have had to sight on it with a telescope to hit it. You knew what you were doing, too, because you turned off the drive as soon as you'd burned through the ship."

Steve's back muscles would no longer support him. He flopped back to horizontal. "All right, you know," he told the ceiling. "Do the others?"

"I doubt it. Killing in self-defense is too far outside their experience. I think Sue's guessed."

"Oooo."

"If she has, she's taking it well," Davis said briskly. "Better than most of them will, when they find out the universe is full of warriors. This is the end of the world, Steve."

"What?"

"I'm being theatrical. But it is. Three hundred years of the peaceful life for everyone. They'll call it the Golden Age. No starvation, no war, no physical sickness other than senescence, no permanent mental sickness at all, even by our rigid standards. When someone over fourteen tries to use his fist on someone else we say he's sick, and we cure him. And now it's over. Peace isn't a stable condition, not for us. Maybe not for anything that lives."

"Can I see the ship from here?"

"Yes. It's just behind us."

Steve rolled out of bed, went to the window.

Someone had steered the ships much closer together. The kzinti ship was a huge red sphere with ugly projections scattered at seeming random over the hull. The beam had sliced it into two unequal halves, sliced it like an ax through an egg. Steve watched, unable to turn aside, as the big half rotated to show its honeycombed interior.

"In a little while," said Jim, "the men will be coming back. They'll be frightened. Someone will probably insist that we arm ourselves against the next attack, using weapons from the other ship. I'll have to agree with him.

"Maybe they'll think I'm sick myself. Maybe I am. But it's the kind of sickness we'll need." Jim looked desperately unhappy. "We're going to become an armed society. And of course we'll have to warn the Earth . . ."

Safe at Any Speed

But how, you ask, *could a car have managed to fail me?*

Already I can see the terror in your eyes at the thought that your car, too, might fail. Here you are with an indefinite lifespan, a potentially immortal being, taking every possible precaution against the abrupt termination of your godhead; and all for nothing. The disruptor field in your kitchen dispose-all could suddenly expand to engulf you. Your transfer booth could make you disappear at the transmitter and forget to deliver you at the receiver. A slidewalk could accelerate to one hundred miles per hour, then slew sideways to throw you against a building. Every boosterspice plant in the Thousand Worlds could die overnight, leaving you to grow old and gray and wrinkled and arthritic. No, it's never happened in human history; but if a man can't trust his *car,* fa' Pete's sake, what *can* he trust?

Rest assured, reader, it wasn't that bad.

For one thing, it all happened on Margrave, a world in the first stages of colonization. I was twenty minutes out of Triangle Lake on my way to the Wiggly River logging region, flying at an altitude of a thousand feet. For several days the logging machines had been cutting trees which were too young, and a mechanic was needed to alter a few settings in the boss brain. I was cruising along on autopilot, playing double-deck complex solitaire in the back seat, with the camera going so that just in case I won one I'd have a film to back up my bragging.

Then a roc swooped down on me, wrapped ten huge talons around my car, and swallowed it.

Right away you'll see that it couldn't happen anywhere but Margrave. In the first place, I wouldn't have been using a car for a two-hour trip on any civilized world. I'd have taken a transfer booth. In the second place, where else can you find rocs?

Anyway, this big damn bird caught me and ate me, and everything went dark. The car flew blithely on, ignoring the roc, but the ride became turbulent as the roc tried to fly away and couldn't. I heard grinding sounds from outside. I tried my radio and got nothing. Either it couldn't reach through all that meat around me, or the trip through the bird's gullet had brushed away my antennas.

There didn't seem to be anything else I could do. I turned on the cabin lights and went on with the game. The grinding noises continued, and now I could see what was causing them. At some time the roc had swallowed several boulders, for the same reason a chicken swallows grit: to help digestion. The rocks were rubbing against the car under peristalsis, trying to break it down into smaller pieces for the murky digestive juices to work on.

I wondered how smart the boss brain was. When it saw a roc glide in for a landing at the logging camp, and when it realized that the bird was incapable of leaving no matter how it shrieked and flapped its wings, would the master computer draw the correct conclusion? Would it realize the bird had swallowed a car? I was afraid not. If the boss brain were that smart it would have been in business for itself.

I never found out. All of a sudden my seat cocoon wrapped itself around me like an overprotective mother, and there was a meaty three-hundred-mile-per-hour Smack!

The cocoon unwrapped itself. My cabin lights still showed red-lit fluid around me, but it was getting redder. The boulders had stopped rolling around. My cards were all over the cabin, like a snowstorm.

Obviously I'd forgotten one teensy little mountain when I programed the autopilot. The roc had been blocking the radar and sonar, with predictable results. A little experimenting showed that my drive had failed under the impact, my radio still wouldn't work, and my emergency flares refused to try to fire through a roc's belly.

There was no way to get out, not without opening my door to a flood of digestive juices. I could have done that if I'd had a vac suit, but how was I to know I'd need one on a two-hour car trip?

There was only one thing to do.

I collected my cards, shuffled, and started a new game.

It was half a year before the roc's corpus decomposed enough to let me out. In that time I won five games of double complex solitaire. I've only got films for four; the camera ran out. I'm happy to say that the emergency foodmaker worked beautifully if a little monotonously, the airmaker never failed, and the clock TV kept perfect time as a clock. As a TV it showed only technicolor ripples of static. The washroom went out along about August, but I got it fixed without much trouble. At 2:00 P.M. on October 24 I forced the door open, hacked my way through the mummified skin and flesh between a couple of roc ribs, and took a deep breath of real air. It smelled of roc. I'd left the cabin door open, and I could hear the airmaker whine crazily as it tried to absorb the smell.

I fired off a few flares, and fifteen minutes later a car dropped to take me home. They say I was the hairiest human being they'd ever seen. I've since asked Mr. Dickson, the president of General Transportation, why he didn't include a depil tube in the emergency stores.

"A castaway is supposed to look like a castaway," he tells me. "If you're wearing a year's growth of hair, your rescuer will know immediately that you've been lost for some time and will take the appropriate steps."

General Transportation has paid me a more than adequate sum in compensation for the fact that my car was unable to handle a roc. (I've heard that they're changing the guarantees for next year's model.) They've promised me an equal sum for writing this article. It seems there are strange and possibly damaging rumors going around concerning my delayed arrival at Wiggly River.

Rest assured, reader. I not only lived through the accident without harm, but came out of it with a substantial profit. Your car is perfectly safe, provided it was built later than 3100 A.D.

How the Heroes Die

Only sheer ruthlessness could have taken him out of town alive. The mob behind Carter hadn't tried to guard the Marsbuggies, since Carter would have needed too much time to take a buggy through the vehicular airlock. They could have caught him there, and they knew it. Some were guarding the personnel lock, hoping he'd try for that. He might have; for if he could have closed the one door in their faces and opened the next, the safeties would have protected him while he went through the third and fourth and outside. On the Marsbuggy he was trapped in the bubble.

There was room to drive around in. Less than half the prefab houses had been erected so far. The rest of the bubbletown's floor was flat fused sand, empty but for scattered piles of foam-plastic walls and ceilings and floors. But they'd get him eventually. Already they were starting up another buggy.

They never expected him to run his vehicle through the bubble wall.

The Marsbuggy tilted, then righted itself. A blast of breathing-air roared out around him, picked up a cloud of fine sand, and hurled it explosively away into the thin, poisoned atmosphere. Carter grinned as he looked behind him. They would die now, all of them. He was the only one wearing a pressure suit. In an hour he could come back and repair the rip in the bubble. He'd have to dream up a fancy story to tell when the next ship came ...

Carter frowned. What were they—

At least ten wind-harried men were wrestling with the wall of a prefab house. As Carter watched, they picked the wall up off the fused sand, balanced it almost upright, and let go. The foam-plastic wall rose into the wind and slapped hard against the bubble, over the ten-foot rip.

Carter stopped his buggy to see what would happen.

Nobody was dead. The air was not shrieking away but leaking away. Slowly, methodically, a line of men climbed into their suits and filed through the personnel lock to repair the bubble.

A buggy entered the vehicular lock. The third and last was starting to life. Carter turned his buggy and was off.

Top speed for a Marsbuggy is about twenty-five miles per hour. The buggy rides on three wide balloon-tired wheels, each mounted at the end of a five-foot arm. What those wheels can't go over, the buggy can generally hop over on the compressed-air jet mounted underneath. The motor and the compressor are both powered by a Litton battery holding a tenth as much energy as the original Hiroshima bomb.

Carter had been careful, as careful as he had had time for. He was carrying a full load of oxygen, twelve four-hour tanks in the air bin behind him, and an extra tank rested against his knees. His batteries were nearly full; he would be out of air long before his power ran low. When the other buggies gave up he could circle round and return to the bubble in the time his extra tank would give him.

His own buggy and the two behind him were the only such vehicles on Mars. At twenty-five miles per hour he fled, and at twenty-five miles per hour they followed. The closest was half a mile behind.

Carter turned on his radio.

He found the middle of a conversation. "—Can't afford it. One of you will come back. We could lose two of the buggies, but not all three."

That was Shute, the bubbletown's research director and sole military man. The next voice, deep and sarcastic, belonged to Rufus Doolittle, the biochemist. "What'll we do, flip a coin?"

"Let me go," the third voice said tightly. "I've got a stake in this."

Carter felt apprehension touch the nape of his neck.

"Okay, Alf. Good luck," said Rufus. "Good hunting," he added maliciously, as if he knew Carter were listening.

"You concentrate on getting the bubble fixed. I'll see that Carter doesn't come back."

Behind Carter, the rearmost buggy swung in a wide loop toward town. The other came on. And it was driven by the linguist, Alf Harness.

Most of the bubble's dozen men were busy repairing the ten-foot rip with heaters and plastic sheeting. It would be a long job but an easy one, for by Shute's orders the bubble had been deflated. The transparent plastic had fallen in folds across the prefab houses, forming a series of interconnected tents. One could move about underneath with little difficulty.

Lieutenant-Major Michael Shute watched the men at work and decided they had things under control. He walked away like a soldier on parade, stooping as little as possible as he moved beneath the dropping folds.

He stopped and watched Gondot operating the airmaker. Gondot noticed him and spoke without looking up.

"Mayor, why'd you let Carter chase Alf alone?"

Shute accepted his nickname. "We couldn't lose both tractors."

"Why not just post them on guard duty for two days?"

"And what if Carter got through the guard? He must be determined to wreck the dome. He'd catch us with our pants down. Even if some of us got into suits, could we stand another rip in the bubble?"

Gondot reached to scratch his short beard. His fingertips rapped helmet plastic and he looked annoyed. "Maybe not. I can fill the bubble anytime you're ready, but then the airmaker'll be empty. We'll be almost out of tanked air by the time they finish mending that rip. Another'd finish us."

Shute nodded and turned away. All the air anyone could use—tons of nitrogen and oxygen—was right outside; but it was in the form of nitrogen dioxide gas. The airmaker could convert it three times as fast as men could use it. But if Carter tore the dome again, that would be too slow.

But Carter wouldn't. Alf would see to that. The emergency was over—this time.

And so Lieutenant-Major Shute could go back to worrying about the emergency's underlying causes.

His report on those causes had been finished a month ago. He had reread it several times since, and always it had seemed complete and to the point. Yet he had the feeling it could be written better. He ought to make it as effective as possible. What he had to say could only be said once, and then his career would be over and his voice silenced.

Cousins had sold some fiction once, writing as a hobby. Perhaps he would help. But Shute was reluctant to involve anyone else in what amounted to his own rebellion.

Yet—he'd have to rewrite that report now, or at least add to it. Lew Harness was dead, murdered. John Carter would be dead within two days. All Shute's responsibility. All pertinent.

The decision wasn't urgent. It would be a month before Earth was in reach of the bubbletown's sending station.

Most of the asteroids spend most of their time between Mars and Jupiter, and it often happens that one of them crosses a planet where theretofore it had crossed only an orbit. There are asteroid craters all over Mars. Old eroded ones, sharp new ones, big ones, little ones, ragged and smooth ones. The bubbletown was at the center of a large, fairly recent crater four miles across: an enormous, poorly cast ashtray discarded on the reddish sand.

The buggies ran over cracked glass, avoiding the occasional tilted blocks, running uphill toward the broken rim. A sky the color of blood surrounded a tiny, brilliant sun set precisely at the zenith.

Inevitably Alf was getting closer. When they crossed the rim and started downhill they would pull apart. It was going to be a long chase.

Now was the time for regrets, if there ever was such a time. But Carter wasn't the type, and he had nothing to be ashamed of anyway. Lew Harness had needed to die; had as much as *asked* to die. Carter was only puzzled that his death should have provoked so violent a reaction. Could they *all* be—the way Lew had been? Unlikely. If he'd stayed and explained—

They'd have torn him apart. Those vulpine faces, with the distended nostrils and the bared teeth!

And now he was being chased by one man. But that man was Lew's brother.

Here was the rim, and Alf was still well behind. Carter slowed as he went over, knowing that the way down would be rougher. He was just going over the edge when a rock ten yards away exploded in white fire.

Alf had a flare pistol.

Carter just stopped himself from scrambling out of the buggy to hide in the rocks. The buggy lurched downward and, like it or not, Carter had to forget his terror to keep the vehicle upright.

The rubble around the crater's rim slowed him still further. Carter angled the buggy for the nearest rise of sloping sand. As he reached it, Alf came over the rim, a quarter mile behind. His silhouette hesitated there against the bloody sky, and another flare exploded, blinding bright and terrifyingly close.

Then Carter was on the straightaway, rolling down sloping sand to a perfectly flat horizon.

The radio said, "Gonna be a long one, Jack."

Carter pushed to transmit. "Right. How many flares do you have left?"

"Don't worry about it."

"I won't. Not the way you're throwing them away."

Alf didn't answer. Carter left the radio band open, knowing that ultimately Alf must talk to the man he needed to kill.

The crater which was home dropped behind and was gone. Endless flat desert rose before the buggies, flowed under the oversized wheels and dropped behind. Gentle crescent dunes patterned the sand, but they were no barrier to a buggy. Once there was a martian well. It stood all alone on the sand, a weathered cylindrical wall seven feet high and ten in circumference, made of cut diamond blocks. The wells, and the slanting script written deep into their "dedication blocks," were responsible for the town's presence on Mars. Since the only martian ever found—a mummy centuries dead, at least— had exploded at the first contact with water, it was generally assumed that the wells were crematoriums. But it wasn't certain. Nothing was certain about Mars.

The radio maintained an eerie silence. Hours rolled past; the sun slid toward the deep red horizon, and still Alf did not speak. It was as if Alf had said everything there was to say to Jack Carter. And that was wrong! Alf should have needed to justify himself!

It was Carter who sighed and gave up. "You can't catch me, Alf."

"No, but I can stay behind you as long as I need to."

"You can stay behind me just twenty-four hours. You've got forty-eight hours of air. I don't believe you'll kill yourself just to kill me."

"Don't count on it. But I won't need to. Noon tomorrow, you'll be chasing me. You need to breathe, just like I do."

"Watch this," said Carter. The O-tank resting against his knee was empty. He tipped it over the side and watched it roll away.

"I had an extra tank," he said. He smiled in relief at his release from that damning weight. "I can live four hours longer than you can. Want to turn back, Alf?"

"No."

"He's not worth it, Alf. He was nothing but a queer."

"Does that mean he's got to die?"

"It does if the son of a bitch propositions me. Maybe you're a little that way yourself?"

"No. And Lew wasn't queer 'til he came here. They should have sent half men, half women."

"Amen."

"You know, lots of people get a little sick to their stomachs about homosexuals. I do myself, and it hurt to see it happening to Lew. But there's only one type who goes looking for 'em so he can beat up on 'em."

Carter frowned.

"Latents. Guys who think they might turn queer themselves if you gave 'em the opportunity. They can't stand queers around because queers are temptation."

"You're just returning the compliment."

"Maybe."

"Anyway, the town has enough problems without—things like that going on. This whole project could have been wrecked by someone like your brother."

"How bad do we need killers?"

"Pretty badly, this time." Suddenly Carter knew that he was now his own defense attorney. If he could convince Alf that he shouldn't be executed, he could convince the rest of them. If he couldn't—then he must destroy the bubble, or die. He went on talking as persuasively as he knew how.

"You see, Alf, the town has two purposes. One is to find out if we can live in an environment as hostile as this one. The other is to contact the martians. Now there are just fifteen of us in town—"

"Twelve. Thirteen when I get back."

"Fourteen if we both do. Okay. Each of us is more or less necessary to the functioning of the town. But I'm needed in both fields. I'm the ecologist, Alf. I not only have to keep the town from dying from some sort of imbalance, I also have to figure out how the martians live, what they live on, how martian life forms depend on each other. You see?"

"Sure. How 'bout Lew? Was he necessary?"

"We can get along without him. He was the radio man. At least a couple of us have training enough to take over communications."

"You make me so happy. Doesn't the same go for you?"

Carter thought hard and fast. Yes, Gondot in particular

could keep the town't life-support system going with little help. But—"Not with the martian ecology. There isn't—"

"There isn't any martian ecology. Jack, has anyone ever found *any* life on Mars besides that man-shaped mummy? You can't be an ecologist without something to make deductions from. You've got nothing to investigate. So what good are you?"

Carter kept talking. He was still arguing as the sun dropped into the sea of sand and darkness closed down with a snap. But he knew now it was no use. Alf's mind was closed.

By sunset the bubble was taut, and the tortured scream of incoming breathing-air had dropped to a tired sigh. Lieutenant-Major Shute unfastened the clamps at his shoulders and lifted his helmet, ready to jam it down fast if the air was too thin. It wasn't. He set the helmet down and signaled thumbs-up to the men watching him.

Ritual. Those dozen men had known the air would be safe. But rituals had grown fast where men worked in space, and the most rigid was that the man in charge fastened his helmet last and unfastened it first. Now suits were being removed. Men moved about their duties. Some moved toward the kitchen to clean up the vacuum-induced havoc so Hurley could get dinner.

Shute stopped Lee Cousins as he went by. "Lee, could I see you a minute?"

"Sure, Mayor." Shute was "the Mayor" to all bubbletown.

"I want your help as a writer," said Shute. "I'm going to send in a quite controversial report when we get within range of Earth, and I'd like you to help me make it convincing."

"Fine. Let's see it."

The ten streetlamps came on, dispelling the darkness which had fallen so suddenly. Shute led the way to his prefab bungalow, unlocked the safe, and handed Cousins the manuscript. Cousins hefted it. "Big," he said. "Might pay to cut it."

"By all means, if you find anything unnecessary."

"I'll bet I can," Cousins grinned. He dropped on the bed and began to read.

Ten minutes later he asked, "Just what *is* the incidence of homosexuality in the Navy?"

"I haven't the faintest idea."

"Then it's not powerful evidence. You might quote a limerick to show that the problem's proverbial. I know a few."

"Good."

A little later Cousins said, "A lot of schools in England *are* coeducational. More every year."

"I know. But the present problem is among men who graduated from boys' schools when they were much younger."

"Make that clearer. Incidentally, was your high-school coeducational?"

"No."

"Any queers?"

"A few. At least one in every class. The seniors used to use paddles on the ones they suspected."

"Did it help?"

"No. Of course not."

"Okay. You've got two sets of circumstances under which a high rate of homosexuality occurs. In both cases you've got three conditions: a reasonable amount of leisure, no women, and a disciplinary pecking order. You need a third example."

"I couldn't think of one."

"The Nazi organization."

"Oh?"

"I'll give you details." Cousins went on reading. He finished the report and put it aside. "This'll cause merry hell," he said.

"I know."

"The worst thing about it is your threat to give the whole thing to the newspapers. If I were you I'd leave that out."

"If you were me you wouldn't," said Shute. "Everyone who had anything to do with WARGOD knew they were risking everything that's happened. They preferred to let us take that risk rather than risk public opinion themselves. There are hundreds of Decency Leagues in the United States. Maybe thousands, I don't know. But they'd all come down on the government like harpies if anyone tried to send a mixed crew to Mars or anywhere else in space. The only way I can make the government act is to give them a greater threat."

"You win. This is a greater threat."

"Did you find anything else to cut out?"

"Oh, hell yes. I'll go through this again with a red pencil. You talk too much, you use too many words that are too long, and you generalize. You'll have to give details or you'll lose impact."

"I'll be ruining some reputations."

"Can't be helped. We've got to have women on Mars, and right now. Rufe and Timmy are building up to a real spitting fight. Rufe thinks he caused Lew's death by leaving him. Timmy keeps taunting him with it."

"All right," said Shute. He stood up. He had been sitting erect throughout the discussion, as if sitting at attention. "Are the buggies still in radio range?"

"They can't hear us, but we can hear them. Timmy's working the radio."

"Good. I'll keep him on it until they go out of range. Shall we get dinner?"

Phobos rose where the sun had set, a scattering of moving dots of light, like a crescent of dim stars. It grew brighter as it rose: a new moon becoming a half-moon in hours. Then it was too high to look at. Carter had to keep his eyes on the triangle of desert lit by his headlights. The headlight beams were the color of earthly sunlight, but to Carter's Mars-adapted eyes they turned everything blue.

He had chosen his course well. The desert ahead was flat for more than seven hundred miles. There would be no low hills rising suddenly before him to trap him into jet-jumping in faint moonlight or waiting for Alf to come down on him. Alf's turnover point would come at high noon tomorrow, and then Carter would have won.

For Alf would turn back toward the bubble, and Carter would go on into the desert. When Alf was safely over the horizon, Carter would turn left or right, go on for an hour, and then follow a course parallel to Alf's. He would be in sight of the bubble an hour later than Alf, with three hours in which to plan.

Then would come the hardest part. Certainly there would be someone on guard. Carter would have to charge past the guard—who might be armed with a flare pistol—tear the bubble open, and somehow confiscate the supply of O-tanks. Ripping the bubble open would probably kill everyone inside, but there would be men in suits outside. He would have to load some of the O-tanks on his buggy and open the stop-cocks of the rest, all before anyone reached him.

What bothered him was the idea of charging a flare pistol ... But perhaps he could just aim the buggy and jump out. He would have to see.

His eyelids were getting heavy, and his hands were cramped. But he dared not slow down, and he dared not sleep.

Several times he had thought of smashing the come-hither in his suit radio. With that thing constantly beeping, Alf could find him anytime he pleased. But Alf could find him anyway. His headlights were always behind, never catching up, never dropping away. If he ever got out of Alf's sight, that come-hither would have to go. But there was no point in letting Alf know that. Not yet.

Stars dropped into the black western horizon. Phobos rose again, brighter this time, and again became too high to watch. Deimos now showed above the steady shine of Alf's headlights.

Suddenly it was day, and there were thin black shadows pointing to a yellow horizon. Stars still glowed in a red-black sky. There was a crater ahead, a glass dish set in the desert, not too big to circle around. Carter angled left. The buggy behind him also angled. If he kept turning like this, Alf couldn't help but gain on him. Carter sucked water and nutrient solution from the nipples in his helmet, and concentrated on steering. His eyes felt gritty, and his mouth belonged to a martian mummy.

"Morning," said Alf.

"Morning. Get plenty of sleep?"

"Not enough. I only slept about six hours, in snatches. I kept worrying you'd turn off and lose me."

For a moment Carter went hot and cold. Then he knew that Alf was needling him. He'd no more slept than Carter had.

"Look to your right," said Alf.

To their right was the crater wall. And—Carter looked again to be sure—there was a silhouette on the rim, a man-shaped shadow against the red sky. With one hand it balanced something tall and thin.

"A martian," Carter said softly. Without thinking he turned his buggy to climb the wall. Two flares exploded in front of him, a second apart, and he frantically jammed the tiller bar hard left.

"God damn it, Alf! That was a *martian!* We've got to go *after* it!"

The silhouette was gone. No doubt the martian had run for its life when it saw the flares.

Alf said nothing. Nothing at all. And Carter rode on, past the crater, with a murderous fury building in him.

It was eleven o'clock. The tips of a range of hills were pushing above the western horizon.

"I'm just curious," Alf said, "but what would you have said to that martian?"

Carter's voice was tight and bitter. "Does it matter?"

"Yah. The best you could have done was scare him. When we get in touch with the martians, we'll do it just the way we planned."

Carter ground his teeth. Even without the accident of Lew Harness' death, there was no telling how long the translation plan would take. It involved three steps: sending pictures of the writings on the crematory wells and other artifacts to Earth, so that computers could translate the language; writing messages in that language to leave near the wells where martians would find them; and then waiting for the martians to make a move. But there was no reason to believe that the script on the wells wasn't from more than one language, or from the same language as it had changed over thousands of years. There was no reason to assume the martians would be interested in strange beings living in a glorified balloon, regardless of whether the invaders knew how to write. And could the martians read their own ancestors' script?

An idea . . . "You're a linguist," said Carter.

No answer.

"Alf, we've talked about whether the town needed Lew, and we've talked about whether the town needs me. How about you? Without you we'd *never* get the well-script translated."

"I doubt that. The Cal Tech computers are doing most of the work, and anyhow I left notes. But so what?"

"If you keep chasing me you'll force me to kill you. Can the town afford to lose you?"

"You can't do it. But I'll make you a deal if you want. It's eleven now. Give me two of your O-tanks, and we'll go back to town. We'll stop two hours from town, leave your buggy, and you'll ride the rest of the way tied up in the air bin. Then you can stand trial."

"You think they'll let me off?"

"Not after the way you ripped the bubble open on your way out. That was a blunder, Jack."

"Why don't you just take one tank?" If Alf did that, Carter would get back with two hours to spare. He knew, now, that he would have to wreck the bubble. He had no alternative. But Alf would be right behind him with the flare gun . . .

"No deal. I wouldn't feel safe if I didn't know you'd run out of air two hours before we got back. You want me to feel safe, don't you?"

It was better the other way. Let Alf turn back in an hour. Let Alf be in the bubble when Carter returned to tear it open.

"Carter turned him down," said Timmy. He hunched over the radio, holding his earphones with both hands, listening with every nerve for voices which had almost died into the distance.

"He's planning something," Gondot said uneasily.

"Naturally," said Shute. "He wants to lose Alf, return to the bubble, and wreck it. What other hope has he?"

"But he'd die too," said Timmy.

"Not necessarily. If he killed us all, he could mend the new rip while he lived on the O-tanks we've got left. I think he could keep the bubble in good enough repair to keep one man alive."

"My *Lord!* What can we do?"

"Relax, Timmy. It's simple math." It was easy for Lieutenant-Major Shute to keep his voice light, and he didn't want Timmy to start a panic. "If Alf turns back at noon, Carter can't get here before noon tomorrow. At four he'll be out of air. We'll just keep everyone in suits for four hours." Privately he wondered if twelve men could repair even a small rip before they used up the bottled air. It would be one tank every twenty minutes ... but perhaps they wouldn't be tested.

"Five minutes of twelve," said Carter. "Turn back, Alf. You'll only get home with ten minutes to spare."

The linguist chuckled. A quarter mile behind, the blue dot of his buggy didn't move.

"You can't fight mathematics, Alf. Turn back."

"Too late."

"In five minutes it will be."

"I started this trip short of an O-tank. I should have turned two hours ago."

Carter had to wet his lips from the water nipple before he answered. "You're lying. Will you stop bugging me? Stop it!"

Alf laughed. "Watch me turn back."

His buggy came on.

It was noon, and the chase would not end. At twenty-five miles per, two Marsbuggies a quarter of a mile apart moved serenely through an orange desert. Chemical stains of green rose ahead and fell behind. Crescent dunes drifted by, as regular as waves on an ocean. The ghostly path of a meteorite touched the northern horizon in a momentary white flash. The hills were higher now, humps of smooth rock like animals sleeping beyond the horizon. The sun burned small and bright in a sky reddened by nitrogen dioxide and, near the horizon, blackened by its thinness to the color of bloody India ink.

Had the chase really started at noon? Exactly noon? But it was twelve-thirty now, and he was *sure* that was too late.

Alf had doomed himself—to doom Carter.

But he *wouldn't*.

"Great minds think alike," he told the radio.

"Really?" Alf's tone said he couldn't have cared less.

"You took an extra tank. Just like me."

"No I didn't, Jack."

"You must have. If there's one thing I'm sure of in life, it's that *you* are *not* the type to kill yourself. All right, Alf, I quit. Let's go back."

"Let's not."

"We'd have three hours to chase that martian."

A flare exploded behind his buggy. Carter sighed raggedly. At two o'clock both buggies would turn back to bubbletown, where Carter would probably be executed.

But suppose I turn back now?

That's easy. Alf will shoot me with the flare gun.

He might miss. If I let him choose my course, I'll die for certain.

Carter sweated and cursed himself, but he couldn't do it. He couldn't deliberately turn into Alf's gun.

At two o'clock the base of the range came over the horizon. The hills were incredibly clear, almost as clear as they would have been on the Moon. But they were horribly weathered, and the sea of sand lapped around them as if eager to finish them off, to drag them down.

Carter rode with his eyes turned behind. His watch hands moved on, minute to minute, and Carter watched in disbelief as Alf's vehicle continued to follow. As the time approached and reached two-thirty, Carter's disbelief faded. It didn't matter, now, how much oxygen Alf had. They had passed Carter's turnover point.

"You've killed me," he said.

No answer.

"I killed Lew in a fistfight. What you've done to me is

much worse. You're killing me by slow torture. You're a demon, Alf."

"Fistfight my aunt's purple asterisk. You hit Lew in the throat and watched him drown in his own blood. Don't tell *me* you didn't know what you were doing. Everybody in town knows you know karate."

"He died in minutes. I'll need a whole day!"

"You don't like that? Turn around and rush my gun. It's right here waiting."

"We could get back to the crater in time to search for that martian. That's why I came to Mars. To learn what's here. So did you, Alf. Come on, let's turn back."

"You first."

But he couldn't. He *couldn't*. Karate can defeat any hand-to-hand weapon but a quarterstaff, and Carter had quarterstaff training too. But he couldn't charge a flare gun! Not even if Alf meant to turn back. And Alf didn't.

A faint whine vibrated through the bubble. The sandstorm was at the height of its fury, which made it about as dangerous as an enraged caterpillar. At worst it was an annoyance. The shrill, barely audible whine could get on one's nerves, and the darkness made streetlamps necessary. Tomorrow the bubble would be covered a tenth of an inch deep in fine, Moon-dry silt. Inside the bubble it would be darker than night until someone blew the silt away with an O-tank.

To Shute the storm was depressing. Here on Mars was Lieutenant-Major Shute, Boy Hero, facing terrifying dangers on the frontiers of human exploration! A sandstorm that wouldn't have harmed an infant. Nobody here faced a single danger that he had not brought with him.

Would it be like this forever? Men traveling enormous distances to face themselves?

There had been little work done since noon today. Shute had given up on that. On a stack of walls sat Timmy, practically surrounding the buggy-pickup radio, surrounded in turn by the bubble's population.

Timmy stood up as Shute approached the group. "They're gone," he announced, sounding very tired. He turned off the radio. The men looked at each other, and some got to their feet.

"Tim! How'd you lose them?"

Timmy noticed him. "They're too far away, Mayor."

"They never turned around?"

"They never did. They just kept going out into the desert. Alf must have gone insane. Carter's not worth dying for."

Shute thought, *But he was once.* Carter had been one of the best: tough, fearless, bright, enthusiastic. Shute had watched him deteriorate under the boredom and the close quarters aboard ship. He had seemed to recover when they reached Mars, when all of them suddenly had work to do. Then, yesterday morning—murder.

Alf. It was hard to lose Alf. Lew had been little loss, but Alf—

Cousins dropped into step beside him. "I've got that red-pencil work done."

"Thanks, Lee. I'll have to do it all over now."

"Don't do it over. Write an addendum. Show how and why three men died. Then you can say, 'I told you so.' "

"You think so?"

"My professional judgment. When's the funeral?"

"Day after tomorrow. That's Sunday. I thought it would be appropriate."

"You can say all three services at once. Good timing."

To all bubbletown, Jack Carter and Alf Harness were dead. But they still breathed—

The mountains came toward them: the only fixed points in an ocean of sand. Alf was closer now, something less than four hundred yards behind. At five o'clock Carter reached the base of the mountains.

They were too high to go over on the air jet. He could see spots where he might have landed the buggy while the pump filled the jet tank for another hop. But for what?

Better to wait for Alf.

Suddenly Carter knew that that was the one thing in the world Alf wanted. To roll up alongside in his buggy. To watch Carter's face until he was sure Carter knew exactly what was to come. And then to blast Carter down in flames from ten feet away, and watch while a bright magnesium-oxidizer flare burned through his suit and skin and vitals.

The hills were low and shallow. Even from yards away he might have been looking at the smooth flank of a sleeping beast—except that this beast was not breathing. Carter took a deep breath, noticing how stale the air had become despite the purifier unit, and turned on the compressed-air jet.

The air of Mars is terribly thin, but it can be compressed; and a rocket will work anywhere, even a compressed-air rocket. Carter went up, leaning as far back in the cabin as he could to compensate for the loss of weight in the O-tanks behind him, to put as little work as possible on gyroscopes meant to spin only in emergencies. He rose fast, and he tilted the buggy to send it skating along the thirty-degree slope of the hill. There were flat places along the slope, but not many. He should reach the first one easily . . .

A flare exploded in his eyes. Carter clenched his teeth and fought the urge to look behind. He tilted the buggy backward to slow him down. The jet pressure was dropping.

He came down like a feather two hundred feet above the desert. When he turned off the jet he could hear the gyros whining. He turned the stabilizer off and let them run down. Now there was only the chugging of the compressor, vibrating through his suit.

Alf was out of his buggy, standing at the base of the mountains, looking up.

"Come on," said Carter. "What are you waiting for?"

"Go on over if you want to."

"What's the matter? Are your gyros fouled?"

"Your brain is fouled, Carter. Go on over." Alf raised one arm stiffly out. The hand showed flame, and Carter ducked instinctively.

The compressor had almost stopped, which meant the tank was nearly full. But Carter would be a fool to take off before it was completely full. You got the greatest acceleration from an air jet during the first seconds of flight. The rest of the flight you got just enough pressure to keep you going.

But—Alf was getting into his buggy. Now the buggy was rising.

Carter turned on his jet and went up.

He came down hard, three hundred feet high, and only then dared to look down. He heard Alf's nasty laugh, and he saw that Alf was still at the foot of the mountains. It had been a bluff!

But *why* wasn't Alf coming after him?

The third hop took him to the top. The first downhill hop was the first he'd ever made, and it almost killed him. He had to do his decelerating on the last remnants of pressure in the jet tank! He waited until his hands stopped shaking, then continued the rest of the way on the wheels. There was no sign of Alf as he reached the foot of the range and started out into the desert.

Already the sun was about to go. Faint bluish stars in a red-black sky outlined the yellow hills behind him.

Still no sign of Alf.

Alf spoke in his ear, gently, almost kindly. "You'll just have to come back, Jack."

"Don't hold your breath."

"I'd rather not have to. That's why I'm telling you this. Look at your watch."

It was about six-thirty.

"Did you look? Now count it up. I started with forty-four hours of air. You started with fifty-two. That gave us ninety-six breathing hours between us. Together we've used up sixty-one hours. That leaves thirty-five between us.

"Now, I stopped moving an hour ago. From where I am it's almost thirty hours back to base. Sometime in the next two and a half hours, you've got to get my air and stop me from breathing. Or I've got to do the same for you."

It made sense. Finally, everything made sense. "Alf, are you listening? Listen," said Carter, and he opened his radio panel and, moving by touch, found a wire he'd located long ago. He jerked it loose. His radio crackled deafeningly, then stopped.

"Did you hear that, Alf? I just jerked my come-hither loose. Now you couldn't find me even if you wanted to."

"I wouldn't have it any other way."

Then Carter realized what he'd done. There was now no possibility of Alf finding him. After all the miles and hours of the chase, now it was Carter chasing Alf. All Alf had to do was wait.

The dark fell on the west like a heavy curtain.

Carter went south, and he went immediately. It would take him an hour or more to cross the range. He would have to leapfrog to the top with only his headlights to guide him. His motor would not take him uphill over such a slope. He could use the wheels going down, with luck, but he would have to do so in total darkness. Deimos would not have risen; Phobos was not bright enough to help.

It had gone exactly as Alf had planned. Chase Carter to the range. If he attacks there, take his tanks and go home. If he chooses to cross, he may be killed. Take his tanks. If he makes it, show him why he has to come back. Time it so he has to come back in darkness. If by some miracle he makes it this time—well, there's always the flare gun.

Carter could give him only one surprise. He would cross six miles south of where he was expected, and approach Alf's buggy from the *southeast*.

Or was Alf expecting that too?

It didn't matter. Carter was beyond free will.

The first jump was like jumping blindfolded from a ship's airlock. He'd pointed the headlights straight down, and as he went up he watched the circle of light expand and dim. He angled east. First he wasn't moving at all. Then the slope slid toward him, far too fast. He back-angled. Nothing seemed to happen. The pressure under him died slowly, but it was dying, and the slope was a wavering blur surrounded by dark.

It came up, clarifying fast.

The landing jarred him from coccyx to cranium. He held himself rigid, waiting for the buggy to tumble end-for-end down the hill. But though the buggy was tilted at a horrifying angle, it stayed.

Carter sagged and buried his helmet in his arms. Two

enormous hanging tears, swollen to pinballs in the low gravity, dropped onto his faceplate and spread. For the first time he regretted all of it. Killing Lew, when a kick to the kneecap would have put him out of action and taught him a permanent, memorable lesson. Snatching the buggy instead of surrendering himself for trial. Driving through the bubble—and making every man on Mars his mortal enemy. Hanging around to watch what would happen—when, perhaps, he could have run beyond the horizon before Alf came out the vehicular airlock. He clenched his fists and pressed them against his faceplate, remembering his attitude of mild interest as he sat watching Alf's buggy roll into the lock.

Time to go. Carter readied himself for another jump. This one would be horrible. He'd be taking off with the buggy canted thirty degrees backward . . .

Wait a minute.

There was something wrong with that picture of Alf's buggy as it rolled toward the lock surrounded by trotting men. Definitely something wrong there. But what?

It would come to him. He gripped the jet throttle and readied his other hand to flip on the gyros the moment he was airborne.

—Alf had planned so carefully. How had he come away with one O-tank too few?

And—if he really had everything planned, *how did Alf expect to get Carter's tanks if Carter crashed?*

Suppose Carter crashed his buggy against a hill, right now, on his second jump. How would Alf know? He wouldn't, not until nine o'clock came and Carter hadn't shown up. Then he'd know Carter had crashed somewhere. But it would be too late!

Unless Alf had lied.

That was it, that was what was wrong with his picture of Alf in the vehicular airlock. Put one O-tank in the air bin and it would stand out like a sore thumb. Fill the air bin and then remove one tank, and the hole in the hexagonal array would show like Sammy Davis III on the Berlin Nazis football team! There had been no such hole.

Let Carter crash now, and Alf would know it with four hours in which to search for his buggy.

Carter swung his headlights up to normal position, then moved the buggy backward in a dead-slow half circle. The buggy swayed but didn't topple. Now he could move down behind his headlights . . .

Nine o'clock. If Carter was wrong then he was dead now. Even now Alf might be unfastening his helmet, his eyes blank with the ultimate despair, still wondering where Carter had got to. But if he was right . . .

Then Alf was nodding to himself, not smiling, merely confirming a guess. Now he was deciding whether to wait another five minutes on the chance that Carter was late, or to start searching now. Carter sat in his dark cabin at the foot of the black mountains, his left hand clutching a wrench, his eyes riveted on the luminous needle of the direction finder.

The wrench had been the heaviest in his toolbox. He'd found nothing sharper than a screwdriver, and that wouldn't have penetrated suit fabric.

The needle pointed straight toward Alf.

And it wasn't moving.

Alf had decided to wait.

How long would he wait?

Carter caught himself whispering, not loudly. *Move, idiot. You've got to search both sides of the range. Both sides and the top. Move. Move!*

Ye gods! Had he shut off his radio? Yes, the switch was down.

Move.

The needle moved. It jerked once, infinitesimally, and was quiet.

It was quiet a long time—seven or eight minutes. Then it jerked in the opposite direction. Alf was searching the wrong side of the hills!

And then Carter saw the flaw in his own plan. Alf must now assume he was dead. And if he, Carter, was dead, then he wasn't using air. Alf had two hours extra, but he thought he had four!

The needle twitched and moved—a good distance. Carter sighed and closed his eyes. Alf was coming over. He had sensibly decided to search this side first; for if Carter was on this side, dead, then Alf would have to cross the range again to reach home.

Twitch.

Twitch. He must be at the top.

Then the long, slow, steady movement down.

Headlights. Very faint, to the north. Would Alf turn north?

He turned south. Perfect. The headlights grew brighter ... and Carter waited, with his buggy buried to the windshield in the sand at the base of the range.

Alf still had the flare gun. Despite all his certainty that Carter was dead, he was probably riding with the gun in his hand. But he was using his headlights, and he was going slowly, perhaps fifteen miles per hour.

He would pass ... twenty yards west ...

Carter gripped the wrench. *Here he comes.*

There was light in his eyes. *Don't see me.* And then there wasn't. Carter swarmed out of the buggy and down the sloping sand. The headlights moved away, and Carter was after them, leaping as a moonie leaps, both feet pushing at once into the sand, a second spent in flying, legs straddled and feet reaching forward for the landing and another leap.

One last enormous kangaroo jump—and he was on the O-tanks, falling on knees and forearms with feet lifted high so the metal wouldn't clang. One arm landed on nothing at all where empty O-tanks were missing. His body tried to roll off onto the sand. He wouldn't let it.

The transparent bubble of Alf's helmet was before him. The head inside swept back and forth, sweeping the triangle created by the headlights.

Carter crept forward. He poised himself over Alf's head, raised the wrench high, and brought it down with all his strength.

Cracks starred out in the plastic. Alf looked up with his

eyes and mouth all wide open, his amazement unalloyed by rage or terror. Carter brought the weight down again.

There were more cracks, longer cracks. Alf winced and— finally—brought up the flare gun. Carter's muscles froze for an instant as he looked into its hellish mouth. Then he struck for what he knew must be the last time.

The wrench smashed through transparent plastic and scalp and skull. Carter knelt on the O-tanks for a moment, looking at the unpleasant thing he'd done. Then he lifted the body out by the shoulders, tumbled it over the side, and climbed into the cabin to stop the buggy.

It took him a few minutes to find his own buggy where he'd buried it in the sand. It took longer to uncover it. That was all right. He had plenty of time. If he crossed the range by 12:30 he would reach bubbletown on the last of his air.

There would be little room for finesse. On the other hand, he would be arriving an hour before dawn. They'd never see him. They would have stopped expecting him, or Alf, at noon tomorrow—even assuming they didn't know Alf had refused to turn back.

The bubble would be empty of air before anyone could get into a suit.

Later he could repair and fill the bubble. In a month Earth would hear of the disaster: how a meteorite had touched down at a corner of the dome, how John Carter had been outside at the time, the only man in a suit. They'd take him home and he could spend the rest of his life trying to forget.

He knew which tanks were his empties. Like every man in town, he had his own method of arranging them in the air bin. He dumped six and stopped. It was a shame to throw away empties. The tanks were too hard to replace.

He didn't know Alf's arrangement scheme. He'd have to test Alf's empties individually.

Already Alf had thrown some away. (To leave space for Carter's tanks?) One by one, Carter turned the valve of each tank. If it hissed, he put it in his own air bin. If it didn't, he dropped it.

One of them hissed. Just one.

Five O-tanks. He couldn't possibly make a thirty-hour trip on five O-tanks.

Somewhere, Alf had left three O-tanks where he could find them again. Just on the off chance: just in case something went terribly wrong for Alf, and Carter captured his buggy, Carter still wouldn't go home alive.

Alf must have left the tanks where he could find them easily. He must have left them near here; for he had never been out of Carter's sight until Carter crossed the range, and furthermore he'd kept just one tank to reach them. The tanks were nearby, and Carter had just two hours to find them.

In fact, he realized, they must be on the other side of the range. Alf hadn't stopped anywhere on this side.

But he could have left them on the hillside during his jumps to the top . . .

In a sudden frenzy of hurry, Carter jumped into his buggy and took it up. The headlights showed his progress to the top and over.

The first red rays of sunlight found Lee Cousins and Rufe Doolittle already outside the bubble. They were digging a grave. Cousins dug in stoic silence. In a mixture of pity and disgust he endured Rufe's constant compulsive flow of words.

". . . first man to be buried on another planet. Do you think Lew would have liked that? No, he'd hate it. He'd say it wasn't worth dying for. He wanted to go home. He would have, too, on the next ship . . ."

The sand came up in loose, dry shovelfuls. Practice was needed to keep it on the shovel. It tried to flow like a viscous liquid.

"I tried to tell the Mayor he'd have liked a well burial. The Mayor wouldn't listen. He said the martians might not—hey!"

Cousins' eyes jerked up, and the movement caught them—a steadily moving fleck on the crater wall. Martian! was his first thought. What else could he be moving out there? And then he saw that it was a buggy.

To Lee Cousins it was like a corpse rising from its grave. The buggy moved like a blind thing down the tilted blocks of old glass, touched the drifted sand in the crater floor, all while he stood immobile. At the corner of his eye he saw Doolittle's shovel flying wide as Doolittle ran for the bubble.

The buggy only grazed the sand, then began reclimbing the crater. Cousins' paralysis left him and he ran for the town's remaining buggy.

The ghost was moving at half speed. He caught it a mile beyond the crater rim. Carter was in the cockpit. His helmet was in his lap clutched in a rigid death-grip.

Cousins reported, "He must have aimed the buggy along his direction finder when he felt his air going. Give him credit," he added, and lifted a shovelful from the second grave. "He did that much. He sent back the buggy."

Just after dawn a small biped form came around a hill to the east. It walked directly to the sprawled body of Alf Harness, picked up a foot in both delicate-looking hands, and began to tug the corpse across the sand, looking rather like an ant tugging a heavy bread crumb. In the twenty minutes it needed to reach Alf's buggy the figure never stopped to rest.

Dropping its prize, the martian climbed the pile of empty O-tanks and peered into the air bin, then down at the body. But there was no way such a small, weak being could lift such a mass.

The martian seemed to remember something. It scrambled down the O-tanks and crawled under the buggy's belly.

Minutes later it came out, dragging a length of nylon line. It tied each end of the line to one of Alf's ankles, then dropped the loop over the buggy's trailer-attachment knob.

For a time the figure stood motionless above Alf's broken helmet, contemplating its work. Alf's head might take a beating, riding that way; but as a specimen Alf's head was useless. Wherever nitrogen dioxide gas had touched moisture, red fuming nitric acid had formed. By now the rest of the body was dry and hard, fairly well preserved.

The figure climbed into the buggy. A little fumbling, surprisingly little, and the buggy was rolling. Twenty yards away it stopped with a jerk. The martian climbed out and walked back. It knelt beside the three O-tanks which had been tied beneath the buggy with the borrowed nylon line, and it opened the stopcocks of each in turn. It leapt back in horrid haste when the noxious gas began hissing out.

Minutes later the buggy was moving south. The O-tanks hissed for a time, then were quiet.

At the Bottom of a Hole

Twelve stories below the roof gardens were citrus groves, grazing pastures, and truck farms. They curved out from the base of the hotel in neat little squares, curved out and up, and up, and up and over. Five miles overhead was the fusion sunlight tube, running down the radius of the slightly bulging cylinder that was Farmer's Asteroid. Five miles above the sunlight tube, the sky was a patchwork of small squares, split by a central wedding ring of lake and by tributary rivers, a sky alive with the tiny red glints of self-guided tractors.

Lucas Garner was half-daydreaming, letting his eyes rove the solid sky. At the Belt government's invitation he had entered a bubbleworld for the first time, combining a vacation from United Nations business with a chance at a brand new experience—a rare thing for a man seventeen decades old. He found it pleasantly kooky to look up into a curved sky of fused rock and imported topsoil.

"There's nothing immoral about smuggling," said Lit Shaeffer.

The surface overhead was dotted with hotels, as if the bubbleworld were turning to city. Garner knew it wasn't. Those hotels, and the scattered hotels in the other bubbleworld, served every Belter's occasional need for an earthlike environment. Belters don't need houses. A Belter's home is the inside of his pressure suit.

Garner returned his attention to his host. "You mean smuggling's like picking pockets on Earth?"

"That's just what I don't mean," Shaeffer said. The Belter reached into his coverall pocket, pulled out something flat and black, and laid it on the table. "I'll want to play that in a minute. Garner, picking pockets is legal on Earth. Has to be, the way you crowd together. You couldn't enforce a law against picking pockets. In the Belt smuggling is against the law, but it isn't immoral. It's like a flatlander forgetting to feed the parking meter. There's no loss of self-respect. If you get caught you pay the fine and forget it."

"Oh."

"If a man wants to send his earnings through Ceres, that's up to him. It costs him a straight thirty percent. If he thinks he can get past the goldskins, that too is his choice. But if we catch him we'll confiscate his cargo, and everybody will be laughing at him. Nobody pities an inept smuggler."

"Is that what Muller tried to do?"

"Yah. He had a valuable cargo, twenty kilos of pure north magnetic poles. The temptation was too much for him. He tried to get past us, and we picked him up on radar. Then he did something stupid. He tried to whip around a hole.

"He must have been on course for Luna when we found him. Ceres was behind him with the radar. Our ships were ahead of him, matching course at two gee. His mining ship wouldn't throw more than point five gee, so eventually they'd pull alongside him no matter what he did. Then he noticed Mars was just ahead of him."

"The hole." Garner knew enough Belters to have learned a little of their slang.

"The very one. His first instinct must have been to change course. Belters learn to avoid gravity wells. A man can get killed half a dozen ways coming too close to a hole. A good autopilot will get him safely around it, or program an in-and-out spin, or even land him at the bottom, God forbid. But miners don't carry good autopilots. They carry cheap autopilots, and they stay clear of holes."

"You're leading up to something," Garner said regretfully. "Business?"

"You're too old to fool."

Sometimes Garner believed that himself. Sometime between the first world war and the blowing of the second bubbleworld, Garner had learned to read faces as accurately as men read print. Often it saved time—and in Garner's view his time was worth saving.

"Go on," he said.

"Muller's second thought was to use the hole. An in-and-out spin would change his course more than he could hope to do with the motor. He could time it so Mars would hide him from Ceres when he curved out. He could damn near touch the surface, too. Mars' atmosphere is as thin as a flatlander's dreams."

"Thanks a lot. Lit, isn't Mars UN property?"

"Only because we never wanted it."

Then Muller had been trespassing. "Go on. What happened to Muller?"

"I'll let him tell it. This is his log." Lit Shaeffer did something to the flat box, and a man's voice spoke.

April 20, 2112

The sky is flat, the land is flat, and they meet in a circle at infinity. No star shows but the big one, a little bigger than it shows through most of the Belt, but dimmed to red, like the sky.

It's the bottom of a hole, and I must have been crazy to risk it. But I'm *here*. I got down alive. I didn't expect to, not there at the end.

It was one crazy landing.

Imagine a universe half of which has been replaced by an ocher abstraction, too distant and far too big to show meaningful detail, moving past you at a hell of a clip. A strange, singing sound comes through the walls, like nothing you've ever heard before, like the sound of the wings of the angel of death. The walls are getting warm. You can hear the thermosystem whining even above the shriek of air whipping around the hull. Then, because you don't have enough problems, the ship shakes itself like a mortally wounded dinosaur.

That was my fuel tanks tearing loose. All at once and nothing first, the four of them sheered their mooring bars and went spinning down ahead of me, cherry red.

That faced me with two bad choices. I had to decide fast. If I finished the hyperbola I'd be heading into space on an unknown course with what fuel was left in my inboard cooling tank. My lifesystem wouldn't keep me alive more than two weeks. There wasn't much chance I could get anywhere in that time, with so little fuel, and I'd seen to it the goldskins couldn't come to *me*.

But the fuel in the cooling tank would get me down. Even the ships of Earth use only a little of their fuel getting in and out of their pet gravity well. Most of it gets burned getting them from place to place fast. And Mars is lighter than Earth.

But what then? I'd still have two weeks to live.

I remembered the old Lacis Solis base, deserted seventy years ago. Surely I could get the old lifesystems working well enough to support one man. I might even find enough water to turn some into hydrogen by electrolysis. It was a better risk than heading out into nowhere.

Right or wrong, I went down.

The stars are gone, and the land around me makes no sense. Now I know why they call planet dwellers "flatlanders." I feel like a gnat on a table.

I'm sitting here shaking, afraid to step outside.

Beneath a red-black sky is a sea of dust punctuated by scattered, badly cast glass ashtrays. The smallest, just outside the port, are a few inches in diameter. The largest are miles across. As I came down the deep-radar showed me fragments of much larger craters deep under the dust. The dust is soft and fine, almost like quicksand. I came down like a feather, but the ship is buried to halfway up the lifesystem.

I set down just beyond the lip of one of the largest craters, the one which houses the ancient flatlander base. From above the base looked like a huge transparent raincoat discarded on the cracked bottom.

It's a weird place. But I'll have to go out sometime; how else can I use the base lifesystem?

My Uncle Bat used to tell me stupidity carries the death penalty.

I'll go outside tomorrow.

April 21, 2112

My clock says it's morning. The Sun's around on the other side of the planet, leaving the sky no longer bloody. It looks almost like space if you remember to look away from gravity, though the stars are dim, as if seen through fogged plastic. A big star has come over the horizon, brightening and dimming like a spinning rock. Must be Phobos, since it came from the sunset region.

I'm going out.

Later:

A sort of concave glass shell surrounds the ship where the fusion flame splashed down. The ship's lifesystem, the half that shows above the dust, rests in the center like a frog on a lilypad in Confinement Asteroid. The splashdown shell is all a spiderweb of cracks, but it's firm enough to walk on.

Not so the dust.

The dust is like thick oil. The moment I stepped onto it I started to sink. I had to swim to where the crater rim slopes out like the shore of an island. It was hard work. Fortunately the splashdown shell reaches to the crater rock at one point, so I won't have to do *that* again.

It's queer, this dust. I doubt you could find its like anywhere in the system. It's meteor debris, condensed from vaporized rock. On Earth dust this fine would be washed down to the sea by rain and turned to sedimentary rock, natural cement. On the Moon there would be vacuum cementing, the bugaboo of the Belt's microminiaturization industries. But here, there's just enough "air" to be adsorbed by the dust surface ... to prevent vacuum cementing ... and not nearly enough to stop a meteorite. Result: it won't cement, nohow. So it behaves like a viscous fluid. Probably the only rigid surfaces are the meteor craters and mountain ranges.

Going up the crater lip was rough. It's all cracked, tilted blocks of volcanic glass. The edges are almost sharp. This crater must be geologically recent. At the bottom, half submerged in a shallow lake of dust, is bubbletown. I can walk okay in this gravity; it's something less than my ship's gee max. But I almost broke my ankles a couple of times getting down over those tilted, slippery, dust-covered blocks. As a whole the crater is a smashed ashtray pieced loosely together like an impromptu jigsaw puzzle.

The bubble covers the base like a deflated tent, with the airmaking machinery just outside. The airmaker is in a great cube of black metal, blackened by seventy years of martian atmosphere. It's huge. It must have been a bitch to lift. How they moved that mass from Earth to Mars with only chemical and ion rockets, I'll never know. Also *why?* What was on Mars that they wanted?

If ever there was a useless world, this is it. It's not close to Earth, like the Moon. The gravity's inconveniently high. There are no natural resources. Lose your suit pressure and it'd be a race against time, whether you died of blowout or of red fuming nitrogen dioxide eating your lungs.

The wells?

Somewhere on Mars there are wells. The first expedition found one in the 1990s. A mummified *something* was nearby. It exploded when it touched water, so nobody ever knew more about it, including just how old it was.

Did they expect to find live martians? If so, so what?

Outside the bubble are two two-seater Marsbuggies. They have an enormous wheelbase and wide, broad wheels, probably wide enough to keep the buggy above the dust while it's moving. You'd have to be careful where you stopped. I won't be using them anyway.

The airmaker will work, I think, if I can connect it to the ship's power system. Its batteries are drained, and its fusion plant must be mainly lead by now. Thousands of tons of breathing-air are all about me, tied up in nitrogen dioxide, NO_2. The airmaker will release oxygen and nitrogen, and will also pick up what little water vapor there is. I'll pull hydrogen out of the water for fuel. But can I get the power? There may be cables in the base.

It's for sure I can't call for help. My antennas burned off coming down.

I looked through the bubble and saw a body, male, a few feet away. He'd died of blowout. Odds are I'll find a rip in the bubble when I get around to looking.

Wonder what happened here?

April 22, 2112

I went to sleep at first sunlight. Mars' rotation is just a fraction longer than a ship's day, which is convenient. I can work when the stars show and the dust doesn't, and that'll keep me sane. But I've had breakfast and done clean-ship chores, and still it'll be two hours before sundown. Am I a coward? I *can't* go out there in the light.

Near the sun the sky is like fresh blood, tinged by nitrogen dioxide. On the other side it's almost black. Not a sign of a star. The desert is flat, broken only by craters and by a regular pattern of crescent dunes so shallow that they can be seen only near the horizon. Something like a straight lunar mountain range angles away into the desert; but it's terribly eroded, like something that died a long time ago. Could it be the tilted lip of an ancient asteroid crater? The Gods must have hated Mars, to put it right in the middle of the Belt. This shattered, pulverized land is like a symbol of age and corruption. Erosion seems to live only at the bottom of holes. Later:

Almost dawn. I can see red washing out the stars.

After sundown I entered the base through the airlock, which still stands. Ten bodies are sprawled in what must have been the village square. Another was halfway into a suit in the administration building, and the twelfth was a few feet from the bubble wall, where I saw him yesterday. A dozen bodies, and they all died of blowout: explosive decompression if you want to be technical.

The circular area under the bubble is only half full of buildings. The rest is a carefully fused sand floor. Other buildings lie in stacks of walls, ceilings, floors, ready to be put up. I suppose the base personnel expected others from Earth.

One of the buildings held electrical wiring. I've hooked a cable to the airmaker battery, and was able to adapt the other end to the contact on my fusion plant. There's a lot of sparking, but the airmaker works. I'm letting it fill the stack of empty O-tanks I found against a pile of walls. The nitrogen dioxide is draining into the bubble.

I know now what happened to the flatlander base.

Bubbletown died by murder. No question of it. When nitrogen dioxide started pouring into the bubble I saw dust blowing out from the edge of town. There was a rip. It was sharp-edged, as if cut by a knife. I can mend it if I can find a bubble repair kit. There must be one somewhere.

Meanwhile I'm getting oxygen and water. The oxygen tanks I can empty into the lifesystem as they fill. The ship takes it back out of the air and stores it. If I can find a way to get the water here I can just pour it into the john. Can I carry it here in the O-tanks?

April 23, 2112

Dawn.

The administration building is also a tape library. They kept a record of the base doings, very complete and so far very boring. It reads like a ship's log sounds, but more gossipy and more detailed. Later I'll read it all the way through.

I found some bubble plastic and contact cement and used them to patch the rip. The bubble still wouldn't inflate. So I went out and found two more rips just like the first. I patched them and looked for more. Found three. When I got them fixed it was nearly sunup.

The O-tanks hold water, but I have to heat them to boil the water to get it out. That's hard work. Question: is it easier to do that or to repair the dome and do my electrolysis inside? How many rips are there?

I've found six. So how many killers were there? No more than three. I've accounted for twelve inside, and according to the log there were fifteen in the second expedition.

No sign of the goldskins. If they'd guessed I was here they'd have come by now. With several months' worth of air in my lifesystem, I'll be home free once I get out of this hole.

April 24, 2112

Two more rips in the bubble, a total of eight. They're about twenty feet apart, evenly spaced around the transparent plastic fabric. It looks like at least one man ran around the dome slashing at the fabric until it wasn't taut enough to cut. I mended the rips. When I left the bubble it was swelling with air.

I'm halfway through the town log, and nobody's seen a martian yet. I was right, that's what they came for. Thus far they've found three more wells. Like the first, these are made of cut diamond building blocks, fairly large, very well worn, probably tens or hundreds of thousands of years old. Two of the four have dirty nitrogen dioxide at the bottoms. The others are dry. Each of the four has a "dedication block" covered with queer, partially eroded writing. From a partial analysis of the script, it seems that the wells were actually crematoriums: a deceased martian would explode when he touched water in the nitrogen dioxide at the bottom. It figures. Martians wouldn't have fire.

I still wonder why they came, the men of the base. What could martians do for them? If they wanted someone to talk to, someone not human, there were dolphins and killer whales right in their own oceans. The trouble they took! And the risks! Just to get from one hole to another!

April 24, 2112

Strange. For the first time since the landing, I did not return to the ship when the sky turned light. When I did start back the sun was up. It showed as I went over the rim. I stood there between a pair of sharp obsidian teeth, staring down at my ship.

It looked like the entrance to Confinement Asteroid.

Confinement is where they take women when they get pregnant: a bubble of rock ten miles long and five miles across, spinning on its axis to produce one gee of outward pull. The children have to stay there for the first year, and the law says they have to spend a month out of each year there until they're fifteen. I've a wife named Letty waiting there now, waiting for the year to pass so she can leave with our daughter Janice. Most miners, they pay the fatherhood fee in one lump sum if they've got the money; it's about sixty thousand commercials, so some have to pay in installments, and sometimes it's the woman who pays; but when they pay they forget about it and leave the women to raise the kids. But I've been thinking about Letty. And Janice. The monopoles in my hold would buy gifts for Letty, and raise Janice with enough left over so she could do some traveling, and *still* I'd have enough commercials left for more children. I'd have them with Letty, if she'd agree. I think she would.

How'd I get onto that? As I was saying before I was so rudely interrupted, my ship looks like the entrance to Confinement—or to Farmer's Asteroid, or any underground city. With the fuel tanks gone there's nothing left but the drive and the lifesystem and a small magnetically insulated cargo hold. Only the top half of the lifesystem shows above the sea of dust, a blunt steel bubble with a thick door, not streamlined like a ship of Earth. The heavy drive tube hangs from the bottom, far beneath the dust. I wonder how deep the dust is.

The splashdown shell will leave a rim of congealed glass around my lifesystem. I wonder if it'll affect my takeoff?

Anyway, I'm losing my fear of daylight.

Yesterday I thought the bubble was inflating. It wasn't. More rips were hidden under the pool of dust, and when the pressure built up the dust blew away and down went the bubble. I repaired four rips today before sunlight caught me.

One man couldn't have made all those slashes.

That fabric's *tough*. Would a knife go through it? Or would you need something else, like an electric carving knife or a laser?

April 25, 2112

I spent most of today reading the bubbletown log.

There *was* a murder. Tensions among fifteen men with no

women around can grow pretty fierce. One day a man named Carter killed a man named Harness, then ran for his life in one of the Marsbuggies, chased by the victim's brother. Neither came back. They must have run out of air.

Three dead out of fifteen leaves twelve.

Since I counted twelve bodies, who's left to slash the dome?

Martians?

In the entire log I find no mention of a martian being seen. Bubbletown never ran across any martian artifact, except the wells. If there are martians, where are they? Where are their cities? Mars was subjected to all kinds of orbital reconaissance in the early days. Even a city as small as bubbletown would have been seen.

Maybe there are no cities. But where do the diamond blocks come from? Diamonds as big as the well material don't form naturally. It takes a respectable technology to make them that big. Which implies cities—I think.

That mummy. Could it have been hundreds of thousands of years old? A man couldn't last that long on Mars, because the water in his body would react with the nitrogen dioxide around him. On the Moon, he could last millions of years. The mummified martian's body chemistry was and is a complete mystery, barring the napalmlike explosion when water touched it. Perhaps it *was* that durable, and perhaps one of the pair who left to die returned to cut the dome instead, and perhaps I'm seeing goblins. This is the place for it. If I ever get out of here, you *try* and catch me near another hole.

April 26, 2112

The sun shows clear and bright above a sharp-edged horizon. I stand at the port looking out. Nothing seems strange anymore. I've lived here all my life. The gravity is settling in my bones; I no longer stumble as I go over the crater lip.

The oxygen in my tanks will take me anywhere. Give me hydrogen and you'll find me on Luna, selling my monopoles without benefit of a middleman. But it comes slowly. I can get hydrogen only by carrying water here in the base O-tanks and then electrolyzing it into the fuel-cooling tank, where it liquifies.

The desert is empty except for a strange rosy cloud that covers one arm of horizon. Dust? Probably. I heard the wind singing faintly through my helmet as I returned to the ship. Naturally the sound can't get through the hull.

The desert is empty.

I can't repair the bubble. Today I found four more rips before giving up. They must circle the bubble all the way 'round. One man couldn't have done it. Two men couldn't.

It looks like martians. But where are they?

They could walk on the sand, if their feet were flat and broad and webbed . . . and there'd be no footprints. The dust hides everything. If there were cities here the dust must have covered them ages ago. The mummy wouldn't have shown webbing; it would have been worn away.

Now it's starlessly black outside. The thin wind must have little trouble lifting the dust. I doubt it will bury me. Anyway the ship would rise to the surface.

Gotta sleep.

April 27, 2112

It's oh four hundred by the clock, and I haven't slept at all. The sun is directly overhead, blinding bright in a clear red sky. No more dust storm.

The martians exist. I'm sure of it. Nobody else was left to murder the base.

But why don't they show themselves?

I'm going to the base, and I'm taking the log with me.

I'm in the village square. Oddly enough, it was easier making the trip in sunlight. You can see what you're stepping on, even in shadow, because the sky diffuses the light a little, like indirect lighting in a dome city.

The crater lip looks down on me from all sides, splintered shards of volcanic glass. It's a wonder I haven't cut my suit open yet, making that trip twice a day.

Why did I come here? I don't know. My eyes feel rusty, and there's too much light. Mummies surround me, with faces twisted by anguish and despair, and with fluids dried on their mouths. Blowout is an ugly death. Ten mummies here, and one by the edge of town, and one in the admin building.

I can see all of the crater lip from here. The buildings are low bungalows, and the square is big. True, the deflated bubble distorts things a little, but not much.

So. The martians came over the lip in a yelling swarm or a silent one, brandishing sharp things. Nobody would have heard them if they yelled.

But ten men were in a position to see them.

Eleven men. There's a guy at the edge . . . no, they might have come from the other direction. But still, ten men. And they just waited here? I don't believe it.

The twelfth man. He's half into a suit. What did he see that they didn't?

I'm going to go look at him.

By God, I was right. He's got two fingers on a zipper, and he's pulling down. He's not half into a suit, he's half out of it!

No more goblins.

But who cut the dome?

The hell with it. I'm sleepy.

April 28, 2112

A day and a half of log to catch up on.

My cooling tank is full, or nearly. I'm ready to try the might of the goldskins again. There's air enough to let me take my time, and less chance of a radar spotting me if I move slowly. Goodby, Mars, lovely paradise for the manic-depressive.

That's not funny. Consider the men in the base.

Item: it took a lot of knives to make those slits.

Item: everyone was inside.

Item: no martians. They would have been seen.

Therefore the slits were made from inside. If someone was running around making holes in the bubble, why didn't someone stop him?

It looks like mass suicide. Facts are facts. They must have spread evenly out around the dome, slashed, and then walked to the town square against a driving wind of breathing-air roaring out behind them. Why? Ask 'em. The two who aren't in the square may have been dissenters; if so, it didn't help them.

Being stuck at the bottom of a hole is not good for a man. Look at the insanity records on Earth.

I am now going back to a minute-to-minute log.

1120

Ready to prime drive. The dust won't hurt the fusion tube, nothing could do that, but backblast might damage the rest of the ship. Have to risk it.

1124

The first shot of plutonium didn't explode. Priming again.

1130

The drive's dead. I can't understand it. My instruments swear the fusion shield is drawing power, and when I push the right button the hot uranium gas sprays in there. What's wrong?

Maybe a break in the primer line. How am I going to find out? The primer line's way down there under the dust.

1245

I've sprayed enough uranium into the fusion tube to make a pinch bomb. By now the dust must be hotter than Washington.

· How am I going to repair that primer line? Lift the ship in my strong, capable hands? Swim down through the dust and do it by touch? I haven't anything that'll do a welding job under ten feet of fine dust.

I think I've had it.

Maybe there's a way to signal the goldskins. A big, black SOS spread on the dust . . . if I could find something black to spread around. Have to search the base again.

1900

Nothing in the town. Signalling devices in plenty, for suits and Marsbuggies and orbital ships, but only the laser was meant to reach into space. I can't fix a seventy-year-old comm laser with spit and wire and good intentions.

I'm going off minute-to-minute. There'll be no takeoff.

April 29, 2112

I've been stupid.

Those ten suicides. What did they do with their knives after they were through cutting? Where did they get them in the first place? Kitchen knives won't cut bubble plastic. A laser might, but there can't be more than a couple of portable lasers in the base. I haven't found any.

And the airmaker's batteries were stone dead.

Maybe the martians kill to steal power. They wouldn't have fire. Then they took my uranium for the same reason, slicing my primer line under the sand and running it into their own container.

But how would they get down there? Dive under the dust?

Oh.

I'm getting out of here.

I made it to the crater. God knows why they didn't stop me. Don't they care? They've *got* my primer fuel.

They're under the dust. They live there, safe from meteors and violent temperature changes, and they build their cities there too. Maybe they're heavier than the dust, so they can walk around on the bottom.

Why, there must be a whole ecology down there! Maybe one-celled plants on top, to get energy from the sun, to be driven down by currents in the dust and by dust storms, to feed intermediate stages of life. Why didn't anybody *look?* Oh, I wish I could *tell* someone!

I haven't time for this. The town O-tanks won't fit my suit valves, and I can't go back to the ship. Within the next twenty-four hours I've got to repair and inflate the bubble, or die of runout.

Later:

Done. I've got my suit off, and I'm scratching like a madman. There were just three slits left to patch, none at all along the edge of the bubble where I found the lone mummy. I patched those three and the bubble swelled up like instant city.

When enough water flows in I'll take a bath. But I'll take it in the square, where I can see the whole rim.

I wonder how long it would take a martian to get over the rim and down here to the bubble?

Wondering won't help. I could still be seeing goblins.

April 30, 2112

The water feels wonderful. At least these early tourists took some luxuries with them.

I can see perfectly in all directions. Time has filmed the bubble a little, merely enough to be annoying. The sky is jet black, cut raggedly in half by the crater rim. I've turned on all the base lights. They light the interior of the crater, dimly, but well enough so I'd see anything creeping down on me. Unfortunately they also dim out the stars.

The goblins can't get me while I'm awake.

But I'm getting sleepy.

Is that a ship? No, just a meteor. The sky's lousy with meteors. I've got nothing to do but talk to myself until something happens.

Later:

I strolled up to the rim to see if my ship was still there. The martians might have dragged it into the dust. They hadn't, and there's no sign of tampering.

Am I seeing goblins? I could find out. All I'd have to do is peep into the base fusion plant. Either there's a pile there, mostly lead by now ... or the pile was stolen seventy years ago. Either way the residual radiation would punish my curiosity.

I'm watching the sun rise through the bubble wall. It has a strange beauty, unlike anything I've seen in space. I've seen Saturn from an infinity of angles when I pulled monopoles in the rings, but it can't compare to this.

Now I know I'm crazy. It's a hole! I'm at the bottom of a lousy hole!

The sun writes a jagged white line along the crater rim. I can see the whole rim from here, no fear of that. No matter how fast they move, I can get into my suit before they get down to me.

It would be good to see my enemy.

Why did they come here, the fifteen men who lived and

died here? I know why I'm here: for love of money. Them too? A hundred years ago the biggest diamonds men could make looked like coarse sand. They may have come after the diamond wells. But travel was fiendishly expensive then. Could they have made a profit?

Or did they think they could develop Mars the way they developed the asteroids? Ridiculous! But they didn't have my hindsight. Any holes *can* be useful ... like the raw lead deposits along Mercury's dawnside crescent. Pure lead, condensed from dayside vapor, free for the hauling. We'd be doing the same with martian diamonds if it weren't so cheap to make them.

Here's the Sun. An anticlimax: I can't look into it, though it's dimmer than the rock miner's Sun. No more postcard scenery 'til

Wups.

I'd never reach my suit. One move and the bubble will be a sieve. Just now they're as motionless as I am, staring at me without eyes. I wonder how they sense me? Their spears are poised and ready. Can they really puncture bubble fabric? But the martians must know their own strength, and they've done this before.

All this time I've been waiting for them to swarm over the rim. They came out of the dust pool in the bottom of the crater. I should have realized the obsidian would be as badly cracked down there as elsewhere.

They *do* look like goblins.

For moments the silence was broken only by the twin humming of a nearby bumblebee and a distant tractor. Then Lit reached to turn off the log. He said, "We'd have saved him if he could have held out."

"You knew he was there?"

"Yah. The Deimos scope watched him land. We sent in a routine request for permission to land on UN property. Unfortunately flatlanders can't move as fast as a drugged snail, and we knew of no reason to hurry them up. A telescope would have tracked Muller if he'd tried to leave."

"Was he nuts?"

"Oh, the martians were real enough. But we didn't know that until way too late. We saw the bubble inflate and stay that way for awhile, and we saw it deflate all of a sudden. It looked like Muller'd had an accident. We broke the law and sent a ship down to get him if he was still alive. And that's why I'm telling you all this, Garner. As First Speaker for the Belt Political Section, I hereby confess that two Belt ships have trespassed on United Nations property."

"You had good reasons. Go on."

"You'd have been proud of him, Garner. He didn't run for his suit; he knew perfectly well it was too far away. Instead, he ran toward an O-tank full of water. The martians must have slashed the moment he turned, but he reached the tank, stepped through one of the holes and turned the O-tank on the martians. In the low pressure it was like using a fire hose. He got six before he fell."

"They burned?"

"They did. But not completely. There are some remains. We took three bodies, along with their spears, and left the others in situ. You want the corpses?"

"Damn right."

"Why?"

"What do you mean, Lit?"

"Why do you want them? We took three mummies and three spears as souvenirs. To you they're not souvenirs. It was a Belter who died down there."

"I'm sorry, Lit, but those bodies are important. We can find out what a martian's made of before we go down. It could make all the difference."

"Go down." Lit made a rude noise. "Luke, why do you want to go down there? What could you possibly *want* from Mars? Revenge? A million tons of dust?"

"Abstract knowledge."

"For what?"

"Lit, you amaze me. Why did Earth go to space in the first place, if not for abstract knowledge?"

Words crowded over each other to reach Lit's mouth. They jammed in his throat, and he was speechless. He spread his hands, made frantic gestures, gulped twice, and said, "It's *obvious!*"

"Tell me slow. I'm a little dense."

"There's *everything* in space. Monopoles. Metal. Vacuum for the vacuum industries. A place to build cheap without all kinds of bracing girders. Free fall for people with weak hearts. Room to test things that might blow up. A place to learn physics where you can watch it happen. Controlled environments—"

"Was it all that obvious before we got here?"

"Of course it was!" Lit glared at his visitor. The glare took in Garner's withered legs, his drooping, mottled, hairless skin, the decades that showed in his eyes—and Lit remembered his visitor's age. ". . . Wasn't it?"

Bordered in Black

Only one figure stood in the airlock, though it was a cargo lock, easily big enough to hold both men. Lean and sandy haired, the tiny figure was obviously Carver Rappaport. A bushy beard now covered half its face. It waited patiently while the ramp was run up, and then it started down.

Turnbull, waiting at the bottom, suppressed growing uneasiness. Something was wrong. He'd known it the moment he heard that the *Overcee* was landing. The ship must have been in the solar system for hours. Why hadn't she called in?

And where was Wall Kameon?

Returning spacers usually sprinted down the ramp, eager to touch honest concrete again. Rappaport came down with slow, methodical speed. Seen close, his beard was ragged, unkempt. He reached bottom, and Turnbull saw that the square features were set like cement.

Rappaport brushed past him and kept walking.

Turnbull ran after him and fell into step, looking and feeling foolish. Rappaport was a good head taller, and where he was walking, Turnbull was almost running. He shouted above the background noise of the spaceport, "Rappaport, where's Kameon?"

Like Turnbull, Rappaport had to raise his voice. "Dead."

"Dead? Was it the ship? Rappaport, did the *ship* kill him?"

"No."

"Then what? Is his body aboard?"

"Turnbull, I don't want to talk about it. No, his body isn't aboard. His—" Rappaport ground the heels of his hands into his eyes, like a man with a blinding headache. "His grave," he said, emphasizing the word, "has a nice black border around it. Let's leave it at that."

But they couldn't, of course.

Two security officers caught up with them near the edge of the field. "Stop him," said Turnbull, and they each took an arm. Rappaport stopped walking and turned.

"Have you forgotten that I'm carrying a destruct capsule?"

"What about it?" For the moment Turnbull really didn't understand what he meant.

"Any more interference and I'll use it. Understand this, Turnbull. I don't care any more. Project Overcee is over. I don't know where I go from here. The best thing we can do is blow up that ship and stay in our own solar system."

"Man, have you gone crazy? What *happened* out there? You—meet aliens?"

"No comment.—No, I'll answer that one. We didn't meet aliens. Now tell your comedian friends to let go."

Turnbull let himself realize that the man wasn't bluffing. Rappaport was prepared to commit suicide. Turnbull, the instinctive politician, weighed changes and gambled.

"If you haven't decided to talk in twenty-four hours we'll let you go. I promise that. We'll keep you here 'til then, by force if necessary. Just to give you an opportunity to change your mind."

Rappaport thought it over. The security men still held his arms, but cautiously, now, standing as far back as they could, in case his personal bomb went off.

"Seems fair," he said at last, "if you're honest. Sure, I'll wait twenty-four hours."

"Good." Turnbull turned to lead the way back to his office. Instead, he merely stared.

The *Overcee* was red hot at the nose, glaring white at the tail. Mechs and techs were running in all directions. As

Turnbull watched, the solar system's first faster-than-light spacecraft slumped and ran in a spreading, glowing pool.

... It had started a century ago, when the first ramrobot left the solar system. The interstellar ramscoop robots could make most of their journey at near lightspeed, using a conical electromagnetic field two hundred miles across to scoop hydrogen fuel from interstellar space. But no man had ever ridden a ramrobot. None ever would. The ramscoop magnetic field did horrible things to chordate organisms.

Each ramrobot had been programed to report back only if it found a habitable world near the star to which it had been assigned. Twenty-six had been sent out. Three had reported back—so far.

... It had started twelve years ago, when a well-known mathematician worked out a theoretical hyperspace over Einsteinian fourspace. He did it in his spare time. He considered the hyperspace a toy, an example of pure mathematics. And when has pure mathematics been anything but good clean fun?

... It had started ten years ago, when Ergstrom's brother Carl demonstrated the experimental reality of Ergstrom's toy universe. Within a month the UN had financed Project Overcee, put Winston Turnbull in charge, and set up a school for faster-than-light astronauts. The vast number of applicants was winnowed to ten "hypernauts." Two were Belters; all were experienced spacers. The training began in earnest. It lasted eight years, while Project Overcee built the ship.

... It had started a year and a month ago, when two men climbed into the almost luxurious lifesystem of the *Overcee*, ran the ship out to Neptune's orbit under escort, and vanished.

One was back.

Now his face was no stonier than Rappaport's. Turnbull had just watched his work of the last ten years melt and run like quicksilver. He was mad clean through; but his mind worked furiously. Part of him, the smaller part, was wondering how he would explain the loss of ten billion dollars worth of ship.

The rest was reviewing everything it could remember about Carver Geoffrey Rappaport and William (Wall) Kameon.

Turnbull entered his office and went straight to the bookshelf, sure that Rappaport was following. He pulled out a leather-bound volume, did something to the binding and poured two paper cups full of amber fluid. The fluid was bourbon, and it was more than ice cold.

Rappaport had seen this bookcase before, yet he wore a faintly puzzled frown as he took a cup. He said, "I didn't think I'd ever anticipate anything again."

"The bourbon?"

Rappaport didn't answer. His first swallow was a gulp.

"Did you destroy your ship?"

"Yes. I set the controls so it would only melt. I didn't want anyone hurt."

"Commendable. And the overcee motor? You left it in orbit?"

"I hard-landed it on the Moon. It's gone."

"That's great. Just great. Carver, that ship cost ten billion dollars to build. We can duplicate it for four, I think, because we won't be making any false starts, but you—"

"Hell you wouldn't." Rappaport swirled the bourbon in his cup, looking down into the miniature whirlpool. He was twenty to thirty pounds lighter than he had been a year ago. "You build another *Overcee* and you'll be making one enormous false start. We were wrong, Turnbull. It's not our universe. There's nothing out there for us."

"It *is* our universe." Turnbull let the quiet certainty show in his politician's voice. He needed to start an argument—he needed to get this man to talking. But the certainty was real, and always had been. It was humanity's universe, ready for the taking.

Over the rim of his cup Rappaport looked at him in exasperated pity. "Turnbull, can't you take my word for it? It's not our universe, and it's not worth having anyway. What's out there is—" He clamped his mouth shut and turned away in the visitor's chair.

Turnbull waited ten seconds to point up the silence. Then he asked, "Did you kill Kameon?"

"Kill Wall? You're out of your mind!"

"Could you have saved him?"

Rappaport froze in the act of turning around. "No," he said. And again, "No. I tried to get him moving, but he wouldn't—stop it! Stop needling me. I can walk out anytime, and you couldn't stop me."

"It's too late. You've aroused my curiosity. What about Kameon's black-bordered grave?"

No answer.

"Rappaport, you seem to think that the UN will just take your word and dismantle Project Overcee. There's not a prayer of that. Probability zero. In the last century we've spent tens of billions of dollars on the ramrobots and the *Overcee*, and now we can rebuild her for four. The only way to stop that is to tell the UN exactly why they shouldn't."

Rappaport didn't answer, and Turnbull didn't speak again. He watched Rappaport's cigarette burning unheeded in the ashtray, leaving a strip of charred wet paper. It was uncharacteristic of the former Carver Rappaport to forget burning cigarettes, or to wear an untrimmed beard and sloppily cut hair. That man had been always clean shaven; that man had lined up his shoes at night, every night, even when staggering drunk.

Could he have killed Kameon for being sloppy?—and then turned messy himself as he lost his self-respect. Stranger things had happened in the days when it took eight months to reach Mars.—No, Rappaport had not done murder; Turnbull would have bet high on that. And Kameon would have won any fair fight. Newspapermen had nicknamed him The Wall when he was playing guard for the Berlin Nazis.

"You're right. Where do I start?"

Turnbull was jerked out of his abstraction. "Start at the beginning. When you went into hyperspace."

"We had no trouble there. Except with the windows. You shouldn't have put windows on the *Overcee*."

"Why not? What did you see?"

"Nothing."

"Well, then?"

"You ever try to find your blind spot? You put two dots on

a piece of paper, maybe an inch apart, and you close one eye, focus on one dot and slowly bring the paper up to your face. At some point the other dot disappears. Looking at the window in overcee is like your blind spot expanding to a two-foot square with rounded corners."

"I assume you covered them up."

"Sure. Would you believe it, we had trouble finding those windows? When you wanted them they were invisible. We got them covered with blankets. Then every so often we'd catch each other looking under the blankets. It bothered Wall worse than me. We could have made the trip in five months instead of six, but we had to keep coming out for a look around."

"Just to be sure the universe was still there."

"Right."

"But you did reach Sirius."

"Yes. We reached Sirius . . ."

Ramrobot #6 had reported from Sirius B, half a century ago. The Sirius stars are an unlikely place to look for habitable worlds, since both stars are blue-white giants. Still, the ramrobots had been programed to test for excessive ultraviolet. Sirius B was worth a look.

The ship came out where Sirius was two bright stars. It turned its sharp nose toward the dimmer star and remained motionless for twenty minutes, a silver torpedo shape in a great, ungainly cradle studded with heavy electromagnetic motors. Then it was gone again.

Now Sirius B was a searing ball of light. The ship began to swing about, like a hound sniffing the breeze, but slowly, ponderously.

"We found four planets," said Rappaport. "Maybe there were more, but we didn't look. Number Four was the one we wanted. It was a cloudy ball about twice the size of Mars, with no moon. We waited until we'd found it before we started celebrating."

"Champagne?"

"Hah! Cigars and drunk pills. And Wall shaved off his grubby beard. My God, we were glad to be out in space again! Near the end it seemed like those blind spots were growing around the edges of the blankets. We smoked our cigars and sucked our drunk pills and yakked about the broads we'd known. Not that we hadn't done *that* before. Then we slept it off and went back to work . . ."

The cloud cover was nearly unbroken. Rappaport moved the telescope a bit at a time, trying to find a break. He found several, but none big enough to show him anything. "I'll try infrared," he said.

"Just get us down," Wall said irritably. He was always irritable lately. "I want to get to work."

"And I want to be sure we've got a place to land."

Carv's job was the ship. He was pilot, astrogator, repairman, and everything but the cook. Wall was the cook. Wall was also the geologist, astrophysicist, biologist, and chemist— the expert on habitable planets, in theory. Each man had been trained nine years for his job, and each had some training as backup man for the other; and in each case the training had been based largely on guesswork.

The picture on the scope screen changed from a featureless disk to a patterned ball as Carv switched to infrared. "Now which is water?" he wondered.

"The water's brighter on the night side and darker on the day side. See?" Wall was looking over his shoulder. "Looks like about forty percent land. Carv, those clouds might cut out enough of the ultraviolet to let people live in what gets through."

"Who'd want to? You couldn't see the stars." Carv turned a knob to raise the magnification.

"Hold it right there, Carv. Look at that. There's a white line around the edge of that continent."

"Dried salt?"

"No. It's warmer than what's around it. And it's just as bright on the night side as on the day."

"I'll get us a closer look."

The *Overcee* was in orbit, three hundred miles up. By now the continent with the "hot" border was almost entirely in shadow. Of the three supercontinents, only one showed a white shoreline under infrared.

Wall hung at the window, looking down. To Rappaport he looked like a great ape. "Can we do a reentry glide?"

"In this ship? The *Overcee* would come apart like a cheap meteor. We'll have to brake to a full stop above the atmosphere. Want to strap down?"

Kameon did, and Carv watched him do it before he went ahead and dropped the overcee motor. *I'll be glad to be out of here,* he thought. *It's getting so Wall and I hate the sight of each other.* The casual, uncaring way Kameon fastened his straps jarred his teeth. He knew that Kameon thought he was finicky to the point of psychasthenia.

The fusion drive started and built up to one gee. Carv swung the ship around. Only the night side showed below, with the faint blue light of Sirius A shining softly off the cloud cover. Then the edge of dawn came up in torn blue-white cloud. Carv saw an enormous rift in the cloud bank and turned ship to shift their path over it.

Mountains and valleys, and a wide river ... Patches of wispy cloud shot by, obscuring the view, but they could see down. Suddenly there was a black line, a twisting ribbon of India ink, and beyond that the ocean.

Only for a moment the ocean showed, and then the rift jogged east and was gone. But the ocean was an emerald green.

Wall's voice was soft with awe. "Carv, there's life in that water."

"You sure?"

"No. It could be copper salts or something. Carv, we've got to get *down* there!"

"Oh, wait your turn. Did you notice that your hot border is black in visible light?"

"Yah. But I can't explain it. Would it be worth our while to turn back after you get the ship slowed?"

Carv fingered his neatly trimmed Vandyke. "It'd be night over the whole continent before we got back there. Let's spend a few hours looking at that green ocean."

The *Overcee* went down on her tail, slowly, like a cautious crab. Layer after layer of cloud swallowed her without trace, and darkness fell as she dropped. The key to this world was the word "moonless." Sirius B-IV had had no oversized moon to strip away most of her atmosphere. Her air pressure would be comfortable at sea level, but only because the planet was too small to hold more air. That same low gravity produced a more gentle pressure gradient, so that the atmosphere reached three times as high as on Earth. There were cloud layers from ground to 130 kilometers up.

The *Overcee* touched down on a wide beach on the western shore of the smallest continent. Wall came out first, then Carv lowered a metal oblong as large as himself and followed it down. They wore lightly pressurized vac suits. Carv did nothing for twenty minutes while Wall opened the box out flat and set the carefully packed instruments into their grooves and notches. Finally Wall signaled, in an emphatic manner. By taking off his helmet.

Carv waited a few seconds, then followed suit.

Wall asked, "Were you waiting to see if I dropped dead?"

"Better you than me." Carv sniffed the breeze. The air was cool and humid, but thin. "Smells good enough. No. No, it doesn't. It smells like something rotting."

"Then I'm right. There's life here. Let's get down to the beach."

The sky looked like a raging thunderstorm, with occasional vivid blue flashes that might have been lightning. They were flashes of sunlight penetrating tier upon tier of cloud. In that varying light Carv and Wall stripped off their suits and went down to look at the ocean, walking with shuffling steps in the light gravity.

The ocean was thick with algae. Algae were a bubbly green blanket on the water, a blanket that rose and fell like breathing as the insignificant waves ran beneath. The smell of rotting vegetation was no stronger here than it had been a quarter of a mile back. Perhaps the smell pervaded the whole planet. The shore was a mixture of sand and green scum so rich that you could have planted crops in it.

"Time I got to work," said Wall. "You want to fetch and carry for me?"

"Later maybe. Right now I've got a better idea. Let's get to hell out of each other's sight for an hour."

"That *is* brilliant. But take a weapon."

"To fight off maddened algae?"

"Take a weapon."

Carv was back at the end of an hour. The scenery had been deadly monotonous. There was water below a green blanket of scum six inches deep; there was loamy sand, and beyond that dry sand; and behind the beach were white cliffs, smoothed as if by countless rainfalls. He had found no target for his laser cutter.

Wall looked up from a binocular mircroscope, and grinned when he saw his pilot. He tossed a depleted pack of cigarettes. "And don't worry about the air plant!" he called cheerfully.

Carv came up beside him. "What news?"

"It's algae. I can't name the breed, but there's not much difference between this and any terrestrial algae, except that this sample is all one species."

"That's unusual?" Carv was looking around him in wonder. He was seeing a new side to Wall. Aboard ship Wall was sloppy almost to the point of being dangerous, at least in the eyes of a Belter like Carv. But now he was at work. His small tools were set in neat rows on portable tables. Bulkier instruments with legs were on flat rock, the legs carefully adjusted to leave their platforms exactly horizontal. Wall handled the binocular microscope as if it might dissolve at a touch.

"It is," said Wall. "No little animalcules moving among the strands. No variations in structure. I took samples from depths up to six feet. All I could find was the one alga. But otherwise—I even tested for proteins and sugars. You could eat it. We came all this way to find pond scum."

They came down on an island five hundred miles south. This time Carv helped with the collecting. They got through faster that way, but they kept getting in each other's way. Six months spent in two small rooms had roused tempers too often. It would take more than a few hours on ground before they could bump elbows without a fight.

Again Carv watched Wall go through his routines. He stood just within voice range, about fifty yards away, because it felt so good to have so much room. The care Wall exercised with his equipment still amazed him. How could he reconcile it with Wall's ragged fingernails and his thirty hours growth of beard?

Well, Wall was a flatlander. All his life he'd had a whole planet to mess up, and not a crowded pressure dome or the cabin of a ship. No flat ever learned real neatness.

"Same breed," Wall called.

"Did you test for radiation?"

"No. Why?"

"This thick air must screen out a lot of gamma rays. That means your algae can't mutate without local radiation from the ground."

"Carv, it had to mutate to get to its present form. How could all its cousins just have died out?"

"That's your field."

A little later Wall said, "I can't get a respectable background reading anywhere. You were right, but it doesn't explain anything."

"Shall we go somewhere else?"

"Yah."

They set down in deep ocean, and when the ship stopped bobbing Carv went out the airlock with a glass bucket. "It's a foot thick out there," he reported. "No place for a Disneyland. I don't think I'd want to settle here."

Wall sighed his agreement. The green scum lapped thickly at the *Overcee*'s gleaming metal hull, two yards below the sill of the airlock.

"A lot of planets must be like this," said Carv. "Habitable, but who needs it?"

"And I wanted to be the first man to found an interstellar colony."

"And get your name in the newstapes, the history books—"

"—And my unforgettable face on every trivis in the solar system. Tell me, shipmate, if you hate publicity so much, why have you been trimming that Vandyke so prettily?"

"Guilty. I like being famous. Just not as much as you do."

"Cheer up then. We may yet get all the hero worship we can stand. This may be something bigger than a new colony."

"What could be bigger than that?"

"Set us down on land and I'll tell you."

On a chunk of rock just big enough to be called an island, Wall set up his equipment for the last time. He was testing for food content again, using samples from Carv's bucket of deep ocean algae.

Carv stood by, a comfortable distance away, watching the weird variations in the clouds. The very highest were moving across the sky at enormous speeds, swirling and changing shape by the minutes and seconds. The noonday light was subdued and pearly. No doubt about it, Sirius B-IV had a magnificent sky.

"Okay, I'm ready." Wall stood up and stretched. "This stuff isn't just edible. I'd guess it would taste as good as the food supplements they were using on Earth before the fertility laws cut the population down to something reasonable. I'm going to taste it now."

The last sentence hit Carv like an electric shock. He was running before it was quite finished, but long before he could get there his crazy partner had put a dollup of green scum in his mouth, chewed and swallowed. "Good," he said.

"You—utter—damned—fool."

"Not so. I knew it was safe. The stuff has an almost cheesy flavor. You could get tired of it fast, I think, but that's true of anything."

"Just *what* are you trying to *prove?*"

"That this alga was tailored as a food plant by biological engineers. Carv, I think we've landed on somebody's private farm."

Carv sat heavily down on a rainwashed white rock. "Better spell that out," he said, and heard that his voice was hoarse.

"I was going to. Suppose there was a civilization that had cheap, fast interstellar travel. Most of the habitable planets they found would be sterile, wouldn't they? I mean, life is an unlikely sort of accident."

"We don't have the vaguest idea how likely it is."

"All right, pass that. Say somebody finds this planet, Sirius B-IV, and decides it would make a nice farm planet. It isn't good for much else, mainly because of the variance in lighting, but if you dropped a specially bred food alga in the ocean, you'd have a dandy little farm. In ten years there'd be oceans of algae, free for the carting. Later, if they *did* decide to colonize, they could haul the stuff inland and use it for fertilizer. Best of all, it wouldn't mutate. Not here."

Carv shook his head to clear it. "You've been in space too long."

"Carv, the plant looks *bred*—like a pink grapefruit. And where did all its cousins go? Now I can tell you. They got poured out of the breeding vat because they weren't good enough."

Low waves rolled in from the sea, low and broad beneath their blanket of cheesy green scum. "All right," said Carv. "How can we disprove it?"

Wall looked startled. "*Dis*prove it? Why would we want to do that?"

"Forget the glory for a minute. If you're right, we're trespassing on somebody's property without knowing anything about the owner—except that he's got dirt-cheap interstellar travel, which would make him a tough enemy. We're also introducing our body bacteria into his pure edible algae culture. And how would we explain, if he suddenly showed up?"

"I hadn't thought of it that way."

"We ought to cut and run right now. It's not as if the planet was worth anything."

"No. No, we can't do that."

"Why not?"

The answer gleamed in Wall's eyes.

Turnbull, listening behind his desk with his chin resting in one hand, interrupted for the first time in minutes. "A good question. I'd have gotten out right then."

"Not if you'd just spent six months in a two-room cell with the end of everything creeping around the blankets."

"I see." Turnbull's hand moved almost imperceptibly, writing, *NO WINDOWS IN OVERCEE #2! Oversized viewscreen?*

"It hadn't hit me that hard. I think I'd have taken off if I'd been sure Wall was right, and if I could have talked him into it. But I couldn't, of course. Just the thought of going home then was enough to set Wall shaking. I thought I might have to knock him on the head when it came time to leave. We had some hibernation drugs aboard, just in case."

He stopped. As usual, Turnbull waited him out.

"But then I'd have been all alone." Rappaport finished his drink, his second, and got up to pour a third. The bourbon didn't seem to affect him. "So we stood there on that rocky beach, both of us afraid to leave and both afraid to stay . . ."

Abruptly Wall got up and started putting his tools away. "We can't disprove it, but we can prove it easily enough. The owners must have left artifacts around. If we find one, we run. I promise."

"There's a big area to search. If we had any sense we'd run now."

"Will you drop that? All we've got to do is find the ramrobot probe. If there's anyone watching this place they must have seen it come down. We'll find footprints all over it."

"And if there aren't any footprints? Does that make the whole planet clean?"

Wall closed his case with a snap. Then he stood, motionless, looking very surprised. "I just thought of something," he said.

"Oh, not again."

"No, this is for real, Carv. The owners must have left a long time ago."

"Why?"

"It must be thousands of years since there were enough algae here to use as a food supply. We should have seen ships taking off and landing as we came in. They'd have started their colony too, if they were going to. Now it's gone beyond that. The planet isn't fit for anything to live on, with the soupy oceans and the smell of things rotting."

"No."

"Dammit, it makes sense!"

"It's thin. It sounds thin even to me, and I *want* to believe it. Also, it's too pat. It's just too close to the best possible solution we could dream up. You want to bet our lives on it?"

Wall hoisted his case and moved toward the ship. He looked like a human tank, moving in a stormy darkness lit by shifting, glaring beams of blue light. Abruptly he said, "There's one more point. That black border. It has to be contaminated algae. Maybe a land-living mutant; that's why it hasn't spread across the oceans. It would have been cleaned away if the owners were still interested."

"All *right*. Hoist that thing up and let's get inside."

"Hmph?"

"You've finally said something we can check. The eastern shore must be in daylight by now. Let's get aboard."

At the border of space they hovered, and the Sun burned small and blinding white at the horizon. To the side Sirius A was a tiny dot of intense brilliance. Below, where gaps in the cloud cover penetrated all the way to the surface, a hair-thin black line ran along the twisting beach of Sirius B-IV's largest continent. The silver thread of a major river exploded into a forking delta, and the delta was a black triangle shot with lines of silvery green.

"Going to use the scope?"

Carv shook his head. "We'll see it close in a few minutes."

"You're in quite a hurry, Carv."

"You bet. According to you, if that black stuff is some form of life, then this farm's been deserted for thousands of years at least. If it isn't, then what is it? It's too regular to be a natural formation. Maybe it's a conveyor belt."

"That's right. Calm me down. Reassure me."

"If it is, we go up fast and run all the way home." Carv pulled a lever and the ship dropped from under them. They fell fast. Speaking with only half his attention, Carv went on. "We've met just one other sentient race, and they had nothing like hands and no mechanical culture. I'm not complaining, mind you. A world wouldn't be fit to live in without dolphins for company. But why should we get lucky twice? I don't want to meet the farmer, Wall."

The clouds closed over the ship. She dropped more slowly with every kilometer. Ten kilometers up she was almost hovering. Now the coast was spread below them. The black border was graded: black as night on Pluto along the sea, shading off to the color of the white sand and rocks along the landward side.

Wall said, "Maybe the tides carry the dead algae inland. They'd decay there. No, that won't work. No moon. Nothing but solar tides."

They were a kilometer up. And lower. And lower.

The black was moving, flowing like tar, away from the drive's fusion flame.

Rappaport had been talking down into his cup, his words coming harsh and forced, his eyes refusing to meet Turnbull's. Now he raised them. There was something challenging in that gaze.

Turnbull understood. "You want me to guess? I won't. What was the black stuff?"

"I don't know if I want to prepare you or not. Wall and I, we weren't ready. Why should you be?"

"All right, Carver, go ahead and shock me."

"It was people."

Turnbull merely stared.

"We were almost down when they started to scatter from the downblast. Until then it was just a dark field, but when they started to scatter we could see moving spects, like ants. We sheered off and landed on the water offshore. We could see them from there."

"Carver, when you say people, do you mean—people? Human?"

"Yes. Human. Of course they didn't act much like it . . ."

A hundred yards offshore, the *Overcee* floated nose up. Even seen from the airlock the natives were obviously human. The telescope screen brought more detail.

They were no terrestrial race. Nine feet tall, men and women both, with wavy black hair growing from the eyebrows back to halfway down the spine, hanging almost to the knees. Their skins were dark, as dark as the darkest Negro, but they had chisel noses and long heads and small, thin-lipped mouths.

They paid no attention to the ship. They stood or sat or lay where they were, men and women and children jammed literally shoulder to shoulder. Most of the seaside population was grouped in large rings with men on the outside and women and children protected inside.

"All around the continent," said Wall.

Carv could no more have answered than he could have taken his eyes off the scope screen.

Every few minutes there was a seething in the mass as some group that was too far back pulled forward to reach the shore, the food supply. The mass pushed back. On the fringes of the circles there were bloody fights, slow fights in which there were apparently no rules at all.

"How?" said Carv. "How?"

Wall said, "Maybe a ship crashed. Maybe there was a caretaker's family here, and nobody ever came to pick them up. They must be the farmer's children, Carv."

"How long have they been here?"

"Thousands of years at least. Maybe tens or hundreds of thousands." Wall turned his empty eyes away from the screen. He swiveled his couch so he was looking at the back wall of the cabin. His dreary words flowed out into the cabin.

"Picture it, Carv. Nothing in the world but an ocean of algae and a few people. Then a few hundred people, then hundreds of thousands. They'd never have been allowed near here unless they'd had the bacteria cleaned out of them to keep the algae from being contaminated. Nothing to make tools out of, nothing but rock and bone. No way of smelting ores, because they wouldn't even have fire. There's nothing to *burn*. They had no diseases, no contraceptives, and no recreation but breeding. The population would have exploded like a bomb. Because nobody would starve to death, Carv. For thousands of years nobody would starve on Sirius B-IV."

"They're starving now."

"Some of them. The ones that can't reach the shore." Wall turned back to the scope screen. "One continual war," he said after awhile. "I'll bet their height comes from natural selection."

Carv hadn't moved for a long time. He had noticed that there were always a few men inside each protective circle, and that there were always men outside going inside and men inside going outside. Breeding more people to guard each circle. More people for Sirius B-IV.

The shore was a seething blackness. In infrared light it would have shown brightly, at a temperature of 98.6° Fahrenheit.

"Let's go home," said Wall.

"Okay."

"And did you?"

"No."

"In God's name, why not?"

"We *couldn't*. We had to see it all, Turnbull. I don't understand it, but we did, both of us. So I took the ship up and dropped it a kilometer inshore, and we got out and started walking toward the sea.

"Right away, we started finding skeletons. Some were clean. A lot of them looked like Egyptian mummies, skeletons with black dried skin stretched tight over the bones. Always there was a continuous low rustle of—well, I guess it was conversation. From the beach. I don't know what they could have had to talk about.

"The skeletons got thicker as we went along. Some of them had daggers of splintered bone. One had a chipped stone fist ax. You see, Turnbull, they were intelligent. They could make tools, if they could find anything to make tools out of.

"After we'd been walking awhile we saw that some of the skeletons were alive. Dying and drying under that overcast blue sky. I'd thought that sky was pretty once. Now it was—horrible. You could see a shifting blue beam spear down on the sand and sweep across it like a spotlight until it picked out a mummy. Sometimes the mummy would turn over and cover its eyes.

"Wall's face was livid, like a dead man's. I knew it wasn't just the light. We'd been walking about five minutes, and the dead and living skeletons were all around us. The live ones all stared at us, apathetically, but still staring, as if we were the only things in the world worth looking at. If they had anything to wonder with, they must have been wondering what it was that could move and still not be human. We couldn't have looked human to them. We had shoes and coveralls on, and we were too small.

"Wall said, 'I've been wondering about the clean skeletons. There shouldn't be any decay bacteria here.'

"I didn't answer. I was thinking how much this looked like a combination of Hell and Belsen. The only thing that might have made it tolerable was the surrealistic blue lighting. We couldn't really believe what we were seeing.

" 'There weren't enough fats in the algae,' said Wall. 'There was enough of everything else, but no fats.'

"We were closer to the beach now. And some of the mummies were beginning to stir. I watched a pair behind a dune who looked like they were trying to kill each other, and then suddenly I realized what Wall had said.

"I took his arm and turned to go back. Some of the long skeletons were trying to get up. I knew what they were thinking. *There may be meat in those limp coverings. Wet meat, with water in it. There just may.* I pulled at Wall and started to run.

"He wouldn't run. He tried to pull loose. I had to leave him. They couldn't catch me, they were too starved, and I was jumping like a grasshopper. But they got Wall, all right. I heard his destruct capsule go off. Just a muffled pop."

"So you came home."

"Uh huh." Rappaport looked up like a man waking from a nightmare. "It took seven months. All alone."

"Any idea why Wall killed himself?"

"You crazy? He didn't want to get *eaten*."

"Then why wouldn't he run?"

"It wasn't that he wanted to kill himself, Turnbull. He just decided it wasn't worthwhile saving himself. Another six months in the *Overcee*, with the blind spots pulling at his eyes and that nightmare of a world constantly on his mind—it wasn't worth it."

"I'll bet the *Overcee* was a pigpen before you blew it up."

Rappaport flushed. "What's that to you?"

"You didn't think it was worthwhile either. When a Belter stops being neat it's because he wants to die. A dirty ship is deadly. The air plant gets fouled. Things float around loose, ready to knock your brains out when the drive goes on. You forget where you put the meteor patches—"

"All right. I made it, didn't I?"

"And now you think we should give up space."

Rappaport's voice went squeaky with emotion. "Turnbull, aren't you convinced *yet*? We've got a paradise here, and you want to leave it for—that. Why? Why?"

"To build other paradises, maybe. Ours didn't happen by accident. Our ancestors did it all, starting with not much more than what was on Sirius B-IV."

"They had a *hell*uva lot more." A faint slurring told that the bourbon was finally getting to Rappaport.

"Maybe they did at that. But now there's a better reason. These people you left on the beach. They need our help. And with a new *Overcee*, we can give it to them. What do they need most, Carver? Trees or meat animals?"

"Animals." Rappaport shuddered and drank.

"Well, that could be argued. But pass it. First we'll have to make soil." Turnbull leaned back in his chair, face upturned, talking half to himself. "Algae mixed with crushed rock.

Bacteria to break the rock down. Earthworms. Then grass
..."

"Got it all planned out, do you? And you'll talk the UN
into it, too. Turnbull, you're good. But you've missed something."

"Better tell me now then."

Rappaport got carefully to his feet. He came over to the
desk, just a little unsteadily, and leaned on it so that he stared
down into Turnbull's eyes from a foot away. "You've been
assuming that those people on the beach really were the
farmer's race. That Sirius B-IV has been deserted for a long,
long time. But what if some kind of carnivore seeded that
planet? Then what? The algae wouldn't be for them. They'd
let the algae grow, plant food animals, then go away until the
animals were jammed shoulder to shoulder along the coast.
Food animals! You understand, Turnbull?"

"Yes. I hadn't thought of that. And they'd breed them for
size ..."

The room was deadly quiet.

"Well?"

"Well, we'll simply have to take that chance, won't we?"

Like Banquo's Ghost

On a hot, lovely fall day I drove out to Stardrive Laboratories. If all went well, that was the day the *Snarkhunter #3* probe would send its final message from Alpha Centauri. The *Times* had assigned me to cover the event.

There were coffee and donuts in the anteroom. A diverse lot milled about and introduced each other and shook hands and talked. Pretty secretaries moved briskly through the crowd. I recognized people I'd talked to when I was here two months ago, and one I knew only from his picture. Jubal Hendricks, Senior, had managed Stardrive Labs thirty years ago, when *Snarkhunter #3* was launched. He'd retired just afterward, but here he was, emaciated and tottering, to watch his project's end.

I headed for the coffee table. The man everyone called Butch saw me coming and drew me a cup. He was five feet tall, the color of mahogany, his bright blond hair cut short in a butch cut.

"How good to see you again, Mr. Lane!" He pumped my hand with enthusiasm. "You do remember me?"

"Of course, Butch, very well indeed." I didn't remember his full name, but then, nobody did. And nobody else seemed to want to talk to him. "How have you been?"

"Very well, Mr. Lane, despite my allergies. I have been taking shots."

"They seem to help," I said. Last time I'd seen him his nose had dripped constantly. "Your accent has improved too."

He laughed self-consciously. "It is nearly eight o'clock. Shall we move into the—" His tongue stumbled, and he had to point.

"The auditorium? Yes, let's."

Two months ago we'd been here to catch the first signals from the *Snarkhunter #3* probe as it entered the vicinity of Alpha Centauri. The probe had been flying since before I was born, but that had been its first message since leaving the solar system. On that occasion it had switched itself on on schedule, then given us the sizes and locations of the Centaurus planets.

The speed of light barred us from controlling the *Snarkhunter* from Earth. The probe had been programed to choose the planet most likely to be earthlike, and to home on it. We had named that planet Centaura, even before we knew it existed . . . thirty years ago, when it was known only that the Centauri suns had planets.

Centaura did exist; we knew that now. For the last two months the *Snarkhunter* should have been moving toward it.

The auditorium hadn't changed much in that time. Stardrive Labs uses the same building for all its publicity on all the probes it currently has flying; but none of those probes had done anything interesting since the *Snarkhunter*'s last report. There were seventy chairs with ashtrays fixed to the backs, set up to face a lighted screen. The screen showed a plot of the *Snarkhunter*'s presumed position with respect to the planet Centaura. Arrows pointed in the directions of Earth and Alpha Centauri A. Naturally the plot was 4.3 years out of date, due to light lag. Hanging from the ceiling were eight TV screens, each presently showing a diagram of the Alpha Centauri A system. In one corner of the big room was a blank sphere eight feet across, with a clear plastic hyperbola mounted near it. *That* was new.

Butch pointed. "The curve is the projected course of the

Snarkhunter. Mr. Hendricks, Junior, tells me they will draw continents on the sphere as the data arrives."

"Naturally," I said. We found seats. I manfully resisted the urge to smoke, that being one of Butch's allergies.

Time stopped.

I took my coffee in gulps. I'd been up at six o'clock, for the first time in years. My eyes felt gummy; my mouth was centuries old.

Most of the seats were empty. Even under the circumstances, the lack of excitement was remarkable. On screen were a blank circle and a hyperbola and a couple of arrows, and a little rectangle showing the time remaining until perihelion. The rectangle changed every five minutes, and a new point appeared on the hyperbola, showing the new position of the *Snarkhunter* instrument package.

From time to time a blurred radio voice echoed in the auditorium.

"I am amazed," Butch said fervently. "To think that it has come so far! Do you think it will fulfill its purpose?"

"As you say, it's come this far."

"I cannot understand why there is so little excitement."

He couldn't, could he? "It's partly the time lag," I said. "Who can get excited about old news?"

"I suppose so. Still, so much hinges on the success of the project."

"My cup's empty. Can I get you some coffee?"

"Oh, no. No, thank you."

I went out and filled my cup, then stayed in the anteroom to smoke a cigarette. Things were happening too slowly. Thirty years the probe had been on its way, but the hours it needed to round Centaura were far too long. Maybe Butch was getting on my nerves.

Not his fault, of course. He was unfailingly polite. You couldn't quarrel with his enthusiasm; it was genuine. It only *seemed* a mockery. And I had to stick with him. Butch's reactions were bigger news by far than the *Snarkhunter* itself.

I spent ten minutes by the coffee dispenser, waiting for interviewees. It was the one sure place to find anyone you wanted to see. I caught Hendricks, Senior, and Hendricks, Junior, Markham who had launched the *Snarkhunter*, and Duryodhana who ran the project now, and several others.

Butch couldn't stand coffee. What had he been doing out here by the coffee dispenser?

Just what I was doing, of course. Waiting for people to speak to him. And nobody wanted to.

I was heading for my seat when the radio cleared its throat.

"We are receiving the carrier wave from *Snarkhunter*. *Snarkhunter* has located Sol and is transmitting correctly. Repeat, location successful. We are now receiving *Snarkhunter*."

The air was full of a two-tone musical note, the sound of the carrier wave, low and sweet.

Butch was hugging his knees in delight. "Wonderful! What is it telling them? Why doesn't he say?"

"The *Snarkhunter* isn't saying anything," I told him. I'd gotten that information from my interviews. "It's just a locator wave to alert us."

"What kind of wave is the probe using?"

"A light beam, a ruby laser. Hear that musical tone? That's the laser, translated into sound and then stepped down to the audible range."

The point on the screen moved another notch. Ten minutes to perihelion.

The radio voice said, "We have received our first burst of data from *Snarkhunter*. Composition of Centaura's atmosphere is as follows. Oxygen sixteen percent, nitrogen eighty-three percent—" It continued detailing carbon dioxide, noble gases, water vapor, ozone, surface pressure, and the planet's surface temperature and magnetic field. Butch hugged his knees and made sounds of pleasure.

"Marvelous!" he enthused. "Marvelous! From such a distance! How sensitive, how versatile the instruments!"

"To me it all seems anticlimactic."

"I fear that is my own fault. I am sorry."

The radio saved me from having to answer. "Decoding of *Snarkhunter*'s transmission is now in progress. In a few

minutes we should have a rough map of Centaura's surface."
It added, *"Snarkhunter* is about to pass behind the planet. It
will reach perihelion three minutes later."

The auditorium became silent. I made a shushing motion
at Butch. We heard only the musical sound of the carrier
wave.

The sound cut off abruptly.

"It will not reappear," Butch said sadly.

"That's a pity. It was programed to take another set of
measurements at perihelion. They would have been a little
more accurate."

The point on the screen moved a notch, to its point of
closest approach to Centaura.

"Is that where you shot it down?"

"Yes, at perihelion," said Butch. "How were we to know it
was not hostile? We would not have believed it was possible
at all. An instrument package, with no external guidance,
finding its way over such a distance!" He stood up. "A
remarkable achievement! Remarkable! To have done so
much with so little!"

"Thanks," I said. Thanks for the pat on the head. "Then
you'll go ahead with the trade?"

"I will have to wait," said Butch, "to see if your map of
our world is accurate. Thus far your measurements have
been excellent. Unbelievably so! If your map is as good, we
have a bargain. We will trade you our faster-than-light drive
for your incredible probes. Together we will explore space!"

"Fine." I had what I came for. I rose to leave.

"It has been a lonely year," said Butch. "I do not think I
knew why until now. Mr. Lane, please don't be offended. Did
my landing a year ago cause your people to regard their own
technology as inferior?"

"Of course. Why wouldn't it? Our lousy little probe took
thirty years to reach Centaura. Your ship took six months!
And here you are, like the ghost at the banquet—oh, damn.
I'm sorry, Butch. I lost my head."

"And so you all tend to avoid me. But my own people felt
the same way, when your probe reached us four point three
years ago. Our faster-than-light drive was a single lucky

discovery. Your probe was the combined result of centuries of single-minded, terribly expensive labor and experimentation. We are awed. We are not capable of such sustained effort. But you cannot believe that, can you?"

I couldn't. And I can't.

One Face

An alarm rang: a rising, falling crescendo, a mechanical shriek of panic. The baritone voice of the ship's Brain blared, "Strac Astrophysics is not in his cabin! Strac Astrophysics, report to your cabin immediately! The *Hogan's Goat* will Jump in sixty seconds."

Verd sat bolt upright, then forced himself to lie down again. The *Hogan's Goat* had not lost a passenger through carelessness in all the nearly two centuries of Verd's captaincy. Passengers were *supposed* to be careless. If Strac didn't reach his room Verd would have to postpone Jump to save his life: a serious breach of custom.

Above the green coffin which was his Jump couch the Brain said, "Strac Astrophysics is in his cabin and protected."

Verd relaxed.

"Five," said the Brain. "Four. Three . . ."

In various parts of the ship, twenty-eight bodies jerked like springs released. "Oof," came a complaint from the Jump couch next to Verd's. "That felt strange. Dam' strange."

"Um," said Verd.

Lourdi Coursefinder tumbled out of her Jump couch. She was a blend of many subdivisions of man, bearing the delicate, willowy beauty born of low-gravity worlds. She was

Verd's wife, and an experienced traveler. Now she looked puzzled and disturbed.

"Jump never felt like that. What do you suppose—?"

Verd grunted as he climbed out. He was a few pounds overweight. His face was beefy, smooth and unlined, fashionably hairless. So was his scalp, except for a narrow strip of black brush which ran straight up from between his brow ridges and continued across his scalp and downward until it faded out near the small of his back. Most of the hair had been surgically implanted. Neither wrinkled skin nor width of hair strip could number a man's years, and superficially Verd might have been anywhere from twenty to four hundred years old. It was in his economy of movement that his age showed. He did things the easy way, the fast way. He never needed more than seconds to find it, and he always took that time. The centuries had taught him well.

"I don't know," he said. "Let's find out what it was. Brain!" he snapped at a wall speaker.

The silence stretched like a nerve.

"Brain?"

One wall arced over to become the ceiling, another jogged inward to leave room for a piece of the total conversion drive, a third was all controls and indicators for the ship's Brain. This was the crew common room. It was big and comfortable, a good place to relax, and no crewman minded its odd shape. Flat ceilings were for passengers.

Verd Spacercaptain, Lourdi Coursefinder, and Parliss Lifesystems sat along one wall, watching the fourth member of the crew.

Chanda Metalminds was a tall, plain woman whose major beauty was her wavy black hair. A strip three inches wide down the center of her scalp had been allowed to grow until it hung to the region of her coccyx. Satin black and satin smooth, it gleamed and rippled as she moved. She stood before the biggest of the Brain screens, which now showed a diagram of the *Hogan's Goat*, and she used her finger as a pointer.

"The rock hit here." Chanda's finger rested almost halfway

back along the spinal maze of lines and little black squares and lighted power scources which represented the Jumper section. The *Hogan's Goat* was a sculptured torpedo, and the Jumper machinery was its rounded nose and its thick spine and its trailing wasplike sting. You could see it in the diagram. the rest of the *Goat* had been designed to fit the Jumper. And the Jumper was cut by a slanting line, bright red, next to Chanda's fingertip.

"It was a chunk of dirty ice, a typical piece of comet head," said Chanda. "The meteor gun never had a chance at it. It was too close for that when we came out of overspace. Impact turned the intruder to plasma in the Jumper. The plasma cone knocked some secondary bits of metal loose, and they penetrated *here*. That rained droplets of high-speed molten metal all through the ship's Brain."

Parliss whistled. He was tall, ash blond, and very young. "That'll soften her up," he murmured irreverently. He winced under Chanda's glare and added, "Sorry."

Chanda held the glare a moment before she continued. "There's no chance of repairing the Brain ourselves. There are too many points of injury, and most of them too small to find. Fortunately the Brain can still solve problems and obey orders. Our worst problem seems to be this motor aphasia. The Brain can't speak, not in any language. I've circumvented that by instructing the Brain to use Winsel code. Since I don't know the extent of the damage precisely, I recommend we land the passengers by tug instead of trying to land the *Goat*."

Verd cringed at the thought of what the tug captains would say. "Is that necessary?"

"Yes, Verd. I don't even know how long the Brain will answer to Winsel code. It was one of the first things I tried. I didn't really expect it to work, and I doubt it would on a human patient."

"Thanx, Chanda." Verd stood up and the Brain surgeon sat down. "All I have to say, group, is that we're going to take a bad loss this trip. The Brain is sure to need expensive repairs, and the Jumper will have to be almost completely torn out. It gave one awful discharge when the meteor hit, and a lot of parts are fused—Lourdi, what's wrong? We can afford it."

Lourdi's face was bloodless. Her delicate surgeon's fingers strangled the arms of her chair.

"Come on," Verd said gently. What could have driven her into such a panic? "We land on Earth and take a vacation while the orbital repair companies do the worrying. What's wrong with that?"

Lourdi gave her head a spastic shake. "We can't do that. Oh, Eye of Kdapt, I didn't dare believe it. Verd, we've got to fix the Jumper out here."

"Not a chance. But—"

"Then we've got trouble." Lourdi had calmed a little, but it was the calm of defeat. "I couldn't ask the Brain to do it, so I used the telescope myself. That's not Sol."

The others looked at her.

"It's not the Sun. It's a greenish-white dwarf, a dead star. I couldn't find the Sun."

Once it had its orders, the Brain was much faster with the telescope than Lourdi. It confirmed her description of the star which was where Sol should have been, and added that it was no star in the Brain's catalogue. Furthermore the Brain could not recognize the volume of space around it. It was still scanning stars, hoping to find its bearings.

"But the rock hit *after* we came out of overspace. *After!*" Verd said between his teeth. "How could we have gone anywhere else?" Nobody was listening.

They sat in the crew common room drinking droobleberry juice and vodka.

"We'll have to tell the passengers something," said Chanda. Nobody answered, though she was dead right. Interstellar law gave any citizen free access to a computer. In space the appropriate computer was a ship's Brain. By now the passengers must have discovered that the Brain was incommunicado.

Lourdi stopped using her glass to make rings on the tabletop. "Chanda, will you translate for me?"

Chanda looked up. "Of course."

"Ask the Brain to find the planet in this system which most resembles Saturn."

"Saturn?" Chanda's homely face lost its hopeful expression. Nonetheless she began tapping on the rim of a Brain speaker with the end of a stylus, tapping in the rhythms of Winsel code.

Almost immediately a line of short and long white dashes began moving left to right across the top of the Brain screen. The screen itself went white, cleared, showed what looked like a picture of Saturn. But the ring showed too many gaps, too well defined. Chanda said, "Fifth major planet from primary. Six moons. Period: 29.46 years. Distance from Sun: 9.45 A.U. Diameter: 72,018 miles. Type: gas giant. So?"

Lourdi nodded. Verd and Parliss were watching her intently. "Ask it to show us the second and third planets."

The second planet was in its quarter phase. The Brain screen showed it looking like a large moon, but less badly pocked, and with a major difference: the intensely bright area across the middle. Chanda translated the marching dots: "Distance: 1.18 A.U. Period: 401.4. Diameter: 7918 miles. No moons. No air."

The third planet—"That's Mars," said Lourdi.

It was.

And the second planet was Earth.

"I believe I know what has happened." Verd was almost shouting. Twenty-seven faces looked back at him across the dining room. He was addressing crew and passengers, and he had to face them in person, for the Brain could no longer repeat his words over the stateroom speakers.

"You know that a Jumper creates an overspace in which the speed of light becomes infinite in the neighborhood of the ship. When—"

"Almost infinite," said a passenger.

"That's a popular misconception," Verd snapped. He found that he did not like public speaking, not under these conditions. With an effort he resumed his speaking voice. "The speed of light goes all the way to infinity. Our speed is kept finite by the braking spine, which projects out of the effective neighborhood. Otherwise we'd go simultaneous: we'd be everywhere at once along a great circle of the universe. The braking spine is that thing like a long stinger that points out behind the ship.

"Well, there was a piece of ice in our way, inside the range of our meteor gun, when we came out of overspace. It went through the Jumper and into the Brain.

"The damage to the Brain is secondary. Something happened to the Jumper while the meteor was in there. Maybe some metal vaporized and caused a short circuit. Anyway the *Goat* Jumped back into the counterpart of overspace." Verd stopped. Was he talking over their heads? "You understand that when we say we travel in an overspace of Einsteinian space, we really mean a *subspace* of that overspace?"

A score of blank faces looked back at him. Doggedly Verd went on. "We went into the counterpart of that subspace. The speed of light went to zero."

A murmur of whispering rose and fell. Nobody laughed.

"The braking spine stuck out, or we'd have been in there until the bitter end of time. Well, then. In a region around the ship, the speed of light was zero. Our mass was infinite, our clocks and hearts stopped, the ship became an infinitely thin disk. This state lasted for no time in ship's time, but when it ended several billion years had passed."

A universal gasp, then pandemonium. Verd had expected it. He waited it out.

"Billion?" "Kdapt stomp it—" "Oh my God." "Practical joke, Marna. I must say—" "Shut up and let him finish!"

The shouting died away. A last voice shouted, "But if our mass was infinite—"

"Only in a region around the ship!"

"Oh," said a dark stick-figure Verd recognized as Strac Astrophysics. Visibly he shrugged off a vision of suns and galaxies snatched brutally down upon his cringing head by the *Goat*'s infinite gravity.

"The zero effect has been used before," Verd continued in the relative quiet. "For suspended animation, for very long-range time capsules, et cetera. To my knowledge it has never happened to a spacecraft. Our position is very bad. The Sun has become a greenish-white dwarf. The Earth has lost all its air and has become a one-face world; it turns one side forever to the Sun. Mercury isn't there anymore. Neither is the Moon.

"You can forget the idea of going home, and say goodby to anyone you knew outside this ship. This is the universe, ourselves and nobody else, and our only duty is to survive. We will keep you informed of developments. Anyone who wishes his passage money refunded is welcome to it."

In a crackle of weak graveyard laughter, Verd bobbed his head in dismissal.

The passengers weren't taking the hint. Hearing the Captain in person was as unique to them as it was to Verd. They sat looking at each other, and a few got up, changed their minds, and sat down again. One called, "What will you do next?"

"Ask the Brain for suggestions," said Verd. "Out, now!"

"We'd like to stay and listen," said the same man. He was short and broad and big footed, probably from one of the heavier planets, and he had the rough-edged compactness of a land tank. "We've the legal right to consult the Brain at any time. If it takes a translator we should have a translator."

Verd nodded. "That's true." Without further comment he turned to Chanda and said, "Ask the Brain what actions will maximize our chance of survival for maximal time."

Chanda tapped her stylus rhythmically against the rim of the Brain speaker.

The dining area was raucous with the sound of breathing and the stealthy shuffling of feet. Everyone seemed to be leaning forward.

The Brain answered in swiftly moving dots of light. Chanda said, "Immediately replace—Eye of Kdapt!" Chanda looked very startled, then grinned around at Verd. "Sorry, Captain. 'Immediately replace Verd Spacercaptain with Strac Astrophysics in supreme command over *Hogan's Goat.*' "

In the confusion that followed, Verd's voice was easily the loudest. "Everybody out! Everybody but Strac Astrophysics."

Miraculously, he was obeyed.

Strac was a long, tall oldster, old in habits and manners and mode of dress. A streak of black-enameled steel wool emphasized his chocolate scalp, and his ears spread like wings. Once Verd had wondered why Strac didn't have them fixed. Later he had stopped wondering. Strac obviously made a fetish of keeping what he was born with. His hairline began not between his eyes, but at the very top of his forehead, and it petered out on his neck. His fingernails grew naturally. They must have needed constant trimming.

He sat facing the members of the crew, waiting without impatience.

"I believe you've traveled on my ship before," said Verd. "Have you ever said or done anything to give the Brain, or any passenger, the idea that you might want to command the *Hogan's Goat?*"

"Certainly not!" Strac seemed as ruffled by the suggestion as Verd himself. "The Brain must be insane," he muttered venomously. Then his own words backlashed him, and in fear he asked, *"Could* the Brain be insane?"

"No," Chanda answered. "Brains of this type can be damaged, they can be destroyed, but if they come up with an answer it's the right one. There's a built-in doubt factor. Any ambiguity gives you an Insufficient Data."

"Then why would it try to take my command?"

"I don't know. Captain, there's something I should tell you."

"What's that?"

"The Brain has stopped answering questions. There seems to be some progressive deterioration going on. It stopped even before the passengers left. If I give it orders in Winsel it obeys, but it won't answer back."

"Oh, Kdapt take the Brain!" Verd rubbed his temples with his fingertips. "Parliss, what did the Brain know about Strac?"

"Same as any other passenger. Name, profession, medical state and history, mass, world of origin. That's all."

"Hmph. Strac, where were you born?"

"The Canyon," said Strac. "Is that germane?"

"I don't know. Canyon is a lonely place to grow up, I imagine."

"It is, in a way. Three hundred thousand is a tiny population for a solar system, but there's no room for more. Above the Canyon rim the air's too thin to breathe. I got out as soon as I could. Haven't been back in nearly a century."

"I see."

"Captain, I doubt that. In the Canyon there's no lack of company. It's the culture that's lonely. Everybody thinks just like everybody else. You'd say there's no cultural cross-fertilization. The pressure to conform is brutal."

"Interesting," said Verd, but his tone dismissed the subject. "Strac, do you have any bright ideas that the Brain might have latched onto somehow? Or do you perhaps have a reputation so large in scientific circles that the Brain might know of it?"

"I'm sure that's not the case."

"Well, do you have any ideas at all? We need them badly."

"I'm afraid not. Captain, just what is our position? It seems that everyone is dead but us. How do we cope with an emergency like that?"

"We don't," said Verd. "Not without time travel, and that's impossible. It is, isn't it?"

"Of course."

"Chanda, exactly what did you ask the Brain? How did you phrase it?"

"Maximize the probability of our surviving for maximum time. That's what you asked for. Excuse me, Captain, but the Brain almost certainly assumed that 'maximum time' meant forever."

"All right. Parliss, how long will the ship keep us going?"

Parliss was only thirty years old, and burdened with youth's habitual unsureness; but he knew his profession well enough. "A long time, Captain. Decades, maybe centuries. There's some boosterspice seeds in our consignment for the Zoo of Earth; if we could grow boosterspice aboard ship we could keep ourselves young. The air plant will work as long as there's sunlight or starlight. But the food converter—well, it can't *make* elements, and eventually they'll get lost somewhere in the circuit, and we'll start getting deficiency diseases, and—hmmm. I could probably keep us alive for a century and a half, and if we institute cannibalism we could—"

"Never mind. Let's call that our limit if we stay in space. We've got other choices, Strac, none of them pleasant.

"We can get to any planet in the solar system using the matter-conversion drive. We've enough solid chemical fuel in the landing rockets to land us on any world smaller than Uranus, or to land and take off from a world the size of Venus or smaller. With the matter-conversion drive we can take off from anywhere, but the photon beam would leave boiling rock behind us. We can do all that, but there's no point to it, because nothing in the solar system is habitable."

"If I may interrupt," said Strac. "Why do we have a matter-conversion drive?"

"Excuse me?"

"The *Hogan's Goat* has the Jumper to move between worlds, and the solids to land and take off. Why does such a ship need another reaction drive? Is the Jumper so imprecise?"

"Oh. No, that's not it. You see, the math of Jumper travel postulates a figure for the mass of a very large neighborhood, a neighborhood that takes in most of the local group of galaxies. That figure is almost twice the actual rest mass in the neighborhood. So we have to accelerate until the external universe is heavy enough for us to use the Jumper."

"I see."

"Even with total mass conversion we have to carry a tremendous mass of fuel. We use neutronium; anything less massive would take up too much room. Then, without the artificial gravity to protect us it would take over a year to reach the right velocity. The drive gives us a good one hundred gee in uncluttered space." Verd grinned at Strac's awed expression. "We don't advertise that. Passengers might start wondering what would happen if the artificial gravity went off.

"Where was I? ... Third choice: we can go on to other stars. Each trip would take decades, but by refueling in each system we could reach a few nearby stars in the hundred and fifty years Parliss gives us. But every world we ever used must be dead by now, and the G-type stars we can reach in the time we've got may have no useful worlds. It would be a gamble."

Strac shifted uneasily. "It certainly would. We don't necessarily need a G-type sun, we can settle under any star that won't roast us with ultraviolet, but habitable planets are rare enough. Can't you order the Brain to search out a habitable planet and go there?"

"No," said Lourdi, from across the room. "The telescope isn't that good, not when it has to peer out of one gravity well into another. The light gets all bent up."

"And finally," said Verd, "if we did land on an Earth-sized planet that looked habitable, and then found out it wasn't, we wouldn't have the fuel to land anywhere else. Well, what do you think?"

Strac appeared to consider. "I think I'll go have a drink. I think I'll have several. I wish you'd kept our little predicament secret a few centuries longer." He rose with dignity and turned to the door, then spoiled the exit by turning back. "By the way, Captain, have you ever been to a one-face world? Or have your travels been confined to the habitable worlds?"

"I've been to the Earth's Moon, but that's all. Why?"

"I'm not sure," said Strac, and he left looking thoughtful. Verd noticed that he turned right. The bar was aft of the dining room, to the left.

Gloom settled over the dining area. Verd fumbled in his belt pouch, brought forth a white tube not much bigger than a cigarette. Eyes fixed morosely on a wall, he hung the tube between his lips, sucked through it, inhaled at the side of his mouth. He exhaled cool, thick orange smoke.

The muscles around his eyes lost a little of their tension.

Chanda spoke up. "Captain, I've been wondering why the Brain didn't answer me directly, why it didn't just give us a set of detailed instructions."

"Me too. Have you got an answer?"

"It must have computed just how much time it had before

its motor aphasia became complete. So instead of trying to give a string of detailed instructions it would never finish, it just named the person most likely to have the right answer. It gave us what it could in the few seconds it had left."

"But why Strac? Why not me, or one of you?"

"I don't know," Chanda said wearily. The damage to the Brain had hit her hard. Not surprising; she had always treated the Brain like a beloved but retarded child. She closed her eyes and began to recite, "Name, profession, mass, world of origin, medical history. Strac, astrophysics, the Canyon . . ."

In the next few days, each member of the crew was busy at his own specialty.

Lourdi Coursefinder spent most of her time at the telescope. It was a powerful instrument, and she had the Brain's limited help. But the worlds of even the nearest stars were only circular dots. The sky was thick with black suns, visible only in the infrared. She did manage to find Earth's Moon— more battered than ever, in a Trojan orbit, trailing sixty degrees behind the parent planet in her path around the Sun.

Parliss Lifesystems spent his waking hours in the ship's library, looking up tomes on the medical aspects of privation. Gradually he was putting together a detailed program that would keep the passengers healthy for a good long time, and alive for a long time after that, with safety factors allowing for breakdown of the more delicate components of the life-support system. Later he planned to prepare a similar program using cannibalism to its best medical advantage. That part would be tricky, involving subtle pyschological effects from moral shock.

Slowly and painfully, with miniature extensible waldos, Chanda searched out the tiny burns in the Brain's cortex and scraped away the charred semiconducting ash. "Probably won't help much," she admitted grimly, "but the ash may be causing short circuits. It can't *hurt* to get it out. I wish I had some fine wire."

Once he was convinced that the Jumper was stone-cold dead, Verd left it alone. That gave him little to do but worry. He worried about the damage to the Brain, and wondered if Chanda was being overoptimistic. Like a surgeon forced to operate on a sick friend, she refused even to consider that the Brain might get worse instead of better. Verd worried, and he checked the wiring in the manual override systems for the various drives, moving along outside the hull in a vac suit.

He was startled by the sight of the braking spine. Its ultrahard metal was as shiny as ever, but it was two-thirds gone. Sublimation, over several billion years.

He worried about the passengers too. Without the constant entertainment provided by the Brain, they would be facing the shock of their disaster virtually unaided. The log had a list of passengers, and Chanda got the Brain to put it on the screen, but Verd could find few useful professions among them.

Strac Astrophysics

Jimm Farmer

Avran Zooman

The other professions were all useless here. Taxer, Carmaker, Adman—he was lucky to find anything at all. "All the same," he told Lourdi one night, "I'd give anything to find a Jak FTLsystems aboard."

"How 'bout a Harlan Alltrades?"

"On this tub? Specializing nonspecialists ride the luxury liners." He twisted restlessly in the air between the sleeping plates. "Wanta buy an aircar? It was owned by a sniveling coward—"

Jimm Farmer was the heavy-planet man, with long, smooth muscles and big broad feet. His Jinxian accent implied that he could probably kick holes in hullmetal. "I've never worked without machinery," he said. "Farming takes an awful lot of machinery. Diggers, plowers, seeders, transplanters, aerators, you name it. Even if you gave me seeds and a world to grow them on, I couldn't do anything by myself." He scratched his bushy eyebrows. For some reason he'd let them grow outward from the end of his hairline, like the crossbar on an upside-down T. "But if all the passengers and crew pitched in and followed directions, and if they didn't mind working like robots, I think we could raise something, if we had a planet with good dirt and some seeds."

"At least we've got the seeds," said Verd. "Thanx, Mr. Farmer."

Verd had first seen Avran Zooman walking through the hall at the beginning of the trip. Zooman was a shocking sight. His thin strip of hair was bleached-bone white and started halfway back on his scalp. His skin had faint lines in it, like the preliminary grooves in tooled leather. Verd had avoided him until now. Obviously the man belonged to one of those strange, nearly extinct religious orders which prohibit the taking of boosterspice.

But he didn't behave like a religious nut. Verd found him friendly, alert, helpful, and likeable. His thick We Made It accent was heavy with stressed esses.

"In this one respect we are lucky," Avran was saying. "Or you are lucky. I should have been lucky enough to miss my ship. I came to protect your cargo, which is a selection of fertile plant seeds and frozen animal eggs for the Zoo of Earth Authority."

"Exactly what's in the consignment?"

"Nearly everything you could think of, Captain. The Central Government wished to establish a zoo to show all the life that Earth has lost as a result of her intense population compression. I suspect they wished to encourage emigration. This is the first consignment, and it contains samples of every variety of nondomestic life on We Made It. There were to be other shipments from other worlds, including some expensive mutations from Wunderland designed to imitate the long extinct 'big cats.' We do not have those, nor the useless decorative plants such as orchids and cactus, but we do have everything we need for farming."

"Have you got an incubator for the animals?"

"Unfortunately not. Perhaps I could show you how to make one out of other machinery." Avran smiled humorously. "But there is a problem. I am fatally allergic to boosterspice extract. Thus I will be dead in less than a century, which unfortunately limits the length of any journey that I can make."

Verd felt his face go numb. He was no more afraid of death than the next man, but—frantically he tried to sort his climbing emotions before they strangled him. Admiration, wonder, shame, horror, fear. How could Avran live so casually with death? How could he have reached such a state of emotional maturity in what could be no more than fifty years? Shame won out, shame at his own reaction, and Verd felt himself flushing.

Avran looked concerned. "Perhaps I should come back later," he suggested.

'No! I'm all right." Verd had found his tabac stick without thinking. He pulled in a deep, cooling draft of orange smoke, and held it in his lungs for a long moment.

"A few more questions," he said briskly. "Does the Zoo consignment have grass seed? Are there any bacteria or algae?"

"Grass, yes. Forty-three varieties. No bacteria, I'm afraid."

"That's not good. It takes bacteria to turn rock dust into fertile soil."

"Yes." Avran considered. "We could start the process with sewage from the ship mixed with intestinal flora. Then add the rock dust. We have earthworms. It might work."

"Good."

"Now I have a question, Captain. What is that?"

Verd followed his pointing finger. "Never seen a tabac stick?"

Avran shook his head.

"There's a funny tranquilizer in tobacco that helps you concentrate, lets you block out distractions. People used to have to inhale tobacco smoke to get it. That caused lung cancer. Now we do it better. Are there tobacco plants in the consignment?"

"I'm afraid not. Can you give up the habit?"

"If I have to. But I'll hate it."

Verd sat for a moment after Avran had left, then got up

and hunted down Parliss. "Avran claims to be allergic to boosterspice. I want to know if it's true. Can you find out?"

"Sure, Captain. It'll be in the medical record."

"Good."

"Why would he lie, Captain?"

"He may have a religious ban on boosterspice. If so, he might think I'd shoot him full of it just because I need him. And he'd be right."

There was no point in interviewing Strac Astrophysics again. Parliss told him that Strac spent most of his time in his room, and that he had found a pocket computer somewhere.

"He must have something in mind," said Parliss.

The next day Parliss came to the cabin. "I've gone through the medical histories," he said. "We're all in good shape, except Avran Zooman and Laspia Waitress. Avran told the truth. He's allergic to boosterspice. Laspia has a pair of cultured arms, no telling how she lost the old ones, and both ulnas have machinery in them. One's a dooper, one's a multirange sonic. I wonder what that sweet girl is doing armed to the teeth like that."

"So do I. Can you sabotage her?"

"I put an extension-recharger in her room. If she tries to shoot anyone she'll find her batteries are drained."

The sixth day was the day of mutiny.

Verd and Parliss were in the crew common room, going over Parliss' hundred-and-fifty-year schedule for shipboard living, when the door opened to admit Chanda. The first hint came from Chanda's taut, determined expression. Then Verd saw that someone had followed her in. He stood up to protest, then stood speechless as a line of passengers trooped into the crew common room, filling it nearly to bursting.

"I'm sorry, Captain," said Chanda. "We've come to demand your resignation."

Verd, still standing, let his eyes run over them. The pretty auburn-haired woman in front, the one who held her arms in an inconspicuously strained attitude—she must be Laspia Waitress. Jimm Farmer was also in the front rank. And Strac Astrophysics, looking acutely embarrassed. Many looked embarrassed, and many looked angry; Verd wasn't sure what they were angry at, or who. He gave himself a few seconds to think. Let 'em wait it out . . .

"On what grounds?" he asked mildly.

"On the grounds that it's the best chance we have to stay alive," said Chanda.

"That's not sufficient grounds. You know that. You need a criminal charge to bring against me: dereliction of duty, sloppiness with the drive beam, murder, violation of religious tenets, drug addiction. Do you wish to make such a charge?"

"Captain, you're talking about impeachment—legal grounds for mutiny. We don't have such grounds. We don't want to impeach you, regardless."

"Well, just what did you think this was, Chanda? An election?"

"We're inviting you to resign."

"Thanx, but I think not."

"We could impeach you, you know." Jimm Farmer was neither angry nor embarrassed; merely interested. "We could charge you with addiction to tabac sticks, try you, and convict you."

"Tabac sticks?"

"Sure, everyone knows they're not addictive. The point is that you can't find a higher court to reverse our decision."

"I guess that's true. Very well, go ahead."

Parliss broke in, in a harsh whisper. "Chanda, what are you *doing?"* His face, scalp, and ears burned sunset red.

The tall woman said, "Quiet, Parl. We're only doing what needs to be done."

"You're crazy with grief over that damn mechanical moron."

Chanda flashed him a smoking glare. Parliss returned it. She turned away, aloofly ignoring him.

Strac spoke for the first time. "Don't make us use force, Captain."

'Why not? Do you idiots realize what you're asking?" Verd's control was going. He'd been a young man when the *Hogan's Goat* was built. In nearly two centuries he'd flown her further than the total distance to Andromeda; nursed her and worried about her and lived his life in her lighted, rushing womb. What he felt must have showed in his face, for the girl with the auburn hair raised her left arm and held it innocently bent, pointed right at him. Probably it was the sonic; no doubt he would have been swathed in calming vibrations if her batteries had worked. But all he felt was nausea and a growing rage.

"I do," Strac said quietly. "We're asking you to make it possible for us to give you back your ship after this is over."

Verd jumped at him. A cold corner of his mind was amazed at himself, but most of him only wanted to get his hands around Strac's bony, fragile throat. He glimpsed Laspia Waitress staring in panic at her forearms, and then a steel hand closed around his ankle and *jerked*. Verd stopped in midair.

It was Jimm Farmer. He had jumped across the room like a kangaroo. Verd looked back over his shoulder and carefully kicked him under the jaw. Jimm looked surprised and hurt. He squeezed!

"All right!" Verd yelped. More softly, "All right. I'll resign."

The autodoc mended two cracked ankle bones, injected mysterious substances into the badly bruised lower terminal of his Achilles tendon, and ordered a week of bed rest.

Strac's plans were compatible. He had ordered the ship to Earth. Since the *Goat* was still moving at nearly lightspeed, and had gone well past the solar system, the trip would take about two weeks.

Verd began to enjoy himself. For the first time since the last disastrous Jump, he was able to stop worrying for more than minutes at a time. The pressure was off. The responsibility was no longer his. He even persuaded Lourdi to cooperate with Strac. At first she would have nothing to do with the mutineers, but Verd convinced her that the passengers depended on her. Professional pride was a powerful argument.

After a week on his back Verd started moving around the ship, trying to get an idea of the state of the ship's morale.

He did little else. He was perversely determined not to interfere with the new Captain.

Once Laspia Waitress stopped him in the hall. "Captain, I've decided to take you into my confidence. I am an ARM, a member of the Central Government Police of Earth. There's a badly wanted man aboard this ship." And before Verd could try to humor her out of it she had produced authentic-looking credentials.

"He's involved in the Free Wunderland conspiracy," she went on. "Yes, it still exists. We had reason to believe he was aboard the *Hogan's Goat*, but I wasn't sure of it until he found some way to disarm me. I still haven't identified him yet. He could be anyone, even—"

"Easy, easy," Verd soothed her. "I did that. I didn't want anyone wandering around my ship with concealed weapons."

Her voice cracked. "You fool! How am I going to arrest him?"

"Why should you? Who would you turn him over to if you did? What harm can he do now?"

"What *harm*? He's a revolutionary, a—a seditionist!"

"Sure. He's fanatically determined to free Wunderland from the tyranny of the Central Government of Earth. But Wunderland and the Central Government have been dead for ages, and we haven't a single Earthman on board. Unless you're one."

He left her sputtering helplessly.

When he thought about it later it didn't seem so funny. Many of the passengers must be clinging to such an outmoded cause, unwilling to face the present reality. When that defense gave out, he could expect cases of insanity.

Surprisingly, Strac had talked to nobody, except to ask questions of the crew members. If he had plans they were all his own. Perhaps he wanted one last look at Earth, ancient grandmother Earth, dead now of old age. Many passengers felt the same.

Verd did not. He and Lourdi had last seen Earth twelve years ago—subjective time—when the *Goat* was getting her life-support systems rejuvenated. They had spent a wonderful two months in Rio de Janeiro, a hive of multicolored human beings moving among buildings that reached like frustrated spacecraft toward the sky. Once they had even seen two firemanes, natives of l'Elephant, shouldering their way unconcerned among the bigger humans, but shying like fawns at the sight of a swooping car. Perhaps firemanes still lived somewhere in the smoky arms of this galaxy or another. Perhaps even humans lived, though they must be changed beyond recognition. But Verd did not want to look on the corpse face of Earth. He preferred to keep his memories unspoiled.

He was not asked.

On the tenth day the *Goat* made turnover. Verd thought of the drive beam sweeping its arc across deserted asteroidal cities. Neutronium converted to a destroying blast of pure light. In civilized space a simple turnover required seconds of calculation on the part of the Brain, just to keep the drive beam pointed safely. Anything that light touched would vanish. But now there was nothing to protect.

On the fifteenth ship's-day morning the Earth was a wide, brilliant crescent, blinding bright where the seas had dried across her sunward face. The Sun shone with eerie greenish-white radiance beyond the polarized windows. Verd and Lourdi were finishing breakfast when Strac appeared outside the one-way transparent door. Lourdi let him in.

"I thought I'd better come personally," said Strac. "I've called for a meeting in the crew common room in an hour. I'd appreciate it if you'd be there, Verd."

"I'd just as soon not," said Verd. "Thanx anyway. Have a roast dove?"

Strac politely declined, and left. He had not repeated his invitation.

"He wasn't just being polite," Lourdi told him. "He needs you."

"Let 'im suffer."

Lourdi took him gently by the ears and turned him to face her—a trick she had developed to get his undivided attention. "Friend, this is the wrong time to play prima donna. You talked me into serving the usurper on grounds that the passengers needed my skills. I'm telling you they need yours."

"Dammit, Lourdi, if they needed me I'd still be captain!"

"They need you as a crewman!"

Verd set his jaw and looked stubborn. Lourdi let go, patted his ears gently, and stepped back. "That's my say. Think it through, Lord and Master."

Six people circled the table. Verd was there, and Lourdi and Parliss and Chanda. Strac occupied the Captain's chair, beneath the Brain screen. The sixth man was Jimm Farmer.

"I know what we have to do now," said Strac. His natural dignity had deepened lately, though his shoulders sagged as if ship's gravity were too much for him, and his thin, dark face had lost the ability to smile. "But I want to consider alternatives first. To that end I want you all to hear the answers to questions I've been asking you individually. Lourdi, will you tell us about the Sun?"

Lourdi stood up. She seemed to know exactly what was wanted.

"It's very old," she said. "Terribly old and almost dead. After our Jumper went funny the Sun seems to have followed the main sequence all the way. For awhile it got hotter and brighter and bigger, until it blew up into a red giant. That's probably when Mercury disappeared. Absorbed.

"Sol could have left the main sequence then, by going nova for example, but if it had there wouldn't be any inner planets. So it stayed a red giant until there wasn't enough fuel to burn to maintain the pressure, and then the structure collapsed.

"The Sun contracted to a white dwarf. What with unradiated heat working its way out, and heat of contraction, and fusion reactions still going on inside, it continued to give off light, and still does, even though for all practical purposes there's no fuel left. You can't burn iron. So now the Sun's a greenish dwarf, and still cooling. In a few million years it'll be a reddish dwarf, and then a black one."

"Only millions?"

"Yes, Strac. Only millions."

"How much radiation is being put out now?"

Lourdi considered. "About the same as in our time, but it's bluer light. The Sun is much hotter than we knew it, but all its light has to radiate through a smaller surface area. Do you want figures?"

"No thanx, Lourdi. Jimm Farmer, could you grow foodstuffs under such a star?"

Peculiar question, thought Verd. He sat up straighter, fighting a horrible suspicion.

Jimm looked puzzled, but answered readily. "If the air was right and I had enough water, sure I could. Plants like ultraviolet. The animals might need protection from sunburn."

Strac nodded. "Lourdi, what's the state of the galaxy?"

"Lousy," she said promptly. "Too many dead stars, and most of what's left are blue-white and white giants. Too hot. I'll bet that any planet in this neighborhood that has the right temperature for life will be a gas giant. The young stars are all in the tips of the galactic arms, and they've been scattered by the spin of the galaxy. We can find *some* young stars in the globular clusters. Do you want to hear about them?"

"We'd never reach them," said Verd. His suspicion was a certainty. He blew orange smoke and waited, silently daring Strac to put his intention into words.

"Right," said Strac. "Chanda, how is the Brain?"

"Very, very sick. It might stop working before the decade's end. It'll never last out the century, crippled as it is." Chanda wasn't looking so good herself. Her eyes were red, underlined with blue shadows. Verd thought she had lost mass. Her hair hadn't had its usual care. She continued, as if to herself, "Twice I've given it ordinary commands and gotten the Insufficient Data sign. That's very bad. It means the Brain is starting to distrust the data in its own memory banks."

"Just how bad *is* that?"

"It's a one-way street, with a wiped mind at the end. There's no way to stop it."

"Thanx, Chanda." Strac was carrying it off, but beneath his battered dignity he looked determined and—frightened. Verd thought he had reason. "Now you know everything," he told them. "Any comments?"

Parliss said, "If we're going star hunting we should stop on Pluto and shovel up an air reserve. It'd give us a few decades leeway."

"Uh huh. Anything else?"

Nobody answered.

"Well, that's that." Strac drew a deep breath, let it out slowly. "There's too much risk in searching the nearby stars. We'll have to make do with what we've got. Chanda, please order the Brain to set us down on the highest flat point in Earth's noon-equator region."

Chanda didn't move. Nobody moved.

"I knew it," Verd said, very quietly. His voice echoed in the greater quiet. The crew common room was like a museum exhibit. Everyone seemed afraid to move. Everyone but Jimm Farmer, who in careful silence was getting to his feet.

"Didn't you understand, Strac?" Verd paused and tried to make his voice persuasive. "The Brain put you in charge because you had more useful knowledge than the rest of us. You were supposed to find a new home for the human race."

They were all staring at Strac with varying degrees of horror. All but Jimm, who stood patiently waiting for the others to make up their minds.

"You were not supposed to give up and take us home to die!" Verd snapped. But Strac was ignoring him. Strac was glaring at them all in rage and contempt.

Parliss, normally Nordic-pale, was white as moonlight. "Strac, it's dead! Leave it! We can find another world—"

"You mewling litter of blind idiots."

Even Jimm Farmer looked shocked.

"Do you think I'd kill us all for a twinge of homesickness? Verd, you know better than that, even if nobody else does. They were on *your* back, twenty-seven adults and all their potential children, all waiting for you to tell them how to die. Then came the mutiny. Now you're free! They've all shifted to *my* back!"

His eyes left Verd's and ranged over his shocked, silent crew. "Idiots blindly taking orders from a damaged mechanical brain. Believing everything you're told. Lourdi!" he snapped. "What does 'one face' mean?"

Lourdi jumped. "It means the body doesn't rotate with respect to its primary."

"It doesn't mean the planet has only one face?"

"Wha-at?"

"The Earth has a back side to it."

"Sure!"

"What does it look like?"

"I don't know." Lourdi thought a moment. "The Brain knows. You remember you asked Chanda to make the Brain use the radar to check the back side. Then she couldn't get the Brain to show us the picture. We can't use the telescope because there's no light, not even infrared. It must be terribly cold. Colder than Pluto."

"You don't know," said Strac. "But I do. We're going down. Chanda?"

"Tell us about it," said Jimm Farmer.

"No," said Verd.

He had not known that he was going to speak. He had known only that they had given Strac the responsibility without the power to match it. But Strac felt the responsibility; he carried it in his bent shoulders and bleak expression, in his deep, painful breathing, in his previous attempts to pass the buck to someone else. Why would Strac want to land on Earth? Verd didn't know. But Strac must know what he was doing. Otherwise he couldn't have moved at all!

Someone had to back him up.

"No." Verd spoke with all the authority he could muster. "Chanda, take her down."

"Tell us about it," Jimm repeated. The authority backing his flat, menacing tone was his own titanic physical strength.

"No. Shut up, Jimm. Or we'll let you make all the decisions from now on."

Jimm Farmer thought it over, suddenly laughed and sat down. Chanda picked up her stylus and began tapping on the speaker.

The *Hogan's Goat* lay on her side, nearly in the center of a wide, ancient asteroid crater. There, marring the rounded spine with its long stinger, was the ragged, heat-stained hole that marked a meteor strike. There, along two-thirds of the length of her belly, was the gash a rock had made in the last seconds of the landing. And at the tail, forward of the braking spine, that static explosion of curved metal strips was where the photon drive had been torn free.

A small, fiercely bright Sun burned down from a black sky.

It had been a bad landing. Even at the start the Brain was a fraction of a second slow in adjusting ship's gravity, so that the floor had bucked queasily under them as they dropped. Then, when they were already falling toward the crater, Strac had suddenly added a new order. The photon drive had to be accessible after landing. Chanda had started tapping—and the ship had flipped on its side.

The *Hogan's Goat* had never been built to land on its side. Many of the passengers sported bruises. Avran Zooman had broken an arm. Without boosterspice the bone would be slow to heal.

A week of grinding labor was nearly over.

Only servomachinery now moved on the crater floor. From Verd's viewpoint most of the activity seemed to center around a gigantic silver tube which was aimed like a cannon at a point ten degrees above the horizon. The drive tube had been towed up against the crater wall, and a mountain of piled, heat-fused earth now buried its lower end. Cables and fuel pipes joined it higher up.

"Hi! Is that you, Captain?"

Verd winced. "I'm on top of the crater wall," he said, because Strac couldn't locate him from the sound of his voice. The indeterminate voice had to be Strac. Only Strac would bellow into a suit radio. "And I'm not the Captain."

Strac floated down beside him. "I thought I'd see the sights."

"Good. Have a seat."

"I find it strange to have to call you Verd," said the astrophysicist. "It used to be just 'Captain.'"

"Serves you right for staging a mutiny—Captain."

"I always knew my thirst for power would get me in trouble."

They watched as a tractor-mounted robot disconnected a fuel pipe from the drive, then rolled back. A moment later a wash of smoky flame burst from the pipe. The flame changed color and intensity a dozen times within a few seconds, then died as abruptly as it had begun. The robot waited for the white heat to leave the pipe, then rolled forward to reconnect it.

Verd asked, "Why are you so calm all of a sudden?"

"My job's over," Strac said with a shrug in his voice. "Now it's in the lap of Kdapt."

"Aren't you taking an awful chance?"

"Oh? You've guessed what I'm trying to do?"

"I hope it wasn't a secret. There's only one thing you could be doing, with the photon drive all laid out and braced like that. You're trying to spin the Earth."

"Why?" Strac baited him.

"You must be hoping there's air and water frozen on the dark side. But it seems like a thin chance. Why were you afraid to explain?"

"You put it that way, then ask why I didn't put it to a vote? Verd, would you have done what I did?"

"No. It's too risky."

"Suppose I tell you that I *know* the air and water is there. It has to be there. I can tell you what it looks like. It's a great shallow cap of ice, stratified out according to freezing points, with water ice on the bottom, then carbon dioxide, all the way up through a thick nitrogen layer to a few shifting pools of liquid helium. Surely you don't expect a one-face world to have a gaseous atmosphere? It would all freeze out on the night side. It has to!"

"It's there? There's air there? Your professional word?"

"My word as an astrophysicist. There's frozen gas back there."

Verd stretched like a great cat. He couldn't help himself. He could actually feel the muscles around his eyes and cheeks rippling as they relaxed, and a great grin crawled toward his ears. "You comedian!" he laughed. "Why didn't you say so?"

"Suppose I kept talking?"

Verd turned to look at him.

"You'll have thought of some of these things yourself. Can we breathe that air? Billions of years have passed. Maybe the composition of the air changed before it froze. Maybe too much of it boiled off into space while the Sun was a red giant. Maybe there's too much, generated by outgasing after the Moon was too far away to skim it off. Lourdi said the Sun is putting out about the right amount of heat, but just how close will it be to a livable temperature? Can Jimm Farmer make us topsoil? There'll be live soil on the night-side, possibly containing frozen live bacteria, but can we get there if we have to?

"Worst of all, can we spin the Earth in the first place? I know the drive's strong enough. I don't know about the Earth. There can't be any radioactivity left in the Earth's core, so the planet should be solid rock all the way to the center. But solid rock flows under pressure. We'll get earthquakes. Kdapt only knows how bad. Well, Captain, would you have taken all those risks?"

"She blows."

The drive was on.

Traces of hydrogen, too thin to stop a meteor, glowed faintly in the destroying light. A beam like a spotlight beam reached out over the sharp horizon, pointing dead east. Anything that light touched would flame and blow away on the wings of a photon wind. The drive nosed a little deeper into its tomb of lava.

The ground trembled. Verd turned on his flying unit, and Strac rose after him. Together they hovered over the quivering Earth. Other silver specks floated above the plain.

In space the drive would be generating over a hundred savage gravities. Here . . . almost none. Almost.

Little quick ripples came running in from the eastern horizon. They ran across the crater floor in parallel lines of dancing dust, coming closer and closer together. Rocks showered down from the old ringwall.

"Maybe I wouldn't have risked it," said Verd. "I don't know."

"That's why the Brain put me in charge. Did you see the oxygen ice as we went by the night side? Or was it too dark? To you this frozen atmosphere is pure imagination, isn't it?"

"I'll take your professional word."

"But I don't need to. I *know* it's there."

Lines of dust danced over the shaking ground. But the ripples were less violent, and were coming less frequently.

"The Brain was damaged," Verd said softly.

"Yes," said Strac, frowning down into the old crater. Suddenly he touched his controls and dropped. "Come on, Verd. In a few days there'll be air. We've got to be ready for wind and rain."

The Meddler

Someone was in my room.

It had to be one of Sinc's boys. He'd been stupid. I'd left the lights off. The yellow light now seeping under the door was all the warning I needed.

He hadn't used the door: the threads were still there. That left the fire escape outside the bedroom window.

I pulled my gun, moved back a little in the corridor to get elbow room. Then—I'd practiced it often enough to drive the management crazy—I kicked the door open and was into the room in one smooth motion.

He should have been behind the door, or crouching behind a table, or hidden in the closet with his eye to the keyhole. Instead he was right out in the middle of the living room, facing the wrong way. He'd barely started to turn when I pumped four GyroJet slugs into him. I saw the impacts twitching his shirt. One over the heart.

He was finished.

So I didn't slow down to watch him fall. I crossed the living-room rug in a diving run and landed behind the couch. He couldn't be alone. There had to be others. If one had been behind the couch he might have gotten me, but there wasn't. I scanned the wall behind me, but there was nothing to hide under. So I froze, waiting, listening.

Where were they? The one I'd shot couldn't have come alone.

I was peeved at Sinc. As long as he'd sent goons to waylay me, he might have sent a few who knew what they were doing. The one I'd shot hadn't had time to know he was in a fight.

"Why did you do that?"

Impossibly, the voice came from the middle of the living room, where I'd left a falling corpse. I risked a quick look and brought my head down fast. The afterimage:

He hadn't moved. There was no blood on him. No gun visible, but I hadn't seen his right hand.

Bulletproof vest? Sinc's boys had no rep for that kind of thing, but that had to be it. I stood up suddenly and fired, aiming between the eyes.

The slug smashed his right eye, off by an inch, and I knew he'd shaken me. I dropped back and tried to cool off.

No noises. Still no sign that he wasn't alone.

"I said, 'Why did you do that?' "

Mild curiosity colored his high-pitched voice. He didn't move as I stood up, and there was no hole in either eye.

"Why did I do what?" I asked cleverly.

"Why did you make holes in me? My gratitude for the gift of metal, of course, but—" He stopped suddenly, like he'd said too much and knew it. But I had other worries.

"Anyone else here?"

"Only we two are present. I beg pardon for invasion of privacy, and will indemnify—" He stopped again, as suddenly, and started over. "Who were you expecting?"

"Sinc's boys. I guess they haven't caught on yet. Sinc's boys want to make holes in *me*."

"Why?"

Could he be that stupid? "To turn me off! To kill me!"

He looked surprised, then furious. He was so mad he gurgled. "I should have been informed! Someone has been unforgivably sloppy!"

"Yah. Me. I thought you must be with Sinc. I shouldn't have shot at you. Sorry."

"Nothing," he smiled, instantly calm again.

"But I ruined your suit . . ." I trailed off. Holes showed in his jacket and shirt, but no blood. "Just what *are* you?"

He stood about five feet four, a round little man in an old-fashioned brown one-button suit. There was not a hair on him, not even eyelashes. No warts, no wrinkles, no character lines. A nebbish, one of these guys whose edges are all round, like someone forgot to put in the fine details.

He spread smoothly manicured hands. "I am a man like yourself."

"Nuts."

"Well," he said angrily, "you would have thought so if the preliminary investigation team had done their work properly!"

"You're a—martian?"

"I am *not* a martian. I am—" He gurgled. "Also I am an anthropologist. Your word. I am here to study your species."

"You're from outer space?"

"Very. The direction and distance are secret, of course. My very existence should have been secret." He scowled deeply. Rubber face, I thought, not knowing the half of it yet.

"I won't talk," I reassured him. "But you came at a bad time. Any minute now, Sinc's going to figure out who it is that's on his tail. Then he'll be on mine, and this dump'll be ground zero. I hate to brush you. I've never met a ... whatever."

"I too must terminate this interview, since you know me for what I am. But first, tell me of your quarrel. Why does Sinc want to make holes in you?"

"His name is Lester Dunhaven Sinclair the third. He runs every racket in this city. Look, we've got time for a drink— maybe. I've got scotch, bourbon—"

He shuddered. "No, I thank you."

"Just trying to set you at ease." I was a little miffed.

"Then perhaps I may adapt a more comfortable form, while you drink—whatever you choose. If you don't mind."

"Please yourself." I went to the rolling bar and poured bourbon and tap water, no ice. The apartment house was dead quiet. I wasn't surprised. I've lived here a couple of years now, and the other tenants have learned the routine. When guns go off, they hide under their beds and stay there.

"You won't be shocked?" My visitor seemed anxious. "If you are shocked, please say so at once."

And he melted. I stood there with the paper cup to my lip and watched him flow out of his one-button suit and take the compact shape of a half-deflated gray beach ball.

I downed the bourbon and poured more, no water. My hands stayed steady.

"I'm a private op," I told the martian. He'd extruded a convoluted something I decided was an ear. "When Sinc showed up about three years ago and started taking over the rackets, I stayed out of his way. He was the law's business, I figured. Then he bought the law, and that was okay too. I'm no crusader."

"Crusader?" His voice had changed. Now it was deep, and it sounded like something bubbling up from a tar pit.

"Never mind. I tried to stay clear of Sinc, but it didn't work. Sinc had a client of mine killed. Morrison, his name was. I was following Morrison's wife, getting evidence for a divorce. She was shacking up with a guy named Adler. I had all the evidence I needed when Morrison disappeared.

"Then I found out Adler was Sinc's right hand."

"Right hand? Nothing was said of hive cultures."

"Huh?"

"One more thing the prelim team will have to answer for. Continue talking. You fascinate me."

"I kept working on it. What could I do? Morrison was my client, and he was dead. I collected plenty of evidence against Adler, and I turned it over to the cops. Morrison's body never turned up, but I had good corpus delicti evidence. Anyway, Sinc's bodies never do turn up. They just disappear.

"I turned what I had over to the cops. The case was squashed. Somehow the evidence got lost. One night I got beat up."

"Beat up?"

"Almost any kind of impact," I told him, "can damage a human being."

"Really!" he gurgled. "All that water, I suppose."

"Maybe. In my line you have to heal fast. Well, that tore it. I started looking for evidence against Sinc himself. A week ago I sent Xeroxes off to the Feds. I let one of Sinc's boys find a couple of the copies. Bribery evidence, nothing exciting, but enough to hurt. I figured it wouldn't take Sinc long to figure out who made them. The Xerox machine I borrowed was in a building he owns."

"Fascinating. I think I will make holes in the Lady of Preliminary Investigation."

"Will that hurt?"

"She is not a—" gurgle. "She is a—" loud, shrill bird whistle.

"I get it. Anyway, you can see how busy I'm going to be. Much too busy to talk about, uh, anthropology. Any minute now I'll have Sinc's boys all over me, and the first one I kill I'll have the cops on me too. Maybe the cops'll come first. I dunno."

"May I watch? I promise not to get in your path."

"Why?"

He cocked his ear, if that was what it was. "An example. Your species has developed an extensive system of engineering using alternating current. We were surprised to find you transmitting electricity so far, and using it in so many ways. Some may even be worth imitating."

"That's nice. So?"

"Perhaps there are other things we can learn from you."

I shook my head. "Sorry, short stuff. This party's bound to get rough, and I don't want any bystanders getting hurt. *What the hell am I talking about.* Holes don't hurt you?"

"Very little hurts me. My ancestors once used genetic engineering to improve their design. My major weaknesses are susceptibility to certain organic poisons, and a voracious appetite."

"Okay, stay then. Maybe after it's all over you can tell me about Mars, or wherever you came from. I'd like that."

"Where I come from is classified. I can tell you about Mars."

"Sure, sure. How'd you like to raid the fridge while we wait? If you're so hungry all the time—hold it."

Sliding footsteps.

They were out there. A handful of them, if they were trying to keep it a secret. And these had to be from Sinc, because all the neighbors were under their beds by now.

The martian heard it too. "What shall I do? I cannot reach human form fast enough."

I was already behind the easy chair. "Then try something else. Something easy."

A moment later I had two matching black leather footstools. They both matched the easy chair, but maybe nobody'd notice.

The door slammed wide open. I didn't pull the trigger, because nobody was there. Just the empty hallway.

The fire escape was outside my bedroom window, but that window was locked and bolted and rigged with alarms. They wouldn't get in that way. Unless—

I whispered, "Hey! How did you get in?"

"Under the door."

So that was all right. The window alarms were still working. "Did any of the tenants see you?"

"No."

"Good." I get enough complaints from the management without *that*.

More faint rustling from outside the door. Then a hand and gun appeared for an instant, fired at random, vanished. Another hole in my walls. He'd had time to see my head, to place me. I ran low for the couch. I was getting set again, both eyes on the door, when a voice behind me said, "Stand up slow."

You had to admire the guy. He'd got through the window alarms without a twitch, into the living room without a sound. He was tall, olive-skinned, with straight black hair and black eyes. His gun was centered on the bridge of my nose.

I dropped the GyroJet and stood up. Pushing it now would only get me killed.

He was very relaxed, very steady. "That's a GyroJet, isn't it? Why not use a regular heater?"

"I like this," I told him. Maybe he'd come too close, or take his eyes off me, or—anything. "It's light as a toy, with no recoil. The gun is just a launching chamber for the rocket slugs, and they pack the punch of a forty-five."

"But, man! The slugs cost a buck forty-five each!"

"I don't shoot that many people."

"At those prices, I believe it. Okay, turn around slow. Hands in the air." His eyes hadn't left me for a moment.

I turned my back. Next would be a sap—

Something metal brushed against my head, feather-light. I whirled, struck at his gun hand and his larynx. Pure habit. I'd moved the instant the touch told me he was in reach.

He was stumbling back with his hand to his throat. I put a fist in his belly and landed the other on his chin. He dropped, trying to curl up. And sure enough, he was holding a sap.

But why hadn't he hit me with it? From the feel of it, he'd laid it gently on top of my head, carefully, as if he thought the sap might shatter.

"All right, stand easy." The hand and gun came through the doorway, attached to six feet of clean living. I knew him as Handel. He looked like any blond brainless hero, but he wasn't brainless, and he was no hero.

He said, "You're going to hate yourself for doing that."

The footstool behind him began to change shape.

"Dammit," I said, "that's not fair."

Handel looked comically surprised, then smiled winningly. "Two to one?"

"I was talking to my footstool."

"Turn around. We've got orders to bring you to Sinc, if we can. You could still get out of this alive."

I turned around. "I'd like to apologize."

"Save it for Sinc."

"No, honest. It wasn't my idea to have someone else mix in this. Especially—" Again I felt something brush against the side of my head. The martian must be doing something to stop the impact.

I could have taken Handel then. I didn't move. It didn't seem right that I could break Handel's neck when he couldn't touch me. Two to one I don't mind, especially when the other guy's the one. Sometimes I'll even let some civic-minded bystander help, if there's some chance he'll live through it. But *this* . . .

"What's not fair?" asked a high, complaining voice.

Handel screamed like a woman. I turned to see him charge into the door jamb, back up a careful two feet, try for the door again and make it.

Then I saw the footstool.

He was already changing, softening in outline, but I got an idea of the shape Handel had seen. No wonder it had softened his mind. I felt it softening my bones, melting the marrow, and I closed my eyes and whispered, "Dammit, you were supposed to *watch*."

"You told me the impact would damage you."

"That's not the point. Detectives are *always* getting hit on the head. We *expect* it."

"But how can I learn anything from watching you if your little war ends so soon?"

"Well, what do you learn if you keep jumping in?"

"You may open your eyes."

I did. The martian was back to his nebbish form. He had fished a pair of orange shorts out of his pile of clothes. "I do not understand your objection," he said. "This Sinc will kill you if he can. Do you want that?"

"No, but—"

"Do you believe that your side is in the right?"

"Yes, but—"

"Then why should you not accept my help?"

I wasn't sure myself. It felt wrong. It was like sneaking a suitcase bomb into Sinc's mansion and blowing it up.

I thought about it while I checked the hall. Nobody there. I closed the door and braced a chair under the knob. The dark one was still with us: he was trying to sit up.

"Look," I told the martian. "Maybe I can explain, maybe I can't. But if I don't get your word to stay out of this, I'll leave town. I swear it. I'll just drop the whole thing. Understand?"

"No."

"Will you promise?"

"Yes."

The spanish type was rubbing his throat and staring at the martian. I didn't blame him. Fully dressed, the martian could have passed for a man, but not in a pair of orange undershorts. No hair or nipples marked his chest, no navel pitted his belly. The hood turned a flashing white smile on me and asked, "Who's he?"

"I'll ask the questions. Who're you?"

"Don Domingo." His accent was soft and spanish. If he was worried, it didn't show. "Hey, how come you didn't fall down when I hit you?"

"I said I'll ask the—"

"Your face is turning pink. Are you embarrassed about something?"

"Dammit, Domingo, where's Sinc? Where were you supposed to take me?"

"The place."

"What place? The Bel Air place?"

"That's the one. You know, you have the hardest head—"

"Never mind that!"

"Okay okay. What will you do now?"

I couldn't call the law in. "Tie you up, I guess. After this is over, I'll turn you in for assault."

"After this is over, you won't be doing much, I think. You will live as long as they shoot at your head, but when—"

"Now *drop* that!"

The martian came out of the kitchen. His hand was flowing around a tin of corned beef, engulfing it tin and all. Domingo's eyes went wide and round.

Then the bedroom exploded.

It was a fire bomb. Half the living room was in flames in an instant. I scooped up the GyroJet, stuck it in my pocket.

The second bomb exploded in the hall. A blast of flame blew the door inward, picked up the chair I'd used to brace the door and flung it across the room.

"No!" Domingo yelled. "Handel was supposed to wait! *Now* what?"

Now we roast, I thought, stumbling back with my arm raised against the flames. A calm tenor voice asked, "Are you suffering from excessive heat?"

"Yes! Dammit, yes!"

A huge rubber ball slammed into my back, hurling me at the wall. I braced my arms to take up some of the impact. It was still going to knock me silly. Just before I reached it, the wall disappeared. It was the outside wall. Completely off balance, I dashed through an eight-foot hole and out into the empty night, six floors above concrete.

I clenched my teeth on the scream. The ground came up—the ground came up—where the hell was the ground? I opened my eyes. Everything was happening in slow motion. A second stretched to eternity. I had time to see strollers turning to crane upward, and to spot Handel near a corner of the building, holding a handkerchief to his bleeding nose. Time to look over my shoulder as Domingo stood against a flaming background, poised in slow-motion in an eight-foot circle cut through the wall of my apartment.

Flame licked him. He jumped.

Slow motion?

He went past me like a falling safe. I saw him hit; I heard him hit. It's not a good sound. Living on Wall Street during November '68, I heard it night after night during the weeks following the election. I never got used to it.

Despite everything my belly and groin were telling me, I was not falling. I was sinking, like through water. By now half a dozen people were watching me settle. They all had their mouths open. Something poked me in the side, and I slapped at it and found myself clutching a .45 slug. I plucked another off my cheek. Handel was shooting at me.

I fired back, not aiming too well. If the martian hadn't been "helping" me I'd have blown his head off without a thought. As it was—anyway, Handel turned and ran.

I touched ground and walked away. A dozen hot, curious eyes bored into my back, but nobody tried to stop me.

There was no sign of the martian. Nothing else followed me either. I spent half an hour going through the usual contortions to shake a tail, but that was just habit. I wound up in a small, anonymous bar.

My eyebrows were gone, giving me a surprised look. I found myself studying my reflection in the bar mirror, looking for other signs that I'd been in a fight.

My face, never particularly handsome, has been dignified by scar tissue over the years, and my light brown hair never wants to stay in place. I had to move the part a year back to match a bullet crease in my scalp. The scars were all there, but I couldn't find any new cuts or bruises. My clothes weren't mussed. I didn't hurt anywhere. It was all unreal and vaguely dissatisfying.

But my next brush with Sinc would be for real.

I had my GyroJet and a sparse handful of rocket slugs in one pocket. Sinc's mansion was guarded like Fort Knox. And Sinc would be expecting me; he knew I wouldn't run.

We knew a lot about each other, considering we'd never met.

Sinc was a teetotaler. Not a fanatic; there was liquor on the premises of his mansion/fort. But it had to be kept out of Sinc's sight.

A woman usually shared his rooms. Sinc's taste was excellent. He changed his women frequently. They never left angry, and that's unusual. They never left poor, either.

I'd dated a couple of Sinc's exes, letting them talk about Sinc if they cared to. The consensus:

Sinc was an all-right guy, a spender, inventive and enthusiastic where it counted.

And neither particularly wanted to go back.

Sinc paid well and in full. He'd bail a man out of jail if the occasion arose. He never crossed anyone. Stranger yet, nobody ever crossed him. I'd had real trouble learning anything about Sinc. Nobody had wanted to talk.

But he'd crossed Domingo. That had caught us both by surprise.

Put it different. Someone had crossed Domingo. Domingo had been waiting for rescue, not bombs. So had I. It was Sinc's policy to pull his boys out if they got burned.

Either Domingo had been crossed against Sinc's orders, or Sinc was serious about wanting me dead.

I meet all kinds of people. I like it that way. By now I knew enough about Sinc to want to know more, much more. I wanted to meet him. And I was damn glad I'd shaken the martian, because . . .

Just what was it that bugged me about the martian?

It wasn't the strangeness. I meet all kinds. The way he shifted shape could throw a guy, but I don't bug easy.

Manners? He was almost too polite. And helpful.

Much too helpful.

That was part of it. The lines of battle had been drawn . . . and then something had stepped in from outer space. He was deus ex machina, the angel who descends on a string to set everything right, and incidentally to ruin the story. Me tackling Sinc with the martian's help was like a cop planting evidence. It was wrong. But more than that, it seemed to rob the thing of all its point, so that nothing mattered.

I shrugged angrily and had another drink. The bartender was trying to close. I drank up fast and walked out in a clump of tired drunks.

My car had tools I could use, but by now there'd be a bomb under the hood. I caught a cab and gave him an address on Bellagio, a couple of blocks from Sinc's place, if you can number anything in that area in "blocks." It's all hills, and the streets can drive you nuts. Sinc's home ground was a lumpy triangle with twisted sides, and big. It must have cost the Moon to landscape. One afternoon I'd walked past it, casing it. I couldn't see anything except through the gate. The fence was covered by thick climbing ivy. There were alarms in the ivy.

I waited till the taxi was gone, then loaded the GyroJet and started walking. That left one rocket slug still in my pocket.

In that neighborhood there was something to duck behind every time a car came by. Trees, hedges, gates with massive stone pillars. When I saw headlights I ducked, in case Sinc's boys were patrolling. A little walking took me to within sight of the ivy fence. Any closer and I'd be spotted.

So I ducked onto the property of one of Sinc's neighbors.

The place was an oddity: a rectangular pool with a dinky poolhouse at one end, a main house that was all right angles, and, between the two, a winding brook with a small bridge across it and trees hanging over the water. The brook must have been there before the house, and some of the trees too. It was a bit of primal wilderness that jarred strangely with all the right angles around it. I stuck with the brook, naturally.

This was the easy part. A burglary rap was the worst that could happen to me.

I found a fence. Beyond was asphalt, streetlamps, and then the ivy barrier to Sinc's domain.

Wire cutters? In the car. I'd be a sitting duck if I tried to go over. It could have been sticky, but I moved along the fence, found a rusty gate, and persuaded the padlock to open for me. Seconds later I was across the street and huddled against the ivy, just where I'd taken the trouble to hunt out a few of the alarms.

Ten minutes later I went over.

Sitting duck? Yes. I had a clear view of the house, huge and mostly dark. In the moment before I dropped, someone would have had a clear view of me, too, framed by lamplight at the top of the fence.

I dropped between inner and outer fence and took a moment to think. I hadn't expected an inner fence. It was four feet of solid brick topped by six feet of wiring; and the wiring had a look of high voltage.

Now what?

Maybe I could find something to short out the fence. But that would alert the house just as I was going over. Still, it might be the best chance.

Or I could go back over the ivy and try the gate defenses. Maybe I could even bluff my way through. Sinc must be as curious about me by now as I was about him. Everything I knew about Sinc was in the present tense. Of his past I knew only that there were no records of his past. But if Sinc had heard about my floating lightly down from a sixth-floor window, not unlike Mary Poppins ... it might be worth a try. At least I'd live long enough to see what Sinc looked like.

Or—

"Hello. How does your war proceed?"

I sighed. He drifted down beside me, still man-shaped, dressed in a dark suit. I saw my mistake when he got closer. He'd altered his skin color to make a suit, shirt, and tie. At a distance it would pass. Even close up, he had nothing that needed hiding.

"I thought I'd got rid of you," I complained. "Are you bigger?" At a guess, his size had nearly doubled.

"Yes. I became hungry."

"You weren't kidding about your appetite."

"The war," he reminded me. "Are you planning to invade?"

"I was. I didn't know about this fence."

"Shall I—?"

"No! No, you shall not whatever you were thinking about. Just watch!"

"What am I to watch? You have done nothing for several minutes."

"I'll think of something."

"Of course."

"But whatever I do, I won't use your help, now or ever. If you want to watch, fine, be my guest. But don't help."

"I do not understand why not."

"It's like bugging a guy's telephone. Sinc has certain rights, even if he is a crook. He's immune from cruel and unusual punishment. The FBI can't bug his phone. You can't kill him unless you try him first, unless he's breaking a law at the time. And he shouldn't have to worry about armed attack by martians!"

"Surely if Sinc himself breaks the rules—"

"There are *rules* for dealing with lawbreakers!" I snapped.

The martian didn't answer. He stood beside me, seven feet tall and pudgy, a dark, manlike shape in the dim light from the house.

"Hey. How do you do all those things you do? Just a talent?"

"No. I carry implements." Something poked itself out of his baby-smooth chest, something hard that gleamed like metal. "This, for instance, damps momentum. Other portable artifacts lessen the pull of gravity, or reprocess the air in my lung."

"You keep them all inside you?"

"Why not? I can make fingers of all sizes inside me."

"Oh."

"You have said that there are rules for dealing with rule breakers. Surely you have already broken those rules. You have trespassed on private property. You have departed the scene of an accident, Don Domingo's death. You have——"

"All right."

"Then——"

"All right, I'll try again." I was wasting too much time. Getting over the fence was important. But so, somehow, was this. Because in a sense the martian was right. This had nothing to do with rules . . .

"It has nothing to do with rules," I told him. "At least, not exactly. What counts is power. Sinc has taken over this city, and he'll want others too, later. He's got too much power. That's why someone has to stop him.

"And you give me too much power. A—a man who has too much power loses his head. I don't trust myself with you on my side. I'm a detective. If I break a law I expect to be jailed for it unless I can explain why. It makes me careful. If I tackle a crook who can whip me, I get bruised. If I shoot someone who doesn't deserve it, I go to prison. It all tends to make me careful. But with you around——"

"You lose your caution," said the dark bulk beside me. He spoke almost musingly, with more of human expression than I'd heard before. "You may be tempted to take more power than is good for you. I had not expected your species to be so wise."

"You thought we were stupid?"

"Perhaps. I had expected you to be grateful and eager for any help I might give. Now I begin to understand your attitude. We, too, try to balance out the amount of power given to individuals. What is that noise?"

It was a rustling, a scampering, barely audible but not at all furtive.

"I don't know."

"Have you decided upon your next move?"

"Yes. I—damn! Those are dogs!"

"What are dogs?"

Suddenly they were there. In the dark I couldn't tell what breed, but they were big, and they didn't bark. In a rustling of claws scrabbling on cement, they rounded the curve of the brick wall, coming from both sides, terribly fast. I hefted the GyroJet and knew there were twice as many dogs as I had shots.

Lights came on, bright and sudden, all over the grounds. I fired, and a finger of flame reached out and touched one of the dogs. He fell, tumbling, lost in the pack.

All the lights went deep red, blood red. The dogs stopped. The noise stopped. One dog, the nearest, was completely off the ground, hovering in mid-leap, his lips skinned back from sharp ruby teeth.

"It seems I have cost you time," the martian murmured. "May I return it?"

"What did you do?"

"I have used the damper of inertia in a projected field. The effect is as if time has stopped for all but us. In view of the length of time I have kept you talking, it is the least I can do."

Dogs to the left and dogs to the right, and lights all the hell over the place. I found men with rifles placed like statues about the wide lawn.

"I don't know if you're right or wrong," I said. "I'll be dead if you turn off that time stopper. But this is the last time. Okay?"

"Okay. We will use only the inertia damper."

"I'll move around to the other side of the house. Then you turn off the gadget. It'll give me some time to find a tree."

We went. I stepped carefully among the statues of dogs. The martian floated behind like a gigantic, pudgy ghost.

The channel between inner and outer fence went all the

way around to the gate at the front of the house. Near the
gate the inner fence pinched against the outer, and ended.
But before we reached that point I found a tree. It was big,
and it was old, and one thick branch stretched above the
fence to hover over our heads.

"Okay, turn off the gadget."

The deep red lights glared a sudden white.

I went up the ivy. Long arms and oversized hands are a
big help to my famous monkey act. No point now in worrying about alarms. I had to balance standing on the outer
fence to reach the branch with my fingers. When I put my
weight on it it dipped three feet and started to creak. I
moved along hand over hand, and swung up into the leaves
before my feet could brush the inner fence. At a comfortable
crotch I settled myself to take stock.

There were at least three riflemen on the front lawn. They
were moving in a search pattern, but they didn't expect to
find anything. All the action was supposed to be in back.

The martian floated into the air and moved across the
fence.

He nicked the top going over. A blue spark snapped, and
he dropped like a sack of wheat. He landed against the
fence, grounded now, and electricity leaped and sizzled.
Ozone and burnt meat mixed in the cold night air. I dropped
out of the tree and ran to him. I didn't touch him. The
current would have killed me.

It had certainly killed him.

And that was something I'd never thought of. Bullets
didn't faze him. He could produce miracles on demand. How
could he be killed by a simple electric fence? If he'd only
mentioned that! But he'd been surprised even to find that we
had electricity.

I'd let a bystander be killed. The one thing I'd sworn I
would never do again . . .

Now he was nothing like human. Metal things poked
gleaming from the dead mass that had been an anthropologist from the stars. The rustle of current had stopped seconds
ago. I pulled one of the metal gadgets out of the mass, slid it
in a pocket, and ran.

They spotted me right away. I took a zigzag course around a fenced tennis court, running for the front door. There were man-length windows on either side of the door. I ran up the steps, brought the GyroJet down in a hurried slashing blow that broke most of the panes in one window, and dove off the steps into a line of bushes.

When things happen that fast, your mind has to fill the gaps between what you saw and what you didn't. All three gunmen chased me frantically up the steps and through the front door, shouting at the tops of their lungs.

I moved along the side of the house, looking for a window.

Somebody must have decided I couldn't go through all that jagged glass. He must have outshouted the others, too, because I heard the hunt start again. I climbed a piece of wall, found a little ledge outside a darkened second-floor window. I got the window up without too much noise.

For the first time on this crazy night, I was beginning to think I knew what I was doing. That seemed odd, because I didn't know much about the layout of the house, and I hadn't the faintest idea where I was. But at least I knew the rules of the game. The variable, the martian, the deus ex machina, was out of the picture.

The rules were: whoever saw me would kill me if he could. No bystanders, no good guys would be here tonight. There would be no complex moral choices. I would not be offered supernatural help, in return for my soul or otherwise. All I had to do was try to stay alive.

(But a bystander had died.)

The bedroom was empty. Two doors led to a closet and a bathroom. Yellow light seeped under a third door. No choice here. I pulled the GyroJet and eased the third door open.

A face jerked up over the edge of a reading chair. I showed it the gun, kept it aimed as I walked around in front of the chair. Nobody else was in the room.

The face could have used a shave. It was beefy, middle-aged, but symmetrical enough except for an oversized nose. "I know you," it said, calmly enough considering the circumstances.

THE MEDDLER 141

"I know you too." It was Adler, the one who'd gotten me into this mess, first by cohabiting with Morrison's wife and then by killing Morrison.

"You're the guy Morrison hired," said Adler. "The tough private eye. Bruce Cheseborough. Why couldn't you let well enough alone?"

"I couldn't afford to."

"You couldn't afford not to. Have some coffee."

"Thanks. You know what'll happen if you yell or anything?"

"Sure." He picked up a water glass, dumped the water in the wastebasket. He picked up a silver thermos and poured coffee into his own coffee cup and into the water glass, moving slowly and evenly. He didn't want to make me nervous.

He himself was no more than mildly worried. That was reassuring, in a way, because he probably wouldn't do anything stupid. But . . . I'd seen this same calm in Don Domingo, and I knew the cause. Adler and Domingo and everyone else who worked for Sinc, they all had perfect faith in him. Whatever trouble they were in, Sinc would get them out.

I watched Adler take a healthy gulp of coffee before I touched the glass. The coffee was black and strong, heavily laced with good brandy. My first gulp tasted so good I damn near smiled at Adler.

Adler smiled back. His eyes were wide and fixed, as if he were afraid to look away from me. As if he expected me to explode. I tried to think of a way he could have dropped something in the coffee without drinking it himself. There wasn't any.

"You made a mistake," I told him, and gulped more coffee. "If my name had been Rip Hammer or Mike Hero, I might have dropped the whole thing when I found out you were with Sinc's boys. But when your name is Bruce Cheseborough, Junior, you can't afford to back out of a fight."

"You should have. You might have lived." He said it without concentrating on it. A puzzled frown tugged at the corners of his eyes and mouth. He was still waiting for something to happen.

"Tell you what. You write me out a confession, and I can leave here without killing anyone. Won't that be nice?"

"Sure. What should I confess to?"

"Killing Morrison."

"You don't expect me to do that."

"Not really."

"I'm going to surprise you." Adler got up, still slow, and went behind the desk. He kept his hands high until I was around behind him. "I'll write your damn confession. You know why? Because you'll never use it. Sinc'll see to that."

"If anyone comes through that door—"

"I know, I know." He started writing. While he was at it, I examined the tool I'd taken from the martian's corpse. It was white shiny metal, with a complex shape that like nothing I'd ever seen. Like the plastic guts in a toy gun, half melted and then cooled, so that all the parts were merged and rounded. I had no idea what it did. Anyway, it was no good to me. I could see slots where buttons or triggers were buried, but they were too small for fingers. Tweezers might have reached them, or a hatpin.

Alder handed me the paper he'd been writing on. He'd made it short and pointed: motive, means, details of time. Most of it I already knew.

"You don't say what happened to the body."

"Same thing that happened to Domingo."

"Domingo?"

"Domingo, sure. When the cops came to pick him up in back of your place, he was gone. Even the bloodstains were gone. A miracle, right?" Adler smiled nastily. When I didn't react he looked puzzled.

"How?" I asked him.

Adler shrugged uncomfortably. "You already know, don't you? I won't write it down. It would bring Sinc in. You'll have to settle for what you've got."

"Okay. Now I tie you up and wend my way homeward."

Adler was startled. He couldn't have faked it. "Now?"

"Sure. You killed my client, not Sinc."

He grinned, not believing me. And he still thought something was about to happen.

I used the bathrobe sash for his arms and a handkerchief for a gag. There were other bathrobes in the closet to finish the job. He still didn't believe I was going to leave, and he was still waiting for something to happen. I left him on the bed, in the dark.

Now what?

I turned off the lights in the sitting room and went to the window. The lawn was alive with men and dogs and far too much light. That was the direct way out.

I had Adler's hide in my pocket. Adler, who had killed my client. Was I still chasing Sinc? Or should I try to get clear with that piece of paper?

Get clear, of course.

I stood by the window, picking out shadows. There was a lot of light, but the shadows of bushes and trees were jet black. I found a line of hedge, lighted on this side; but I could try the other. Or move along *that* side of the tennis court, then hop across to *that* odd-looking statue—

The door opened suddenly, and I whirled.

A man in dark slacks and a smoking jacket stood facing my gun. Unhurriedly, he stepped through the door and closed it behind him.

It was Sinc. Lester Dunhaven Sinclair III was a man in perfect condition, not a pound overweight or underweight, with gymnasium muscles. I guessed his age at thirty-four or so. Once before I'd seen him, in public, but never close enough to see what I saw now: that his thick blond hair was a wig.

He smiled at me. "Cheseborough, isn't it?"

"Yah."

"What did you do with my . . . lieutenant?" He looked me up and down. "I gather he's still with us."

"In the bedroom. Tied up." I moved around to lock the door to the hall.

I understood now why Sinc's men had made him into

something like a feudal overlord. He measured up. He inspired confidence. His confidence in himself was total. Looking at him, I could almost believe that nothing could stand against him.

"I gather you were too intelligent to try the coffee. A pity," said Sinc. He seemed to be examining my gun, but with no trace of fear. I tried to think it was a bluff, but I couldn't. No man could put across such a bluff. His twitching muscles would give him away. I began to be afraid of Sinc.

"A pity," he repeated. "Every night for the past year Adler has gone to bed with a pot of coffee spiked with brandy. Handel too."

What was he talking about? The coffee hadn't affected me at all. "You've lost me," I said.

"Have I?" Smiling as if he'd won a victory, Sinc began to gurgle. It was eerily familiar, that gurgle. I felt the rules changing again, too fast to follow. Smiling, gurgling rhythmically, Sinc put a hand in his pants pocket and pulled out an automatic. He took his time about it.

It was not a big gun, but it was a gun; and the moment I knew that, I fired.

A GyroJet rocket slug burns its solid fuel in the first twenty-five feet, and moved from there on momentum. Sinc was twenty-five feet away. Flame reached out to tap him on the shoulder joint, and Sinc smiled indulgently. His gun was steady on the bridge of my nose.

I fired at his heart. No effect. The third shot perforated the space between his eyes. I saw the hole close, and I knew. Sinc was cheating too.

He fired.

I blinked. Cold fluid trickled down from my forehead, stung my eyes, dribbled across my lips. I tasted rubbing alcohol.

"You're a martian too," I said.

"No need for insult," Sinc said mildly. He fired again. The gun was a squirtgun, a plastic kid's toy shaped like an automatic. I wiped the alcohol out of my eyes and looked at him.

"Well," said Sinc. "Well." He reached up, peeled his hair off, and dropped it. He did the same with his eyebrows and eyelashes. "Well, where is he?"

"He told me he was an . . . anthropologist. Was he lying?"

"Sure, Cheseborough. He was the Man. The Law. He's tracked me over distances you couldn't even write down." Sinc backed up against a wall. "You wouldn't even understand what my people called my crime. And you've no reason to protect him. He used you. Every time he stopped a bullet for you, it was to make me think you were him. That's why he helped you put on a floating act. That's why he disposed of Domingo's body. You were his stalking-horse. I'm supposed to kill you while he's sneaking up on me. He'll sacrifice you without a qualm. Now *where is he?*"

"Dead. He didn't know about electric fences."

A voice from the hall, Handel's voice, bellowed, "Mr. Sinclair! Are you all right in there?"

"I have a guest," Sinc called out. "He has a gun."

"What do we do?"

"Don't do anything," Sinc called to him. And then he started to laugh. He was losing his human contours, "relaxing" because I already knew what he was.

"I wouldn't have believed it," he chuckled. "He tracked me all that way to die on an electric fence!" His chuckles cut off like a broken tape, making me wonder how real they were, how real his laughter could be with his no doubt weird breathing system. "The current couldn't kill him, of course. It must have shorted his airmaker and blown the battery."

"The spiked coffee was for him," I guessed. "He said he could be killed by organic poisons. He meant alcohol."

"Obviously. And all I did was give you a free drink," he chuckled.

"I've been pretty gullible. I believed what your women told me."

"*They* didn't know." He did a pretty accurate double take. "You thought . . . Cheseborough, have I made rude comments about your sex life?"

"No. Why?"

"Then you can leave mine alone."

He had to be kidding. No he didn't; he could take any shape he liked. Wow, I thought. Sinc's really gone native. Maybe he *was* laughing, or thought he was.

Sinc moved slowly toward me. I backed away, holding the useless gun.

"You realize what happens now?"

I took a guess. "Same thing that happened to Domingo's body. All your embarrassing bodies."

"Exactly. Our species is known for its enormous appetite." He moved toward me, the squirt gun forgotten in his right hand. His muscles had sagged and smoothed. Now he was like the first step in making a clay model of a man. But his mouth was growing larger, and his teeth were two sharp-edged horseshoes.

I fired once more.

Something smashed heavily against the door. Sinc didn't hear it. Sinc was melting, losing all form as he tried to wrap himself around his agony. From the fragments of his shattered plastic squirt gun, rubbing alcohol poured over what had been his hand and dripped to the floor.

The door boomed again. Something splintered.

Sinc's hand was bubbling, boiling. Sinc, screaming, was flowing out of his slacks and smoking jacket. And I ... I snapped out of whatever force was holding me rooted, and I picked up the silver thermos and poured hot spiked coffee over whatever it was that writhed on the floor.

Sinc bubbled all over. White metal machinery extruded itself from the mass and lay on the rug.

The door crackled and gave. By then I was against the wall, ready to shoot anything that looked my way. Handel burst into the room and stopped dead.

He stood there in the doorway, while the stars grew old and went out. Nothing, I felt, could have torn his eyes from that twitching, bubbling mass. Gradually the mass stopped moving ... and Handel gulped, got his throat working, shrieked, and ran from the room.

I heard the meaty thud as he collided with a guard, and I

heard him babbling, "Don't go in there! Don't . . . oh, don't
. . ." and then a sob, and the sound of uneven running feet.

I went into the bedroom and out the window. The grounds
still blazed with light, but I saw no motion. Anyway, there
was nothing out there but dogs and men.

Dry Run

By habit Simpson was a one-hand driver. On this day he drove with both hands wrapped tight around the wheel, strangling it. He looked straight ahead, down the curving length of the freeway, and he stayed in the right-center lane.

He wanted a cigarette; yet he was almost afraid to let go of the wheel. The air-conditioning nozzle blew icy air up at his face and down at his belt buckle; icy because of the way he was perspiring. He felt the weakness in his bowels, and he cursed silently, trying to relax.

The dog in the trunk—

Too late now, too late to change his mind—

He stabbed a finger at the cigarette lighter, missed—Jesus! He'd only been driving the Buick for five years!—found it and pushed it in. He fumbled a Camel from the central glove compartment, one-handed, without looking. Traffic was not too heavy. It was past seven o'clock, though the July Sun was still a falling glory below red streamers of cloud. A few cars had their lights on, unnecessarily. Were the drivers afraid they'd forget later? The cars in this lane were doing sixty to sixty-five. Usually Simpson chose the fast lane. This time was different. No risks on this trip.

Too late now, too late to back out. He wouldn't if he could. He lit the cigarette, dragged, put the lighter back, and gripped the wheel again with both hands. The cigarette bent and flattened between his fingers.

Red taillights. This lane was slowing. He touched the brake with his foot, eased down, harder. Hard! He tried to push the brake through the floor. He stopped a foot behind a vintage Cadillac, and stalled. Simpson swore and turned the ignition hard over. The motor caught instantly.

It didn't matter. Nobody was moving.

Overhead were the swooping concrete noodles of the Santa Monica Freeway ramps. A carpet of cars was stalled underneath, stalled for as far ahead as Simpson could see. Then there was motion in the distance. He waited.

The vintage Cadillac jerked half a car length forward. Simpson followed. Another ripple of motion, another car length forward.

The freeway shouldn't be this crowded. Seven-thirty on a week-night? He'd picked his time carefully enough. What was happening?

The Cad moved again. Its driver looked back over his shoulder: angry, middle-aged, sweaty, and somewhat overweight. He looked like he'd bite anyone who came close enough.

Simpson felt the same way. He eased forward . . .

Murray Simpson was six inches too tall for the driver's seat of the Buick. He banged his elbows and knees getting in and out. The driver's seat cramped his legs, bending them too far at the knee, even when it was as far back as it would go.

In repose he always looked unhappy. He had that kind of face. His most genuine laughter looked forced. See him now, stalled in a traffic jam on the San Diego Freeway in a car too small for him. Stalled partway through a murder plan which was too complex to begin with . . .

He looked frantic. His brown eyes burned; his no-color hair had lost all semblance of civilization. His forgotten cigarette burned threateningly between white knuckles.

Ahead of the blue Cadillac was a Jaguar convertible whose custom paint job glowed with fiery tangerine brilliance. Ahead of that, a long gray anonymous Detroit car with huge delta fins. The gray car was stalled.

Someone behind Simpson was honking madly.

Cars poured into the gap in his lane, the gap ahead of the stalled car.

At Hermosa Beach the red tide was in. Trillions and quadrillions of plankton made a dirty red-and-brown soup of the ocean. By night the breakers glowed with cold blue fire. By night and day, the ocean air stank of too much life.

In the trunk of the Buick, Simpson's dun-colored Great Dane lay dead with a hole in his head. He was beginning to stiffen.

No room to get out of this lane. Simpson clenched his teeth and clung to his temper. Part of him wanted to stamp on the throttle and swoop out into the next lane, and damn the car that got in his way! But there was Harvey in the trunk, with his head in a Baggy. Simpson lit another cigarette.

What was Janet doing now? Who was she with? Did Simpson know him? No; Janet wasn't stupid, nor was the divorce yet final. Anyone with her now would be female.

Had she missed Harvey yet? Was she searching for him now, wondering how he'd got out, hoping he hadn't reached the street?

How would Janet look in the trunk of the Buick, with her head in a Baggy to hold the blood?

Cars swept by on the left and right, going ten and fifteen miles per hour.

A woman in a peach-colored dress got out of the gray car and opened the hood. She fiddled in the guts of the motor, then got back in. The gray car lurched forward.

She'd fixed it! Amazing!

And the whole lane crawled off at ten miles per hour, southbound on the San Diego Freeway. Toward the beaches. Toward Simpson's tiny house on the Strand at Hermosa Beach.

Driving was torture. Ripples crawled backward along the lines of cars. Some deadhead in front was moving in spurts, and the spurts became waves traveling backward, communicating their motion to every car behind him. Accelerator, brake, accelerator, brake. Brake! Accelerate. Maddeningly slow. There was the car that had blocked the lanes, twisted across the right lanes with its side smashed in, a police car alongside. Now the lanes moved faster.

On Simpson's left they were getting up to speed. Simpson saw a gap. He twisted the wheel, depressed the throttle, and looked quickly over his shoulder. Nobody coming . . . he stamped on the throttle and brought his eyes back to the road.

Every car in his lane must have stopped dead the moment he turned his head. His foot was still on the throttle when he hit.

Discontinuity. He knew he was about to crash . . . and he was getting out to look at the damage. He'd bumped his head, and his ribs must have smacked hard into the steering wheel, but he had no trouble walking.

He walked through a nightmare.

The Buick's hood looked like a squashed banana. The fat man in the Cadillac was getting out, rubbing his thick neck, his eyes squinted against pain. Whiplash, thought Simpson, and moved toward him.

Then the weakness came, and Simpson dropped hard on his knees. The shock should have hurt, but it didn't. "Sorry," Simpson told the man. *Sorry about your car, your neck. Sorry to be such a fool. Sorry, I feel weak. Sorry.* He fainted.

He knew he had fainted, though he had not felt his chin hit concrete. Now, without transition, he was totally alert. But alert to what?

There was darkness around him, and a lack of sensation. No sound. Nothing to see or feel. No up or down. The position of his body was a mystery. He visualized himself in a hospital bed, his spinal cord severed at the neck, his eyes bandaged. The thought should have frightened him. It didn't.

Once he'd smoked marijuana. It was unplanned; he'd seen some friends smoking a small-bowled cigarette pipe, using a mechanical roller to make their own cigarettes, and curiosity had got the better of him. He remembered the awful taste at the back of his nose, and the deep, all-embracing peace, and a queer somatic hallucination: the feeling that all the mass of his body had withdrawn into his feet, below a line drawn at the ankles. It seemed that he could lean as far as he liked in any direction, and he would not fall, because his center of mass was only an inch above the floor.

The deep peace was the same, but now his body was entirely massless. As before, his memory was unimpaired. The body in the trunk, the crash ... how, now, could he keep Harvey's death a secret? ... But it didn't seem to matter.

Suddenly he knew why.

He was dead. Murray Simpson was a dead issue, an embarrassing mass of tissue associated with an equally embarrassing mass of torn metal. And that didn't matter either.

The voice spoke close in front of him. "That was silly, Simpson."

Simpson tried to move. Massless body? He had no body at all. He was a viewpoint. Blind, motionless, without sensation ... he waited.

"The worst possible time to die is when you're involved in a murder." There was no character to that voice, no accent, no timbre, no emphasis, no loudness or softness. It was neither sharp nor dull, neither hoarse nor smooth. A voice with no *handle*. Like print in a typewriter, that voice.

Simpson said, "Murder?" To his own horror, his voice was exactly like the other's.

"Do you deny it?"

"I admit to killing a dog. My own dog, Harvey, a Great Dane."

"Not your own. Harvey belonged to you and to Janet Grey Simpson, your wife. Your wife has had possession of Harvey for seven months, ever since the two of you separated. Do you deny your intent to commit murder?"

Life after death. Reward and punishment? Simpson said, "I refuse to answer. Are you my judge?"

"No. Another will judge you. I collect only evidence, and you."

Simpson didn't answer. The strange peace was still with him, and he felt that he'd already found the right answer.

"Well, we must find out," said the voiceless voice.

What a weird nightmare, Simpson thought, and tried to pull himself awake. *I dreamed I was in an accident ... at the worst possible time ... I'd already killed Harvey ... poor Harvey. Why would I pick Harvey?* There were voices around him.

Cold reality touched him, icy cold, icy and rough against his cheek. He lay on hard concrete. His chin hurt, and his belly hurt below the edge of his rib cage.

He looked up into the face of a policeman. "Am I dying?"

"Ambulance will be here ... moment."

The car! Harvey! He tried to say, "What did you do with the car?"

The policeman spoke calmly. " ... Take it to ... get it whenever ... address ..." His voice faded in and out. And out.

He woke again, thinking, *nightmare!* And again it was too real. There was a cloth under his cheek. Someone had been a good Samaritan.

He asked nobody, "Am I dying?"

"Just take it easy." Two men folded his arms around him and picked him up in a peculiar grip that supported his innards. The pain under his ribs was not great, but it felt unnatural, terrifying.

"I think he could walk himself," said one.

"I don't dare," Simpson got out, trying to convey his fear. *Something broken in my belly or in my skull. Broken, bleeding, slowly bleeding away my life with nothing to show on the outside.* He was convinced he was dying. It was all that remained of a part of the nightmare that he could not visualize at all.

The men put him on a stretcher and unfolded him into prone position.

The rest of it was hazy. The ride in the ambulance, the doctor asking him questions, the same questions asked earlier by the police. Questions he answered without thought, almost without memory. He didn't become fully aware until an intern said, "Nothing broken. Just bruises."

Simpson was startled. "Are you sure?"

"Have your own doctor take a look tomorrow. For tonight you'll be all right. No broken bones. Is that the only pain, under your ribs?"

"My chin hurts.

"Oh, that's just a scrape. Did you faint?"

"Yes."

"Probably got it then. You're lucky, you know. Your spleen is right under those bruised ribs."

"Jesus."

"You think you can get up? Your wife is coming for you."

Janet, coming here? Janet! "I'll take a taxi," said Simpson. He rolled onto his side, sat up on the high operating table and climbed down to the floor, treating himself like a sackful of expensive raw eggs. "Where did they take my car?"

"The police gave me the address." The man tapped his pockets. One crackled. "Here."

Simpson took the slip, looked at it and shoved it in his pocket. There was a chance he could get the car transferred to his own company before the police looked in the trunk. Or was there? They might have looked already.

What would the police do about a Great Dane with a bullet in his head?

Undoubtedly they'd tell Janet.

He must get the car tomorrow.

The intern showed him to a telephone and loaned him a cigarette. After he called the cab, someone else showed him where to wait. He'd waited five minutes when Janet came.

Her hair was back to auburn. The dress she wore was severe, almost a suit, and it was new. She looked competent and sure of herself.

"How did you know?" he asked her.

"How do you think? The police called my house. They must have found the number on your license, if you didn't tell them."

"I've got a taxi coming."

"Let it come. You're going with me. How did you manage to bang yourself up?"

"There was a traffic jam. I got—"

"Can you stand up?"

She was always interrupting. Once he'd thought she did it deliberately. Once she had, perhaps, but now it was a habit she'd never lose.

He stood. The pain under his ribs made him walk carefully. He dreaded what it would feel like tomorrow.

"I'll take you to the beach," she said.

"Okay."

He lived in the beach house now. Janet had been awarded the main house.

He reached the car by leaning on Janet's shoulder. The touch of her was disturbing, and her perfume roused sharp memories. Aside from premarital prostitutes, he had never carnally known a woman other than Janet. Now she distracted him, and he kept landing hard on his feet and jarring his ribs. But her strength was an asset in settling him into the passenger seat.

"Now. How did it happen?"

He told her, in detail. Reaction made him want to babble. Somehow he managed to leave the dog out of it. But he told her how sure he had been that he was going to die, and he spoke of his surprise when the intern told him he wasn't. By the time he finished they were back on the freeway.

The lights, the flying lights ... He planted his feet and tried to push himself through the seat. Janet didn't notice.

"Harvey's missing," she said.

He should have said, "Oh?"

Instead, he stopped with the word on his lips. He had suddenly realized that it didn't matter. It hadn't mattered since the accident, though he hadn't realized it until now.

"I killed Harvey," he said.

She glanced across at him, with distaste. She didn't believe him.

"He's in the trunk of my car. That's why I was in such a hurry tonight."

"That's ridiculous. You *like* Harvey."

"It was a sort of dry run. I was planning to kill you."

"I don't understand."

"I had it all planned out," he said. "There's a red tide down at the beach. Maybe you knew."

"No." She was beginning to believe him, he thought.

"At night it's lovely. The breakers glow like blue fire. In the daytime it stinks, and the water's filthy. I could bury a body anywhere on the beach, and nobody would notice the smell. But I had to know I could go through with it. Wouldn't I be seven kinds of idiot if I murdered you and then froze up?"

"Yes," she said, very coldly.

"So I went up to the house and shot Harvey. It was a sort of a dry run. If it had worked, you would have been next. The gun in the pillow, the drive to the beach—"

"What an idiotic idea. Didn't it occur to you that they'd search harder for a missing woman than a missing dog?"

"Well—"

"And why Harvey? Why not pick up a dog at the pound? Suppose they were searching for my body on the beach and found Harvey's instead. They'd trace him straight to you! Then they'd know they were on the right track!"

"I—"

"I suppose you planned to use the same gun on us both?"

"Yes, I did, as a—"

"And how long do you think a red tide lasts, anyway?"

"The ocean always stinks. There's always a breeze, too."

"Remember the seal that washed up last year? It probably weighed less than seventy pounds. Remember the smell? Think how much worse—"

"All right, all right! It was a stupid plan!"

The angry silence was very, very familiar. It didn't help Simpson to know that his wife was probably right. It never had.

They turned toward the beach. Janet asked, "Why would you want to kill me?"

"The alimony's bleeding me white."

"That's all?"

"No. Personal reasons."

She laughed. He had wondered before: was her laughter always scornful, or did it only sound that way? "My God, Murray! Surely you can tell me, your intended victim!" She sobered suddenly. "Never mind. I don't want to know why. Do you still plan to kill me?"

"No. Not after that."

"The accident."

"Of course. I don't have the nerve. Suppose I ... did it, and then froze up? My car's in a police lot with a dog's body in the trunk. Well, that won't get me killed. But suppose it was you?"

"That's almost funny," said Janet.

"Want a real laugh? I may never drive the freeway again, either. I was so *sure* I was dying ..."

"I think I'd better tell someone else about this conversation, just in case."

"Go ahead then," said Simpson. And he had an odd thought: this was his last chance to go through with it. Before she told someone.

And then, an odder thought. Her tone: too light. She still didn't believe him. He was beginning to doubt it himself. Had he really intended to kill Janet?

She'd hurt him badly. She'd hurt him by leaving him: she, the only woman for Murray Simpson. She might as well have taken his testicles along. And he wanted to hurt her, badly.

They had reached the house. Janet pulled into the garage and shut off the ignition. "Do you always leave the door open?"

"Sometimes I forget."

Very uncomfortably, Janet asked, "Shall I come in and make you some coffee?"

"No. No, thanks." Simpson opened the door and got out.

And felt it end.

Deep peace. Massless body, without sensation. The darkness of the blind.

Simpson said, "What happened?"

"You didn't kill her," said the voice without character.

"No, of course not. Am I dead again?"

"You are dead, still."

"How?"

"Loss of blood through a ruptured spleen, symptoms masked by shock. Your most recent memories were a dry run. Simpson, you did not kill your wife."

With abstracted logic, Simpson said, "But I would have, if there hadn't been an accident."

"That is debatable. In any case, it was your own accident. You caused it without help."

"Deliberately?" Simpson didn't know.

"Your judge will decide. Shall we go?"

"Yes."

They went.

Convergent Series

It was a girl in my anthropology class who got me interested in magic. Her name was Ann, and she called herself a white witch, though I never saw her work an effective spell. She lost interest in me and married somebody, at which point I lost interest in her; but by that time magic had become the subject of my thesis in anthropology. I couldn't quit, and wouldn't if I could. Magic fascinated me.

The thesis was due in a month. I had a hundred pages of notes on primitive, medieval, oriental, and modern magic. Modern magic meaning psionics devices and such. Did you know that certain African tribes don't believe in natural death? To them, *every* death is due to witchcraft, and in every case the witch must be found and killed. Some of these tribes are actually dying out due to the number of witchcraft trials and executions. Medieval Europe was just as bad in many ways, but they stopped in time ... I'd tried several ways of conjuring Christian and other demons, purely in a spirit of research, and I'd put a Taoist curse on Professor Pauling. It hadn't worked. Mrs. Miller was letting me use the apartment-house basement for experiments.

Notes I had, but somehow the thesis wouldn't move. I knew why. For all I'd learned, I had nothing original to say about anything. It wouldn't have stopped everyone (remember the guy who counted every *i* in *Robinson Crusoe?*) but it stopped me. Until one Thursday night—

I get the damndest ideas in bars. This one was a beaut. The bartender got my untouched drink as a tip. I went straight home and typed for four solid hours. It was ten minutes to twelve when I quit, but I now had a complete outline for my thesis, based on a genuinely new idea in Christian witchcraft. All I'd needed was a hook to hang my knowledge on. I stood up and stretched . . .

. . . And knew I'd have to try it out.

All my equipment was in Mrs. Miller's basement, most of it already set up. I'd left a pentagram on the floor two nights ago. I erased that with a wet rag, a former washcloth, wrapped around a wooden block. Robes, special candles, lists of spells, new pentagram . . . I worked quietly so as not to wake anyone. Mrs. Miller was sympathetic; her sense of humor was such that they'd have burned her three centuries ago. But the other residents needed their sleep. I started the incantations exactly at midnight.

At fourteen past I got the shock of my young life. Suddenly there was a demon spread-eagled in the pentagram, with his hands and feet and head occupying all five points of the figure.

I turned and ran.

He roared, "Come back here!"

I stopped halfway up the stairs, turned, and came back down. To leave a demon trapped in the basement of Mrs. Miller's apartment house was out of the question. With that amplified basso profundo voice he'd have wakened the whole block.

He watched me come slowly down the stairs. Except for the horns he might have been a nude middle-aged man, shaved and painted bright red. But if he'd been human you wouldn't have wanted to know⁀ him. He seemed built for all of the Seven Deadly Sins. Avaricious green eyes. Enormous gluttonous tank of a belly. Muscles soft and drooping from sloth. A dissipated face that seemed permanently angry. Lecherous—never mind. His horns were small and sharp and polished to a glow.

He waited until I reached bottom. "That's better. Now what kept you? It's been a good century since anyone called up a demon."

"They've forgotten how," I told him. "Nowadays everyone thinks you're supposed to draw the pentagram on the floor."

"The floor? They expect me to show up lying on my *back?*" His voice was thick with rage.

I shivered. My bright idea. A pentagram was a prison for demons. Why? I'd thought of the five points of a pentagram, and the five points of a spread-eagled man ...

"Well?"

"I know, it doesn't make sense. Would you go away now, please?"

He stared. "You *have* forgotten a lot." Slowly and patiently, as to a child, he began to explain the implications of calling up a demon.

I listened. Fear and sick hopelessness rose in me until the concrete walls seemed to blur. "I am in peril of my immortal soul—" This was something I'd never considered, except academically. Now it was worse than that. To hear the demon talk, my soul was already lost. It had been lost since the moment I used the correct spell. I tried to hide my fear, but that was hopeless. With those enormous nostrils he must have smelled it.

He finished, and grinned as if inviting comment.

I said, "Let's go over that again. I only get one wish."

"Right."

"If you don't like the wish I've got to choose another."

"Right."

"That doesn't seem fair."

"Who said anything about fair?"

"—Or traditional. Why hasn't anyone heard about this deal before?"

"This is the standard deal, Jack. We used to give a better deal to some of the marks. The others didn't have time to talk because of that twenty-four-hour clause. If they wrote anything down we'd alter it. We have power over written things which mention us."

"That twenty-four-hour clause. If I haven't taken my wish

in twenty-four hours, you'll leave the pentagram and take my soul anyway?"

"That's right."

"And if I do use the wish, you have to remain in the pentagram until my wish is granted, or until twenty-four hours are up. Then you teleport to Hell to report same, and come back for me immediately, reappearing in the pentagram."

"I guess teleport's a good word. I vanish and reappear. Are you getting bright ideas?"

"Like what?"

"I'll make it easy on you. If you erase the pentagram I can appear anywhere. You can erase it and draw it again somewhere else, and I've still got to appear inside it."

A question hovered on my tongue. I swallowed it and asked another. "Suppose I wished for immortality?"

"You'd be immortal for what's left of your twenty-four hours." He grinned. His teeth were coal black. "Better hurry. Time's running out."

Time, I thought. Okay. All or nothing.

"Here's my wish. Stop time from passing outside of me."

"Easy enough. Look at your watch."

I didn't want to take my eyes off him, but he just exposed his black teeth again. So—I looked down.

There was a red mark opposite the minute hand on my Rolex. And a black mark opposite the hour hand.

The demon was still there when I looked up, still spread-eagled against the wall, still wearing that knowing grin. I moved around him, waved my hand before his face. When I touched him he felt like marble.

Time had stopped, but the demon had remained. I felt sick with relief.

The second hand on my watch was still moving. I had expected nothing less. Time had stopped for me—for twenty-four hours of interior time. If it had been exterior time I'd have been safe—but of course that was too easy.

I'd thought my way into this mess. I should be able to think my way out, shouldn't I?

I erased the pentagram from the wall, scrubbing until

every trace was gone. Then I drew a new one, using a flexible metal tape to get the lines as straight as possible, making it as large as I could get it in the confined space. It was still only two feet across.

I left the basement.

I knew where the nearby churches were, though I hadn't been to one in too long. My car wouldn't start. Neither would my roommate's motorcycle. The spell which enclosed me wasn't big enough. I walked to a Mormon temple three blocks away.

The night was cool and balmy and lovely. City lights blanked out the stars, but there was a fine werewolf's moon hanging way above the empty lot where the Mormon temple should have been.

I walked another eight blocks to find the B'nai B'rith Synagogue and the All Saints Church. All I got out of it was exercise. I found empty lots. For me, places of worship didn't exist.

I prayed. I didn't believe it would work, but I prayed. If I wasn't heard was it because I didn't expect to be? But I was beginning to feel that the demon had thought of everything, long ago.

What I did with the rest of that long night isn't important. Even to me it didn't feel important. Twenty-four hours, against eternity? I wrote a fast outline on my experiment in demon raising, then tore it up. The demons would only change it. Which meant that my thesis was shot to hell, whatever happened. I carried a real but rigid Scotch terrier into Professor Pauling's room and posed it on his desk. The old tyrant would get a surprise when he looked up. But I spent most of the night outside, walking, looking my last on the world. Once I reached into a police car and flipped the siren on, thought about it, and flipped it off again. Twice I dropped into restaurants and ate someone's order, leaving money which I wouldn't need, paper-clipped to notes which read "The Shadow Strikes."

The hour hand had circled my watch twice. I got back to the basement at twelve ten, with the long hand five minutes from brenschluss.

That hand seemed painted to the face as I waited. My candles had left a peculiar odor in the basement, an odor overlaid with the stink of demon and the stink of fear. The demon hovered against the wall, no longer in a pentagram, trapped halfway through a wide-armed leap of triumph.

I had an awful thought.

Why had I believed the demon? Everything he'd said might have been a lie. And probably was! I'd been tricked into accepting a gift from the devil! I stood up, thinking furiously— I'd already accepted the gift, but—

The demon glanced to the side and grinned wider when he saw the chalk lines gone. He nodded at me, said, "Back in a flash," and was gone.

I waited. I'd thought my way into this, but—

A cheery bass voice spoke out of the air. "I knew you'd move the pentagram. Made it too small for me, didn't you? Tsk, tsk. Couldn't you guess I'd change my size?"

There were rustlings, and a shimmering in the air. "I know it's here somewhere. I can feel it. Ah."

He was back, spread-eagled before me, two feet tall and three feet off the ground. His black know-it-all grin disappeared when he saw the pentagram wasn't there. Then—he was seven inches tall, eyes bugged in surprise, yelling in a contralto voice. "Whereinhell's the—"

He was two inches of bright red toy soldier. "—Pentagram?" he squealed.

I'd won. Tomorrow I'd get to a church. If necessary, have somebody lead me in blindfold.

He was a small red star.

A buzzing red housefly.

Gone.

It's odd, how quickly you can get religion. Let one demon tell you you're damned ... Could I really get into a church? Somehow I was sure I'd make it. I'd gotten this far; I'd outthought a demon.

Eventually he'd look down and see the pentagram. Part of it was in plain sight. But it wouldn't help him. Spread-eagled like that, he couldn't reach it to wipe it away. He was trapped for eternity, shrinking toward the infinitesimal but doomed never to reach it, forever trying to appear inside a pentagram which was forever too small. I had drawn it on his bulging belly.

The Deadlier Weapon

He was standing just off Overland Drive, at the mouth of the on ramp to the Santa Monica Freeway, eastbound. He waited with an air of ready confidence, and his thumbsmanship seemed practiced. His placement was perfect. A few yards further up the ramp, and no car could have stopped for him without being hit by the car behind. A few yards closer, and no driver would have known which route he wanted: the freeway, or the street going past the ramp.

That was what caught my attention: the perfect placement, not too far, not too near. A traveler, for sure. I dropped my arm out the window to signal, hit the brakes, and pulled up an easy foot and a half beyond him.

He was running before the car stopped. I pulled the lock knob and he threw the door open and was in, grinning, wasting no time. Good again. Nobody waits for a lazy hitchhiker; you trot or you don't ride. As soon as he was in I swung between two cars and headed up the ramp, accelerating.

The traffic wasn't bad, not at three in the afternoon. Still, when you enter a freeway you concentrate on the traffic. Everything else gets ignored. I hardly knew what my passenger looked like; I'd seen only a poised silhouette with its thumb raised against the afternoon sky. But I gave him points again. He didn't speak until I was firmly settled in the middle-right lane and could afford to relax a little.

I don't pick up riders often. When I do, I follow the whim of the moment. The ones who look chatty when I want peace and quiet, and the ones who look glum or taciturn when I'm after conversation—these get left standing. I like the unusual ones, the ones who seem to have a kind of salesmanship.

Six months ago there'd been a college girl on Wilshire, carrying a bright red Christmas package almost as big as she was. She was homesick for Kansas. She'd told me what freezing rains are like, when water falls from the sky at night and freezes where it hits, so that in the morning all the trees and bushes are tinkling crystal, crackling in the wind. That would be something to see. But I expect I never will.

Once there'd been a Negro on the freeway, carrying a gas can and smoking. As soon as he was in the car he'd tipped the ash off his cigarette into the gas can. "Okay," I'd said, to prove I was alert. "So you didn't run out of gas. Where you heading?"

"San Francisco," he'd told me. He'd started in Louisiana.

There was the guy who did run out of gas, stranded on the left of the freeway with his wife and four kids. "Oh, the kids are no trouble on a trip," he'd told me. "We know how to keep them interested. We play a game. The first kid to spot an Edsel gets a double ice-cream cone, immediately."

"Must make for frequent stops."

"How long since you last saw an Edsel?"

Right. I'd never seen two in the same day.

The hitchhiker said, "Thanks for the lift."

Traffic was fast and easy, the cars evenly spaced. I risked a look to the side.

He was young, somewhere in his mid-twenties. His nose was a touch too large and a touch too pointed, and his brown hair a touch too long. Gray plastic sunglasses, dark blue windbreaker over a white shirt, serviceable gray slacks. Shoes which looked rugged enough but which were not hiking shoes. He'd shaved recently. Despite the long hair, he looked too neat to have been on the road long. Perhaps he was just starting a trip.

"That's okay," I said. "You've used that thumb a lot, haven't you?"

"That's true." I heard a click then, but it didn't register until later. His voice was college educated, with a little too much tenor.

"How far you going this time?"

"Just far enough."

An odd answer. I glanced over at him and found the point of a knife just touching my larynx. "Watch the road," he said.

I turned back. Now I remembered the click. The knife was a switchblade with a six-inch blade, not very clean, but sharp, with the marks of a whetstone along the edge. I'd caught all of that in one glance.

"Neither of us is going to get hurt," the man with the knife said soothingly. He held the point at the side of my neck, just touching. "When you get the chance, you're going to pull over to the side, and I'm going to take your watch and the money in your wallet. Nothing else. I'll leave the wallet. I don't want your credit cards."

The lane to my left was clear. "Imagine how relieved I must be to hear it," I said, and eased over.

My passenger pushed gently with the knife point. "Wrong direction," he told me. "You want to go right."

I shifted into the far left lane, a little too fast. The knife point was an itch over my carotid artery. My hands wanted to scratch it, and I had to fight to keep them on the wheel. "You've done this before," I said, keeping my voice light.

"What makes you think so?"

"Your wording seems too practiced. On the one hand, the knife. On the other, you've told me just what you'll take, and you'll leave me the rest. The other cars will be going too fast to notice us, right?"

"That's right." He'd kept his voice soft and slow while making his pitch, but now an edge crept in. "This isn't rush hour. Even if someone notices something, he'll be a mile past us before he decides to stop and do something about it.

Now—" He put on a touch more pressure, and the itch became a burn. "Move over."

"Don't do that," I said. At the increase in pressure I'd turned to look him full in the face. He set his jaw and held the stare, and the knife was still at my throat. Except for that, and one other thing, it would have been a comic scene: two grown men trying to outstare each other.

"Watch the road," he said, not soothingly. And then, "I said watch the road. Dammit, watch the damn road!"

Suddenly he turned and braced himself against the padded dash with both hands. I looked forward, hit the brake and swerved. A navy blue Riviera missed us by a foot and dropped behind, weaving, the driver shouting soundlessly and leaning on his horn.

"Keep that knife out of my neck," I said. Some of the itch remained, and I reached up to scratch it. For my trouble I got a sharp stab of pain, and a film of blood on my fingertips. "And you can tell me something else. How do I know you won't kill me before you take my wallet?"

"Cooperate and you won't get hurt."

"Why not?"

He lost patience. With a smooth, quick motion, too fast for me to grab at his arm even if I'd wanted to, he had the knife tip at my neck. "Now pull over. Yeee!" He jerked back as if he'd touched something red hot.

Because I'd been less quick, but I didn't have as far to move. At the touch of the knife I'd yanked the wheel sixty degrees left and instantly back again. I pulled the car out of the emergency lane at the left of the freeway, fighting the drag of the gravel.

"Don't do that," I told him.

"What's *with* you?"

"Just in a bad mood, I guess."

He was backed up against the right front door of the Cadillac. He held the knife at ready, as if he were the defender and I the attacker. He licked his lips and asked, "Do you always drive this way when you're in a bad mood?"

"I've never been in this bad a mood before." I was trying

to sound neither frightened nor belligerent. My smile must have looked peculair, twisted, as if I'd put it on wrong.

"Look, all I want is your—"

"Shut up."

"You can keep your watch."

"Imagine my gratitude. Now will you shut up? You've got nothing to do with this."

"I—" He couldn't speak; he was half strangling on his own indignation. And I saw the overpass ahead, and I came alert, more than alert.

I'd passed here before, ignoring the scenery. Now I peered forward to get details. Some major highway crossed the freeway here. The overpass rose gently up a landscaped slope, leaped across eight lanes of empty space, and dropped as gently back. Halfway across the gap, between the east-bound and westbound lanes, were massive concrete pillars. Ramps curved out to join freeway with highway, and there were green signs to tell what turnoff this was, if I'd cared.

"What's wrong?" my passenger said edgily, and I realized how rigidly I was sitting and how hard I was gripping the wheel. I didn't relax. "See that bridge?"

"Sure."

"Okay."

"What about it?"

"Nothing." I wasn't even trying to smile now.

"All I want is some cash," the hitchhiker explained patiently. "You pull over to the side and stop, and—"

"And you cut my throat and take the car too. The cops get nothing but a missing-person report."

"No, no, no. Honest. All I want—"

"I don't care what you want."

"What do *you* want? Do you want to live?" Amazing, how his voice had lost those soothing overtones.

I didn't answer. The overpass was closer.

The hitchhiker clamped his lips together, nerving himself to something. Suddenly, snakelike, he reached with the knife. I jerked the wheel, and he pulled back against the door. The wheel damn near jerked out of my hands as we hit gravel. To make it worse, the freeway was curving right. I fought us around, and the bridge was almost on us.

There were no cars near me. Maybe they didn't like the way I drove.

Still the freeway curved right, gently as always. I didn't curve with it. I had the accelerator on the floor, and we went faster and faster, the hitchhiker and the Cadillac and me, edging over onto the gravel. Up ahead, the gravel safety lane ended, and there was the concrete supporting pillar of the bridge, with two big red-faceted reflectors shining in the midafternoon sunlight.

I aimed the car right at the reflectors.

My passenger seemed frozen. Only his head moved, swiveling to look at the supporting pillar and then back to my face and then to the pillar and back to me. The pillar was coming up like a cream-colored wall. I was terrified. I made no attempt to hide it. Considering the way the wheel was jumping, trying to pull across the gravel and into the divider fence before we could reach the bridge support, I must have looked like a man wrestling an alligator. There was sweat in my eyes, and at the last moment I whipped the edge of my right hand across my forehead and back to the wheel. Now my hand was dripping wet.

The concrete came at me.

I whipped the wheel hard over, putting my whole body into it. The car slewed, tried to move sideways, tried to roll over. We were going to hit sideways, through the fragile guard rail and into the supporting pillar. Then, with utmost reluctance, the car moved skidding to the right. Suddenly the concrete was behind us. My passenger made a high, whimpering sound.

"Hesitation marks," I gasped. I couldn't get enough air. Reality was a blur. Was I about to faint? I certainly didn't want to faint.

"You're crazy. Crazy!"

I fumbled for a cigarette and managed to get it to my mouth. "There's always hesitation marks. A man shoots himself in the head, you find holes in the wall where he jerked the gun away the first four times. If he cuts his throat you find three or four slashes where he didn't cut deep enough." I was gasping out the words, fighting for air. I had to have air.

"You're out of your mind."

"The thing is, if I have to die, I might as well pick the way I want to go. Right?"

"What are you talking about?"

"I was going to marry a girl."

"Congratulations." If my passenger was trying for sarcasm, it didn't come through. He only sounded scared. He sat facing straight toward me, with one leg on the seat and his back hard up against the door, watching.

"Thanks. Thanks a whole hell of a lot. Only she decided I wasn't her type. She—she tried to tell me we'd both known it all along. We'd just been fooling ourselves, she said. Liar."

"They do that," said my passenger.

"Everybody does that. You know how my dad told me he and Mom were getting divorced?" My cigarette was still in my mouth, unlit. I reached and stabbed at the car lighter. "I was fifteen. They called me into the living room and—"

"I don't *care* what your father told you when you were fifteen!"

"I do. My dad walked a few times around the room and then finally he said, 'I suppose you know your mother and I are separated.' Liar. They'd kept it from me because they thought it might interfere with my finals at school."

All I saw of him, I saw with the corner of my eye. But I saw him start to say something, stop, close his eyes tight to think.

The lighter popped out.

He blurted, "You're *crazy!* You can't *kill* yourself just because some bitch gives you the shaft!"

I pulled the lighter out and reached across the seat to touch it to the tip of his nose. He never moved to stop me. He couldn't believe what I was doing, not until he actually felt the heat. Then he screamed and threw his arms over his face. He missed grabbing my arm because I'd already pulled it back and was lighting my cigarette.

"She's not a bitch," I told him. "And if she was, you

wouldn't be the one to say it. Keep your dirty mouth off her."

"Let me off," said the hitchhiker. He'd forgotten he had the knife. He'd tried it before and it hadn't worked.

"Why should I?"

"I never tried to kill you. It's not fair."

"Who said anything about fair?" My grin felt natural now. After all, we were even. The blood on my neck matched the burn on his nose.

"Look, you don't want to kill yourself. You don't want to die. You're just kidding yourself. Just wait. Just wait until tomorrow. You'll feel different, really you will. I've felt like that myself, I really have but it always went away, sometimes it lasted for days but it always—"

"It's too late."

"It's not too late! You're still alive!"

"This isn't my car."

"What?"

"Do I look like a Cadillac driver?"

Eyes see what they're trained to see, what they expect to see. A polo shirt is just a T-shirt with a collar, except for the material. Pants are pants, except to the guy who wears them. He knows if they bind, or if they're too loose, or if they're tailored to fit just right. If the seat looks shiny, then they're too old, but how can you tell when he's sitting down?

"You stole it," he said.

I bobbed my head a couple of times, jerkily.

"Let me out."

"I don't want to get knifed."

"Please."

"Fasten your seat belt."

"Why?" But he knew. He knew.

"We're going to have an accident."

"Let me out first. Look, I—will you please look?"

I found I was strangling the wheel again. Because up ahead was where the freeway became a bowl of concrete noodles. I'd driven this route before. Here in downtown Los Angeles was where the Santa Monica Freeway led into the Harbor, Santa Ana, and San Bernardino Freeways. The ramps led up and over and around and under each other, and most of the time there was nothing but empty space to left and right. Speeding cars and empty space, separated by fragile metal rails and common sense.

My passenger knew it too. He was swiveling his head, toward the road, toward me, toward the road, toward me. Then he snapped out of it. He yelled, "Will you *look at me?*"

I looked, and he twitched, because now I wasn't watching the road. He was holding the knife out the window, holding it with two fingers around the tip of the handle. He let it drop, ostentatiously, and I saw it bounce once in the mirror. "I dropped the knife," he said. "You saw it. Now let me out."

I nodded. I braked and swung to the left. The car lurched and jerked and tried to pull free and slowed and stopped, not too far from where there wouldn't have been gravel to stop on. Cars whizzed past, and the wind of their passing sounded like blows against the side of the Cadillac.

"Out."

"Not here! I'll be killed!"

I touched the accelerator and the car jumped forward. He was out and around the side and behind the trunk in one smooth, lithe motion, and if there'd been a car coming it would have hit him. I touched the accelerator again to get beyond him, then reached across to slam the door he'd left open.

At the next gap in the traffic I was off, accelerating hard to keep from being hit from behind. The last I saw of the hitchhiker, he was hunched over the guard rail, actually using it for support, not looking at the four lanes of traffic he'd have to pass alive.

I edged to the right across four lanes of hurtling cars, being careful. I saw no point in getting killed now. I took the next turnoff, slowing, feeling my hands begin to shake. My cigarette was still going, and I dragged on it, practically breathing through it. Amazingly, it was mostly unburned. I turned in at the first gas station I saw, stopped alongside the pumps, and rested my head on the wheel. I rubbed my forehead against the smooth surface, harder and harder, because the sensation told me I was still alive.

"What can we do for you? I said—hey. Mister, are you all right?"

"I'm fine. Where's a telephone?"

"Over there." They were in plain sight. I couldn't have missed them if I'd bothered to look first.

"Good. Fill it up. I've got to call the police."

I had trouble getting the coin in the slot.

"About his height," I told the desk sergeant. "Five eleven, say. You wouldn't call him skinny, but he's not fat. Brown hair, a little too long, parted on the left. Long, thin face. By the time you get to him he should have a great big blister on the end of his nose."

"Why?"

"At one point I touched him there with a cigarette lighter."

"You did!" Hah! I'd surprised him. At first he'd sounded like someone who could never be surprised by anything. "Go on, Mr. Ruch."

"He's wearing dark glasses, a dark blue windbreaker, gray slacks. I left him stranded on the wrong side of the eastbound lane, just west of the Olympic turnoff."

"We'll find him, Mr. Ruch. Can you come down to the station and give us a signed statement?" He told me how to get there.

"Okay, fine, but will you give me an hour and a half? I need a drink."

"I can believe that. No hurry, Mr. Ruch. But we do need that statement."

One fast drink stopped my shakes, at least on the outside. I thought I could trust my voice now, so I called Carla in Garden Grove. "I've had some car trouble, honey. Nothing expensive, but I won't be home for dinner. Tell Stan and Eva I'm sorry, and I'll be in around eight if I'm lucky."

"Oh, that's a shame. What kind of trouble?"

"Tell you later."

"You have to get up early tomorrow, remember? Rehearsal."

"No problem. I'll be home in plenty of time."

By the time I got home I'd know how to tell Carla the truth in a way that wouldn't scare the pants off her.

Two drinks and I began to giggle, thinking about the blister on the end of the hitchhiker's nose, thinking about the hopeful look on his face when he dropped the knife out the window, how he had to make so *damn* sure I was watching him. Giggles was too much of a good thing, so I had a sandwich and a glass of milk to drown the second drink.

... I could legitimately tell Carla that the hitchhiker had never had a chance. It would reassure her, and it was true. I'd been better armed from the beginning. He'd had nothing but a knife. I had had a car. Much deadlier.

I reached the station half an hour late. They'd changed desk men. I was explaining why I was there when they brought in the hitchhiker.

He wasn't struggling. He seemed completely exhausted. He actually had trouble walking. But his head came up when he saw me. The tip of his nose was a small white bubble surrounded by angry red flesh.

"So you didn't have the guts!" he snarled. "You chickened out! You yellow-bellied—" He paused to think up an adequately insulting noun, ignoring the police officer who jerked warningly at his arm.

"I couldn't go through with it," I admitted, and looked sheepishly down at the toes of my shoes. Why tell him? He had enough troubles.

Death by Ecstasy

First came the routine request for a Breach of Privacy permit. A police officer took down the details and forwarded the request to a clerk, who saw that the tape reached the appropriate civic judge. The judge was reluctant, for privacy is a precious thing in a world of eighteen billion; but in the end he could find no reason to refuse. On November 2, 2123, he granted the permit.

The tenant's rent was two weeks in arrears. If the manager of Monica Apartments had asked for eviction he would have been refused. But Owen Jennison did not answer his doorbell or his room phone. Nobody could recall seeing him in many weeks. Apparently the manager only wanted to know that he was all right.

And so he was allowed to use his passkey, with an officer standing by.

And so they found the tenant of 1809.

And when they had looked in his wallet, they called me.

I was at my desk at ARMs Headquarters, making useless notes and wishing it were lunchtime.

At this stage the Loren case was all correlate-and-wait. It involved an organlegging gang, apparently run by a single man, yet big enough to cover half the North American west coast. We had considerable data on the gang—methods of

177

operation, centers of activity, a few former customers, even a tentative handful of names—but nothing that would give us an excuse to act. So it was a matter of shoving what we had into the computer, watching the few suspected associates of the ganglord Loren, and waiting for a break.

The months of waiting were ruining my sense of involvement.

My phone buzzed.

I put the pen down and said, "Gil Hamilton."

A small dark face regarded me with soft black eyes. "I am Detective-Inspector Julio Ordaz of the Los Angeles Police Department. Are you related to an Owen Jennison?"

"Owen? No, we're not related. Is he in trouble?"

"You do know him, then."

"Sure I know him. Is he here, on Earth?"

"It would seem so." Ordaz had no accent, but the lack of colloquialisms in his speech made him sound vaguely foreign. "We will need positive identification, Mr. Hamilton. Mr. Jennison's ident lists you as next of kin."

"That's funny. I—back up a minute. Is Owen dead?"

"Somebody is dead, Mr. Hamilton. He carried Mr. Jennison's ident in his wallet."

"Okay. Now, Owen Jennison was a citizen of the Belt. This may have interworld complications. That makes it ARMs business. Where's the body?"

"We found him in an apartment rented under his own name. Monica Apartments, Lower Los Angeles, room 1809."

"Good. Don't move anything you haven't moved already. I'll be right over."

Monica Apartments was a nearly featureless concrete block, eighty stories tall, a thousand feet across the edges of its square base. Lines of small balconies gave the sides a sculptured look, above a forty-foot inset ledge that would keep tenants from dropping objects on pedestrians. A hundred buildings just like it made Lower Los Angeles look lumpy from the air.

Inside, a lobby done in anonymous modern. Lots of metal and plastic showing; lightweight, comfortable chairs without arms; big ashtrays; plenty of indirect lighting; a low ceiling; no wasted space. The whole room might have been stamped out with a die. It wasn't supposed to look small, but it did, and that warned you what the rooms would be like. You'd pay your rent by the cubic centimeter.

I found the manager's office, and the manager, a soft-looking man with watery blue eyes. His conservative paper suit, dark red, seemed chosen to render him invisible, as did the style of his brown hair, worn long and combed straight back without a part. "Nothing like this has ever happened here," he confided as he led me to the elevator banks. "Nothing. It would have been bad enough without his being a Belter, but *now*—" He cringed at the thought. "Newsmen. They'll *smother* us."

The elevator was coffin-sized, but with the handrails on the inside. It went up fast and smooth. I stepped out into a long, narrow hallway.

What would Owen have been doing in a place like this? Machinery lived here, not people.

Maybe it wasn't Owen. Ordaz had been reluctant to commit himself. Besides, there's no law against picking pockets. You couldn't enforce such a law on this crowded planet. Everyone on Earth was a pickpocket.

Sure. Someone had died carrying Owen's wallet.

I walked down the hallway to 1809.

It was Owen who sat grinning in the armchair. I took one good look at him, enough to be sure, and then I looked away and didn't look back. But the rest of it was even more unbelievable.

No Belter could have taken that apartment. I was born in Kansas; but even I felt the awful anonymous chill. It would have driven Owen bats.

"I don't believe it," I said.

"Did you know him well, Mr. Hamilton?"

"About as well as two men can know each other. He and I spent three years mining rocks in the main asteroid belt. You don't keep secrets under those conditions."

"Yet you didn't know he was on Earth."

"That's what I can't understand. Why the blazes didn't he phone me if he was in trouble?"

"You're an ARM," said Ordaz. "An operative in the United Nations Police."

He had a point. Owen was as honorable as any man I knew; but honor isn't the same in the Belt. Belters think flatlanders are all crooks. They don't understand that to a flatlander, picking pockets is a game of skill. Yet a Belter sees smuggling as the same kind of game, with no dishonesty involved. He balances the 30 percent tariff against possible confiscation of his cargo, and if the odds are right he gambles.

Owen could have been doing something that would look honest to him but not to me.

"He could have been in something sticky," I admitted. "But I can't see him killing himself over it. And ... not here. He wouldn't have come here."

1809 was a living room and a bathroom and a closet. I'd glanced into the bathroom, knowing what I would find. It was the size of a comfortable shower stall. An adjustment panel outside the door would cause it to extrude various appurtenances in memory plastic, to become a washroom, a shower stall, a toilet, a dressing room, a steam cabinet. Luxurious in everything but size, as long as you pushed the right buttons.

The living room was more of the same. A King bed was invisible behind a wall. The kitchen alcove, with basin and oven and grill and toaster, would fold into another wall; the sofa, chairs, and tables would vanish into the floor. One tenant and three guests would make a crowded cocktail party, a cozy dinner gathering, a closed poker game. Card table, dinner table, coffee table were all there, surrounded by the appropriate chairs; but only one set at a time would emerge from the floor. There was no refrigerator, no freezer, no bar. If a tenant needed food or drink he phoned down, and the supermarket on the third floor would send it up.

The tenant of such an apartment had his comfort. But he owned nothing. There was room for him; there was none for his possessions. This was one of the inner apartments. An age ago there would have been an air shaft; but air shafts took up expensive room. The tenant didn't even have a window. He lived in a comfortable box.

Just now the items extruded were the overstuffed reading armchair, two small side tables, a footstool, and the kitchen alcove. Owen Jennison sat grinning in the armchair. Naturally he grinned. Little more than dried skin covered the natural grin of his skull.

"It's a small room," said Ordaz, "but not too small. Millions of people live this way. In any case a Belter would hardly be a claustrophobe."

"No. Owen flew a singleship before he joined us. Three months at a stretch, in a cabin so small you couldn't stand up with the airlock closed. Not claustrophobia, but—" I swept my arm about the room. "What do you see that's his?"

Small as it was, the closet was nearly empty. A set of street clothes, a paper shirt, a pair of shoes, a small brown overnight case. All new. The few items in the bathroom medicine chest had been equally new and equally anonymous.

Ordaz said, "Well?"

"Belters are transients. They don't own much, but what they do own, they guard. Small possessions, relics, souvenirs. I can't believe he wouldn't have had *something*."

Ordaz lifted an eyebrow. "His space suit?"

"You think that's unlikely? It's not. The inside of his pressure suit is a Belter's home. Sometimes it's the only home he's got. He spends a fortune decorating it. If he loses his suit, he's not a Belter anymore.

"No, I don't insist he'd have brought his suit. But he'd have had *something*. His phial of Marsdust. The bit of nickel-iron they took out of his chest. Or, if he left all his souvenirs home, he'd have picked up things on Earth. But in this room—there's *nothing*."

"Perhaps," Ordaz suggested delicately, "he didn't notice his surroundings."

And somehow that brought it all home.

Owen Jennison sat grinning in a water-stained silk dressing gown. His space-darkened face lightened abruptly beneath his chin, giving way to normal suntan. His blond hair, too long, had been cut Earth style; no trace remained of the Belter strip cut he'd worn all his life. A month's growth of untended beard covered half his face. A small black cylinder protruded from the top of his head. An electric cord trailed from the top of the cylinder and ran to a wall socket.

The cylinder was a droud, a current addict's transformer.

I stepped closer to the corpse and bent to look. The droud was a standard make, but it had been altered. Your standard current addict's droud will pass only a trickle of current into the brain. Owen must have been getting ten times the usual charge, easily enough to damage his brain in a month's time.

I reached out and touched the droud with my imaginary hand.

Ordaz was standing quietly beside me, letting me make my examination without interruption. Naturally he had no way of knowing about my restricted psi powers.

Restricted was the operative word. I had two psychic powers: telekinesis and esper. With the esper sense I could sense the shapes of objects at a distance; but the distance was the reach of an extra right arm. I could lift small objects, if they were no further away than the fingertips of an imaginary right hand. The restriction was a flaw in my own imagination. Since I could not believe my imaginary hand would reach further than that . . . it wouldn't.

Even so limited a psi power can be useful. With my imaginary fingertips I touched the droud in Owen's head, then ran them down to a tiny hole in his scalp, and further.

It was a standard surgical job. Owen could have had it done anywhere. A hole in his scalp, invisible under the hair, nearly impossible to find even if you knew what you were looking for. Even your best friends wouldn't know, unless they caught you with the droud plugged in. But the tiny hole marked a bigger plug set in the bone of the skull. I touched the ecstasy plug with my imaginary fingertips, then ran them down the hair-fine wire going deep into Owen's brain, down into the pleasure center.

No, the extra current hadn't killed him. What had killed

Owen was his lack of will power. He had been unwilling to get up.

He had starved to death sitting in that chair. There were plastic squeezebottles all around his feet, and a couple still on the end tables. All empty. They must have been full a month ago. Owen hadn't died of thirst. He had died of starvation, and his death had been planned.

Owen my crewmate. Why hadn't he come to me? I'm half a Belter myself. Whatever his trouble, I'd have gotten him out somehow. A little smuggling—what of it? Why had he arranged to tell me only after it was over?

The apartment was so clean, so clean. You had to bend close to smell the death; the air conditioning whisked it all away.

He'd been very methodical. The kitchen was open so that a catheter could lead from Owen to the sink. He'd given himself enough water to last out the month; he'd paid his rent a month in advance. He'd cut the droud cord by hand, and he'd cut it short, deliberately tethering himself to a wall socket beyond reach of the kitchen.

A complex way to die, but rewarding in its way. A month of ecstasy, a month of the highest physical pleasure man can attain. I could imagine him giggling every time he remembered he was starving to death. With food only a few footsteps away . . . but he'd have to pull out the droud to reach it. Perhaps he postponed the decision, and postponed it again . . .

Owen and I and Homer Chandrasekhar, we had lived for three years in a cramped shell surrounded by vacuum. What was there to know about Owen Jennison that I hadn't known? Where was the weakness we didn't share? If Owen had done this, so could I. And I was afraid.

"Very neat," I whispered. "Belter neat."

"Typically Belter, would you say?"

"I would not. Belters don't commit suicide. Certainly not this way. If a Belter had to go, he'd blow his ship's drive and die like a star. The neatness is typical. The result isn't."

"Well," said Oradaz. "Well." He was uncomfortable. The

facts spoke for themselves, yet he was reluctant to call me a liar. He fell back on formality.

"Mr. Hamilton, do you identify this man as Owen Jennison?"

"It's him." He'd always been a touch overweight, yet I'd recognized him the moment I saw him. "But let's be sure." I pulled the dirty dressing gown back from Owen's shoulder. A near-perfect circle of scar tissue, eight inches across, spread over the left side of his chest. "See that?"

"We noticed it, yes. An old burn?"

"Owen's the only man I know who could show you a meteor scar on his skin. It blasted him in the shoulder one day while he was outside the ship. Sprayed vaporized pressure-suit steel all over his skin. The doc pulled a tiny grain of nickel-iron from the center of the scar, just below the skin. Owen always carried that grain of nickel-iron. Always," I said, looking at Ordaz.

"We didn't find it."

"Okay."

"I'm sorry to put you through this, Mr. Hamilton. It was you who insisted we leave the body in situ."

"Yes. Thank you."

Owen grinned at me from the reading chair. I felt the pain, in my throat and in the pit of my stomach. Once I had lost my right arm. Losing Owen felt the same way.

"I'd like to know more about this," I said. "Will you let me know the details as soon as you get them?"

"Of course. Through the ARMs office?"

"Yes." This wasn't ARMs business, despite what I'd told Ordaz; but ARMs prestige would help. "I want to know why Owen died. Maybe he just cracked up . . . culture shock or something. But if someone hounded him to death, I'll have his blood."

"Surely the administration of justice is better left to—" Ordaz stopped, confused. Did I speak as an ARM or as a citizen?

I left him wondering.

The lobby held a scattering of tenants, entering and leaving elevators or just sitting around. I stood outside the elevator for a moment, searching passing faces for the erosion of personality that must be there.

Mass-produced comfort. Room to sleep and eat and watch tridee, but no room to *be* anyone. Living here, one would own nothing. What kind of people would live like that? They should have looked all alike, moved in unison, like the string of images in a barber's mirrors.

Then I spotted wavy brown hair and a dark red paper suit. The manager? I had to get close before I was sure. His face was the face of a permanent stranger.

He saw me coming and smiled without enthusiasm. "Oh, hello, Mr. . . . uh . . . Did you find . . ." He couldn't think of the right question.

"Yes," I said, answering it anyway. "But I'd like to know some things. Owen Jennison lived here for six weeks, right?"

"Six weeks and two days, before we opened his room."

"Did he ever have visitors?"

The man's eyebrows went up. We'd drifted in the direction of his office, and I was close enough to read the name on the door: JASPER MILLER, *Manager*. "Of course not," he said. "Anyone would have noticed that something was wrong."

"You mean he took the room for the express purpose of dying? You saw him once, and never again?"

"I suppose he might . . . no, wait." The manager thought deeply. "No. He registered on a Thursday. I noticed the Belter tan, of course. Then on Friday he went out. I happened to see him pass."

"Was that the day he got the droud? No, skip it, you wouldn't know that. Was it the last time you saw him go out?"

"Yes, it was."

"Then he could have had visitors late Thursday or early Friday."

The manager shook his head, very positively.

"Why not?"

"You see, Mr., uh . . ."

"Hamilton."

"We have a holo camera on every floor, Mr. Hamilton. It

takes a picture of each tenant the first time he goes to his room, and then never again. Privacy is one of the services a tenant buys with his room." The manager drew himself up a little as he said this. "For the same reason, the holo camera takes a picture of anyone who is *not* a tenant. The tenants are thus protected from unwarranted intrusions."

"And there were no visitors to any of the rooms on Owen's floor?"

"No, sir, there were not."

"Your tenants are a solitary bunch."

"Perhaps they are."

"I suppose a computer in the basement decides who is and is not a tenant."

"Of course."

"So for six weeks Owen Jennison sat alone in his room. In all that time he was totally ignored."

Miller tried to turn his voice cold, but he was too nervous. "We try to give our guests privacy. If Mr. Jennison had wanted help of any kind he had only to pick up the house phone. He could have called me, or the pharmacy, or the supermarket downstairs."

"Well, thank you, Mr. Miller. That's all I wanted to know. I wanted to know how Owen Jennison could wait six weeks to die while nobody noticed."

Miller swallowed. "He was dying all that time?"

"Yah."

"We had no way of knowing. How could we? I don't see how you can blame us."

"I don't either," I said, and brushed by. Miller had been close enough, so I had lashed out at him. Now I was ashamed. The man was perfectly right. Owen could have had help if he'd wanted it.

I stood outside, looking up at the jagged blue line of sky that showed between the tops of the buildings. A taxi floated into view, and I beeped my clicker at it, and it dropped.

I went back to ARM Headquarters. Not to work—I couldn't have done any work, not under the circumstances—but to talk to Julie.

Julie. A tall girl, pushing thirty, with green eyes and long hair streaked red and gold. And two wide brown forceps marks above her right knee; but they weren't showing now. I looked into her office, through the one-way glass, and watched her at work.

She sat in a contour couch, smoking. Her eyes were closed. Sometimes her brow would furrow as she concentrated. Sometimes she would snatch a glance at the clock, then close her eyes again.

I didn't interrupt her. I knew the importance of what she was doing.

Julie. She wasn't beautiful. Her eyes were a little too far apart, her chin too square, her mouth too wide. It didn't matter. Because Julie could read minds.

She was the ideal date. She was everything a man needed. A year ago, the day after the night I killed my first man, I had been in a terribly destructive mood. Somehow Julie had turned it into a mood of manic exhilaration. We'd run wild through a supervised anarchy park, running up an enormous bill. We'd hiked five miles without going anywhere, facing backward on a downtown slidewalk. At the end we'd been utterly fatigued, too tired to think ... But two weeks ago it had been a warm, cuddly, comfortable night. Two people happy with each other; no more than that. Julie was what you needed, anytime, anywhere.

Her male harem must have been the largest in history. To pick up on the thoughts of a male ARM, Julie had to be in love with him. Luckily there was room in her for a lot of love. She didn't demand that we be faithful. A good half of us were married. But there had to be love for each of Julie's men, or Julie couldn't protect him.

She was protecting us now. Each fifteen minutes, Julie was making contact with a specific ARM agent. Psi powers are notoriously undependable, but Julie was an exception. If we got in a hole, Julie was always there to get us out ... provided some idiot didn't interrupt her at work.

So I stood outside, waiting, with a cigarette in my imaginary hand.

The cigarette was for practice, to stretch the mental muscles. In its way my "hand" was as dependable as Julie's mind-touch, possibly because of its very limitations. Doubt your psi powers and they're gone. A rigidly defined third arm was more reasonable than some warlock ability to make objects move by wishing at them. I knew how an arm felt, and what it would do.

Why do I spend so much time lifting cigarettes? Well, it's the biggest weight I can lift without strain. And there's another reason . . . something taught me by Owen.

At ten minutes to fifteen Julie opened her eyes, rolled out of the contour couch, and came to the door. "Hi, Gil," she said sleepily. "Trouble?"

"Yah. A friend of mine just died. I thought you'd better know." I handed her a cup of coffee.

She nodded. We had a date tonight, and this would change its character. Knowing that, she probed lightly.

"Jesus!" she said, recoiling. "How . . . how horrible. I'm terribly sorry, Gil. Date's off, right?"

"Unless you want to join the ceremonial drunk."

She shook her head vigorously. "I didn't know him. It wouldn't be proper. Besides, you'll be wallowing in your own memories, Gil. A lot of them will be private. I'd cramp your style if you knew I was there to probe. Now if Homer Chandrasekhar were here, it'd be different."

"I wish he were. He'll have to throw his own drunk. Maybe with some of Owen's girls, if they're around."

"You know what I feel," she said.

"Just what I do."

"I wish I could help."

"You always help." I glanced at the clock. "Your coffee break's about over."

"Slave driver." Julie took my earlobe between thumb and forefinger. "Do him proud," she said, and went back to her soundproof room.

She always helps. She doesn't even have to speak. Just knowing that Julie has read my thoughts, that someone understands . . . that's enough.

All alone at three in the afternoon, I started my ceremonial drunk.

The ceremonial drunk is a young custom, not yet tied down by formality. There is no set duration. No specific toasts must be given. Those who participate must be close friends of the deceased, but there is no set number of participants.

I started at the Luau, a place of cool blue light and running water. Outside it was fifteen-thirty in the afternoon, but inside it was evening in the Hawaiian Islands of centuries ago. Already the place was half full. I picked a corner table with considerable elbow room and dialed for a Luau grog. It came, cold, brown, and alcoholic, its straw tucked into a cone of ice.

There had been three of us at Cubes Forsythe's ceremonial drunk, one black Ceres night four years ago. A jolly group we were, too; Owen and me and the widow of our third crewman. Gwen Forsythe blamed us for her husband's death. I was just out of the hospital with a right arm that ended at the shoulder, and I blamed Cubes and Owen and myself, all at once. Even Owen had turned dour and introspective. We couldn't have picked a worse trio, or a worse night for it.

But custom called, and we were there. Then as now, I found myself probing my own personality for the wound that was a missing crewman, a missing friend. Introspecting.

Gilbert Hamilton. Born of flatlander parents, in April, 2093, in Topeka, Kansas. Born with two arms and no sign of wild talents.

Flatlander: a Belter term referring to earthmen, and particularly to earthmen who had never seen space. I'm not sure my parents ever looked at the stars. They managed the third largest farm in Kansas, ten square miles of arable land between two wide strips of city paralleling two strips of turnpike. We were city people, like all flatlanders, but when the crowds got to be too much for my brothers and me, we had vast stretches of land to be alone in. Ten square miles of playground, with nothing to hamper us but the crops and automachinery.

We looked at the stars, my brothers and I. You can't see stars from the city; the lights hide them. Even in the fields you couldn't see them around the lighted horizon. But straight overhead, they were there: black sky scattered with bright dots, and sometimes a flat white moon.

At twenty I gave up my UN citizenship to become a Belter. I wanted stars, and the Belt government holds title to most of the solar system. There are fabulous riches in the rocks, riches belonging to a scattered civilization of a few hundred thousand Belters; and I wanted my share of that, too.

It wasn't easy. I wouldn't be eligible for a singleship license for ten years. Meanwhile I would be working for others, and learning to avoid mistakes before they killed me. Half the flatlanders who join the Belt die in space before they can earn their licenses.

I mined tin on Mercury and exotic chemicals from Jupiter's atmosphere. I hauled ice from Saturn's rings and quicksilver from Europa. One year our pilot made a mistake pulling up to a new rock, and we damn near had to walk home. Cubes Forsythe was with us then. He managed to fix the com laser and aim it at Icarus to bring us help. Another time the mechanic who did the maintenance job on our ship forgot to replace an adsorber, and we all got roaring drunk on the alcohol that built up in our breathing-air. The three of us caught the mechanic six months later. I hear he lived.

Most of the time I was part of a three-man crew. The members changed constantly. When Owen Jennison joined us he replaced a man who had finally earned his singleship license, and couldn't wait to start hunting rocks on his own. He was too eager. I learned later that he'd made one round trip and half of another.

Owen was my age, but more experienced, a Belter born and bred. His blue eyes and blond cockatoo's crest were startling against the dark of his Belter tan, the tan that ended so abruptly where his neck ring cut off the space-intense sunlight his helmet let through. He was permanently chubby, but in free fall it was as if he'd been born with wings. I took to copying his way of moving, much to Cubes' amusement.

I didn't make my own mistake until I was twenty-six.

We were using bombs to put a rock in a new orbit. A contract job. The technique is older than fusion drives, as old as early Belt colonization, and it's still cheaper and faster than using a ship's drive to tow the rock. You use industrial fusion bombs, small and clean, and you set them so that each explosion deepens the crater to channel the force of later blasts.

We'd set four blasts already, four white fireballs that swelled and faded as they rose. When the fifth blast went off we were hovering nearby on the other side of the rock.

The fifth blast shattered the rock.

Cubes had set the bomb. My own mistake was a shared one, because any of the three of us should have had the sense to take off right then. Instead, we watched, cursing, as valuable oxygen-bearing rock became near-valueless shards. We watched the shards spread slowly into a cloud ... and while we watched, one fast-moving shard reached us. Moving too slowly to vaporize when it hit, it nonetheless sheared through a triple crystal-iron hull, slashed through my upper arm, and pinned Cubes Forsythe to a wall by his heart.

A couple of nudists came in. They stood blinking among the booths while their eyes adjusted to the blue twilight, then converged with glad cries on the group two tables over. I watched and listened with an eye and an ear, thinking how different flatlander nudists were from Belter nudists. These all looked alike. They all had muscles, they had no interesting scars, they carried their credit cards in identical shoulder pouches, and they all shaved the same areas.

... We always went nudist in the big bases. Most people did. It was a natural reaction to the pressure suits we wore day and night while out in the rocks. Get him into a shirtsleeve environment, and your normal Belter sneers at a shirt. But it's only for comfort. Give him a good reason and your Belter will don shirt and pants as quickly as the next guy.

But not Owen. After he got that meteor scar, I never saw him wear a shirt. Not just in the Ceres domes, but anywhere there was air to breathe. He just had to show that scar.

A cool blue mood settled on me, and I remembered ...

... Owen Jennison lounging on a corner of my hospital

bed, telling me of the trip back. I couldn't remember anything after that rock had sheared through my arm.

I should have bled to death in seconds. Owen hadn't given me the chance. The wound was ragged; Owen had sliced it clean to the shoulder with one swipe of a com laser. Then he'd tied a length of fiberglass curtain over the flat surface and knotted it tight under my remaining armpit. He told me about putting me under two atmospheres of pure oxygen as a substitute for replacing the blood I'd lost. He told me how he'd reset the fusion drive for four gees to get me back in time. By rights we should have gone up in a cloud of starfire and glory.

"So there goes my reputation. The whole Belt knows how I rewired our drive. A lot of 'em figure if I'm stupid enough to risk my own life like that, I'd risk theirs too."

"So you're not safe to travel with."

"Just so. They're starting to call me Four Gee Jennison."

"You think you're got problems? I can just see how it'll be when I get out of this bed. 'You do something stupid, Gil?' The hell of it is, it *was* stupid."

"So lie a little."

"Uh huh. Can we sell the ship?"

"Nope. Gwen inherited a third interest in it from Cubes. She won't sell."

"Then we're effectively broke."

"Except for the ship. We need another crewman."

"Correction. *You* need *two* crewmen. Unless you want to fly with a one-armed man. I can't afford a transplant."

Owen hadn't tried to offer me a loan. That would have been insulting, even if he'd had the money. "What's wrong with a prosthetic?"

"An iron arm? Sorry, no. I'm squeamish."

Owen had looked at me strangely, but all he'd said was, "Well, we'll wait a bit. Maybe you'll change your mind."

He hadn't pressured me. Not then, and not later, after I'd left the hospital and taken an apartment while I waited to get used to a missing arm. If he thought I would eventually settle for a prosthetic, he was mistaken.

Why? It's not a question I can answer. Others obviously

feel differently; there are millions of people walking around with metal and plastic and silicone parts. Part man, part machine, and how do they themselves know which is the real person?

I'd rather be dead than part metal. Call it a quirk. Call it, even, the same quirk that makes my skin crawl when I find a place like Monica Apartments. A human being should be all human. He should have habits and possessions peculiarly his own, he should not try to look like or to behave like anyone but himself, and he should not be half robot.

So there I was, Gil the Arm, learning to eat with my left hand.

An amputee never entirely loses what he's lost. My missing fingers itched. I moved to keep from barking my missing elbow on sharp corners. I reached for things, then swore when they didn't come.

Owen had hung around, though his own emergency funds must have been running low. I hadn't offered to sell my third of the ship, and he hadn't asked.

There had been a girl. Now I'd forgotten her name. One night I was at her place waiting for her to get dressed—a dinner date—and I'd happened to see a nail file she'd left on a table. I'd picked it up. I'd almost tried to file my nails, but remembered in time. Irritated, I had tossed the file back on the table—and missed.

Like an idiot I'd tried to catch it with my right hand.

And I'd caught it.

I'd never suspected myself of having psychic powers. You have to be in the right frame of mind to use a psi power. But who had ever had a better opportunity than I did that night, with a whole section of brain tuned to the nerves and muscles of my right arm, and no right arm?

I'd held the nail file in my imaginary hand. I'd felt it, just as I'd felt my missing fingernails getting too long. I had run my thumb along the rough steel surface; I had turned the file in my fingers. Telekinesis for lift, esper for touch.

"That's it," Owen had said the next day. "That's all we need. One crewman, and you with your eldritch powers. You practice, see how strong you can get that lift. I'll go find a sucker."

"He'll have to settle for a sixth of net. Cubes' widow will want her share."

"Don't worry. I'll swing it."

"Don't worry!" I'd waved a pencil stub at him. Even in Ceres' gentle gravity, it was as much as I could lift—then. "You don't think TK and esper can make do for a real arm, do you?"

"It's better than a real arm. You'll see. You'll be able to reach through your suit with it without losing pressure. What Belter can do that?"

"Sure."

"What the hell do you want, Gil? Someone should give you your arm back? You can't have that. You lost it fair and square, through stupidity. Now it's your choice. Do you fly with an imaginary arm, or do you go back to Earth?"

"I can't go back. I don't have the fare."

"Well?"

"Okay, okay. Go find us a crewman. Someone I can impress with my imaginary arm."

I sucked meditatively on a second Luau grog. By now all the booths were full, and a second layer was forming around the bar. The voices made a continuous hypnotic roar. Cocktail hour had arrived.

... He'd swung it, all right. On the strength of my imaginary arm, Owen had talked a kid named Homer Chandrasekhar into joining our crew.

He'd been right about my arm, too.

Others with similar senses can reach further, up to halfway around the world. My unfortunately literal imagination had restricted me to a psychic hand. But my esper fingertips were more sensitive, more dependable. I could lift more weight. Today, in Earth's gravity, I can lift a full shot glass.

I found I could reach through a cabin wall to feel for breaks in the circuits behind it. In vacuum I could brush dust from the outside of my faceplate. In port I did magic tricks.

I'd almost ceased to feel like a cripple. It was all due to

Owen. In six months of mining I had paid off my hospital bills and earned my fare back to Earth, with a comfortable stake left over.

"Finagle's Black Humor!" Owen had exploded when I told him. "Of all places, why Earth?"

"Because if I can get my UN citizenship back, Earth will replace my arm. Free."

"Oh. That's true," he'd said dubiously.

The Belt had organ banks too, but they were always undersupplied. Belters didn't give things away. Neither did the Belt government. They kept the prices on transplants as high as they would go. Thus they dropped the demand to meet the supply, and kept taxes down to boot.

In the Belt I'd have had to buy my own arm. And I didn't have the money. On Earth there was social security, and a vast supply of transplant material.

What Owen had said couldn't be done, I'd done. I'd found someone to hand me my arm back.

Sometimes I'd wondered if Owen held the choice against me. He'd never said anything, but Homer Chandrasekhar had spoken at length. A Belter would have earned his arm or done without. Never would he have accepted charity.

Was that why Owen hadn't tried to call me?

I shook my head. I didn't believe it.

The room continued to lurch after my head stopped shaking. I'd had enough for the moment. I finished my third grog and ordered dinner.

Dinner sobered me for the next lap. It was something of a shock to realize that I'd run through the entire lifespan of my friendship with Owen Jennison. I'd known him for three years, though it had seemed like half a lifetime. And it was. Half my six-year lifespan as a Belter.

I ordered coffee grog and watched the man pour it: hot, milky coffee laced with cinnamon and other spices, and high-proof rum poured in a stream of blue fire. This was one of the special drinks served by a human headwaiter, and it was the reason they kept him around. Phase two of the ceremonial drunk: blow half your fortune, in the grand manner.

But I called Ordaz before I touched the drink.

"Yes, Mr. Hamilton? I was just going home for dinner."

"I won't keep you long. Have you found out anything new?"

Ordaz took a closer look at my phone image. His disapproval was plain. "I see that you have been drinking. Perhaps you should go home now, and call me tomorrow."

I was shocked. "Don't you know *anything* about Belt customs?"

"I do not understand."

I explained the ceremonial drunk. "Look, Ordaz, if you know that little about the way a Belter thinks, then we'd better have a talk. Soon. Otherwise you're likely to miss something."

"You may be right. I can see you at noon, over lunch."

"Good. What have you got?"

"Considerable, but none of it is very helpful. Your friend landed on Earth two months ago, arriving on the *Pillar of Fire,* operating out of Outback Field, Australia. He was wearing a haircut in the style of Earth. From there—"

"That's funny. He'd have had to wait two months for his hair to grow out."

"That occurred even to me. I understand that a Belter commonly shaves his entire scalp, except for a strip two inches wide running from the nape of his neck forward."

"The strip cut, yah. It probably started when someone decided he'd live longer if his hair couldn't fall in his eyes during a tricky landing. But Owen could have let his hair grow out during a singleship mining trip. There'd be nobody to see."

"Still, it seems odd. Did you know that Mr. Jennison has a cousin on Earth? One Harvey Peele, who manages a chain of supermarkets."

"So I wasn't his next of kin, even on Earth."

"Mr. Jennison made no attempt to contact him."

"Anything else?"

"I've spoken to the man who sold Mr. Jennison his droud

and plug. Kenneth Graham owns an office and operating room on Gayley in Near West Los Angeles. Graham claims that the droud was a standard type, that your friend must have altered it himself."

"Do you believe him?"

"For the present. His permits and his records are all in order. The droud was altered with a soldering iron, an amateur's tool."

"Uh huh."

"As far as the police are concerned, the case will probably be closed when we locate the tools Mr. Jennison used."

"Tell you what. I'll wire Homer Chandrasekhar tomorrow. Maybe he can find out things—why Owen landed without a strip haircut, why he came to Earth at all."

Ordaz shrugged with his eyebrows. He thanked me for my trouble and hung up.

The coffee grog was still hot. I gulped at it, savoring the sugary, bittery sting of it, trying to forget Owen dead and remember him in life. He was always slightly chubby, I remembered, but he never gained a pound and he never lost a pound. He could move like a whippet when he had to.

And now he was terribly thin, and his death-grin was ripe with obscene joy.

I ordered another coffee grog. The waiter, a showman, made sure he had my attention before he lit the heated rum, then poured it from a foot above the glass. You can't drink that drink slowly. It slides down too easily, and there's the added spur that if you wait too long it might get cold. Rum and strong coffee. Two of these and I'd be drunkenly alert for hours.

Midnight found me in the Mars Bar, running on scotch and soda. In between I'd been barhopping. Irish coffee at Bergin's, cold and smoking concoctions at the Moon Pool, scotch and wild music at Beyond. I couldn't get drunk, and I couldn't find the right mood. There was a barrier to the picture I was trying to rebuild.

It was the memory of the last Owen, grinning in an armchair with a wire leading down into his brain.

I didn't know that Owen. I had never met the man, and never would have wanted to. From bar to nightclub to restaurant I had run from the image, waiting for the alcohol to break the barrier between present and past.

So I sat at a corner table, surrounded by 3D panoramic views of an impossible Mars. Crystal towers and long, straight blue canali, six-legged beasts and beautiful, impossibly slender men and women, looked out at me across never-never land. Would Owen have found it sad or funny? He'd seen the real Mars, and had not been impressed.

I had reached that stage where time becomes discontinuous, where gaps of seconds or minutes appear between the events you can remember. Somewhere in that period I found myself staring at a cigarette. I must have just lighted it, because it was near its original two-hundred-millimeter length. Maybe a waiter had snuck up behind me. There it was, at any rate, burning between my middle and index fingers.

I stared at the coal as the mood settled on me. I was calm, I was drifting, I was lost in time . . .

. . . We'd been two months in the rocks, our first trip out since the accident. Back we came to Ceres with a holdful of gold, 50 percent pure, guaranteed suitable for rustproof wiring and conductor plates. At nightfall we were ready to celebrate.

We walked along the city limits, with neon blinking and beckoning on the right, a melted rock cliff to the left, and stars blazing through the dome overhead. Homer Chandrasekhar was practically snorting. On this night his first trip out culminated in his first homecoming: and homecoming is the best part.

"We'll want to split up about midnight," he said. He didn't need to enlarge on that. Three men in company might conceivably be three singleship pilots, but chances are they're a ship's crew. They don't have their singleship licenses yet; they're too stupid or too inexperienced. If we wanted companions for the night—

"You haven't thought this through," Owen answered. I saw

Homer's double take, then his quick look at where my shoulder ended, and I was ashamed. I didn't need my crewmates to hold my hand, and in this state I'd only slow them down.

Before I could open my mouth to protest, Owen went on. "Think it through. We've got a draw here that we'd be idiots to throw away. Gil, pick up a cigarette. No, not with your left hand—"

I was drunk, gloriously drunk and feeling immortal. The attenuated martians seemed to move in the walls, the walls that seemed to be picture windows on a Mars that never was. For the first time that night, I raised my glass in toast.

"To Owen, from Gil the Arm. Thanks."

I transferred the cigarette to my imaginary hand.

By now you've got the idea I was holding it in my imaginary fingers. Most people have the same impression, but it isn't so. I held it clutched ignominiously in my fist. The coal couldn't burn me, of course, but it still felt like a lead ingot.

I rested my imaginary elbow on the table, and that seemed to make it easier—which is ridiculous, but it works. Truly, I'd expected my imaginary arm to disappear after I got the transplant. But I'd found I could dissociate from the new arm to hold small objects in my invisible hand, to feel tactile sensations in my invisible fingertips.

I'd earned the title Gil the Arm, that night in Ceres. It had started with a floating cigarette. Owen had been right. Everyone in the place eventually wound up staring at the floating cigarette smoked by the one-armed man. All I had to do was find the prettiest girl in the room with my peripheral vision, then catch her eye.

That night we had been the center of the biggest impromptu party ever thrown in Ceres Base. It wasn't planned that way at all. I'd used the cigarette trick three times, so that each of us would have a date. But the third girl already had an escort, and he was celebrating something; he'd sold some kind of patent to an Earth-based industrial firm. He was throwing money around like confetti. So we let him stay. I did tricks, reaching esper fingers into a closed box to tell what was inside, and by the time I finished all the tables had been pushed together and I was in the center, with Homer and Owen and three girls. Then we got to singing old songs, and the bartenders joined us, and suddenly everything was on the house.

Eventually about twenty of us wound up in the orbiting mansion of the First Speaker for the Belt Government. The goldskin cops had tried to bust us up earlier, and the First Speaker had behaved very rudely indeed, then compensated by inviting them to join us ...

And that was why I used TK on so many cigarettes.

Across the width of the Mars Bar, a girl in a peach-colored dress sat studying me with her chin on her fist. I got up and went over.

My head felt fine. It was the first thing I checked when I woke up. Apparently I'd remembered to take a hangover pill.

A leg was hooked over my knee. It felt good, though the pressure had put my foot to sleep. Fragrant dark hair spilled beneath my nose. I didn't move. I didn't want her to know I was awake.

It's damned embarrassing when you wake up with a girl and can't remember her name.

Well, let's see. A peach dress neatly hung from a doorknob ... I remembered a whole lot of traveling last night. The girl at the Mars Bar. A puppet show. Music of all kinds. I'd talked about Owen, and she'd steered me away from that because it depressed her. Then—

Hah! Taffy. Last name forgotten.

"Morning," I said.

"Morning," she said. "Don't try to move, we're hooked together ..." In the sober morning light she was lovely. Long black hair, brown eyes, creamy untanned skin. To be lovely this early was a neat trick, and I told her so, and she smiled.

My lower leg was dead meat until it started to buzz with renewed circulation, and then I made faces 'until it calmed down. Taffy kept up a running chatter as we dressed. "That third hand is strange. I remember you holding me with two strong arms and stroking the back of my neck with the third. *Very* nice. It reminded me of a Fritz Leiber story."

" 'The Wanderer.' The panther girl."

"Mm hmm. How many girls have you caught with that cigarette trick?"

"None as pretty as you."

"And how many girls have you told that to?"

"Can't remember. It always worked before. Maybe this time it's for real."

We exchanged grins.

A minute later I caught her frowning thoughtfully at the back of my neck. "Something wrong?"

"I was just thinking. You really crashed and burned last night. I hope you don't drink that much all the time."

"Why? You worried about me?"

She blushed, then nodded.

"I should have told you. In fact, I think I did, last night. I was on a ceremonial drunk. When a good friend dies it's obligatory to get smashed."

Taffy looked relieved. "I didn't mean to get—"

"Personal? Why not. You've the right. Anyway, I like—" *maternal types*, but I couldn't say that. "People who worry about me."

Taffy touched her hair with some kind of complex comb. A few strokes snapped her hair instantly into place. Static electricity?

"It was a good drunk," I said. "Owen would have been proud. And that's all the mourning I'll do. One drunk and—" I spread my hands. "Out."

"It's not a bad way to go," Taffy mused reflectively. "Current stimulus, I mean. I mean, if you've got to bow out—"

"Now drop that!" I don't know how I got so angry so fast. Ghoul-thin and grinning in a reading chair, Owen's corpse was suddenly vivid before me. I'd fought that image for too many hours. "Walking off a bridge is enough of a cop-out," I snarled. "Dying for a month while current burns out your brain is nothing less than sickening."

Taffy was hurt and bewildered. "But your friend did it, didn't he? You didn't make him sound like a weakling."

"Nuts," I heard myself say. "He didn't do it. He was—"

Just like that, I was sure. I must have realized it while I was drunk or sleeping. Of *course* he hadn't killed himself. *That* wasn't Owen. And current addiction wasn't Owen either.

"He was murdered," I said. "Sure he was. Why didn't I see it?" And I made a dive for the phone.

"Good morning, Mr. Hamilton." Detective-Inspector Ordaz looked very fresh and neat this morning. I was suddenly aware that I hadn't shaved. "I see you remembered to take your hangover pills."

"Right. Ordaz, has it occurred to you that Owen might have been murdered?"

"Naturally. But it isn't possible."

"I think it might be. Suppose he—"

"Mr. Hamilton."

"Yah?"

"We have an appointment for lunch. Shall we discuss it then? Meet me at Headquarters at twelve hundred."

"Okay. One thing you might take care of this morning. See if Owen registered for a nudist's license."

"Do you think he might have?"

"Yah. I'll tell you why at lunch."

"Very well."

"Don't hang up. You said you'd found the man who sold Owen his droud-and-plug. What was his name again?"

"Kenneth Graham."

"That's what I thought." I hung up.

Taffy touched my shoulder. "Do—do you really think he might have been—killed?"

"Yah. The whole setup depended on him not being able to—"

"No. Wait. I don't want to know about it."

I turned to look at her. She really didn't. The very subject of a stranger's death was making her sick to her stomach.

"Okay. Look, I'm a jerk not to at least offer you breakfast but I've got to get on this right away. Can I call you a cab?"

When the cab came I dropped a ten-mark coin in the slot and helped her in. I got her address before it took off.

ARM Headquarters hummed with early morning activity. Hellos came my way, and I answered them without stopping to talk. Anything important would filter down to me eventually.

As I passed Julie's cubicle I glanced in. She was hard at work, limply settled in her contour couch, jotting notes with her eyes closed.

Kenneth Graham.

A hookup to the basement computer formed the greater part of my desk. Learning how to use it had taken me several months. I typed an order for coffee and donuts, then: INFORMATION RETRIEVAL. KENNETH GRAHAM. LIMITED LICENSE: SURGERY. GENERAL LICENSE: DIRECT CURRENT STIMULUS EQUIPMENT SALES. ADDRESS: NEAR WEST LOS ANGELES.

Tape chattered out of the slot, an instant response, loop after loop of it curling on my desk. I didn't need to read it to know I was right.

New technologies create new customs, new laws, new ethics, new crimes. About half the activity of the United Nations Police, the ARMs, dealt with control of a crime that hadn't existed a century ago. The crime of organlegging was the result of thousands of years of medical progress, of millions of lives selflessly dedicated to the ideal of healing the sick. Progress had brought these ideals to reality, and, as usual, had created new problems.

1900 A.D. was the year Karl Landsteiner classified human blood into four types, giving patients their first real chance to survive a transfusion. The technology of transplants had grown with the growing of the twentieth century. Whole blood, dry bone, skin, live kidneys, live hearts could all be transferred from one body to another. Donors had saved tens of thousands of lives in that hundred years, by willing their bodies to medicine.

But the number of donors was limited, and not many died

in such a way that anything of value could be saved.

The deluge had come something less than a hundred years ago. One healthy donor (but of course there was no such animal) could save a dozen lives. Why, then, should a condemned murderer die to no purpose? First a few states, then most of the nations of the world had passed new laws. Criminals condemned to death must be executed in a hospital, with surgeons to save as much as could be saved for the organ banks.

The world's billions wanted to live, and the organ banks were life itself. A man could live forever as long as the doctors could shove spare parts into him faster than his own parts wore out. But they could do that only as long as the world's organ banks were stocked.

A hundred scattered movements to abolish the death penalty died silent, unpublicized deaths. Everybody gets sick sometime.

And still there were shortages in the organ banks. Still patients died for the lack of parts to save them. The world's legislators had responded to steady pressure from the world's people. Death penalties were established for first, second, and third degree murder. For assault with a deadly weapon. Then for a multitude of crimes: rape, fraud, embezzlement, having children without a license, four or more counts of false advertising. For nearly a century the trend had been growing, as the world's voting citizens acted to protect their right to live forever.

Even now there weren't enough transplants. A woman with kidney trouble might wait a year for a transplant: one healthy kidney to last the rest of her life. A thirty-five-year-old heart patient must live with a sound but forty-year-old heart. One lung, part of a liver, prosthetics that wore out too fast or weighed too much or did too little ... there weren't enough criminals. Not surprisingly, the death penalty *was* a deterrent. People stopped committing crimes rather than face the donor room of a hospital.

For instant replacement of your ruined digestive system, for a *young* healthy heart, for a whole liver when you'd ruined yours with alcohol ... you had to go to an organlegger.

There are three aspects to the business of organlegging.

One is the business of kidnap-murder. It's risky. You can't fill an organ bank by waiting for volunteers. Executing condemned criminals is a government monopoly. So you go out and *get* your donors: on a crowded city slidewalk, in an air terminal, stranded on a freeway by a car with a busted capacitor ... anywhere.

The selling end of the business is just as dangerous, because even a desperately sick man sometimes has a conscience. He'll buy his transplant, then go straight to the ARMs, curing his sickness and his conscience by turning in the whole gang. Thus the sales end is somewhat anonymous, but as there are few repeat sales, that hardly matters.

Third is the technical, medical aspect. Probably this is the safest part of the business. Your hospital is big, but you can put it anywhere. You wait for the donors, who arrive still alive; you ship out livers and glands and square feet of live skin, correctly labeled for rejection reactions.

It's not as easy as it sounds. You need doctors. Good ones. That was where Loren came in. He had a monopoly.

Where did he get them? We were still trying to find out. Somehow, one man had discovered a foolproof way to recruit talented but dishonest doctors practically en masse. Was it really one man? All our sources said it was. And he had half the North American west coast in the palm of his hand.

Loren. No holographs, no fingerprints or retina prints, not even a description. All we had was that one name, and a few possible contacts.

One of these was Kenneth Graham.

The holograph was a good one. Probably it had been posed in a portrait shop. Kenneth Graham had a long Scottish face with a lantern jaw and a small, dour mouth. In the holo he was trying to smile and look dignified simultaneously. He only looked uncomfortable. His hair was sandy and close cut. Above his light gray eyes his eyebrows were so light as to be nearly invisible.

My breakfast arrived. I dunked a donut and bit it, and found out I was hungrier than I'd thought.

A string of holos had been reproduced on the computer tape. I ran through the others fairly quickly, eating with one hand and flipping the key with the other. Some were fuzzy; they had been taken by spy beams through the windows of Graham's shop. None of the prints were in any way incriminating. Not one showed Graham smiling.

He had been selling electrical joy for twelve years now.

A current addict has an advantage over his supplier. Electricity is cheap. With a drug, your supplier can always raise the price on you; but not with electricity. You see the ecstasy merchant once, when he sells you your operation and your droud, and never again. Nobody gets hooked by accident. There's an honesty to current addiction. The customer always knows just what he's getting into, and what it will do for him—and to him.

Still, you'd need a certain lack of empathy to make a living the way Kenneth Graham did. Else he'd have had to turn away his customers. Nobody becomes a current addict gradually. He decides all at once, and he buys the operation before he has ever tasted its joy. Each of Kenneth Graham's customers had reached his shop after deciding to drop out of the human race.

What a stream of the hopeless and the desperate must have passed through Graham's shop! How could they help but haunt his dreams? And if Kenneth Graham slept well at night, then—

Then, small wonder if he had turned organlegger.

He was in a good position for it. Despair is characteristic of the would-be current addict. The unknown, the unloved, the people nobody knew and nobody needed and nobody missed, these passed in a steady stream through Kenneth Graham's shop.

So a few didn't come out. Who'd notice?

I flipped quickly through the tape to find out who was in

charge of watching Graham. Jackson Bera. I called down through the desk phone.

"Sure," said Bera, "we've had a spy beam on him about three weeks now. It's a waste of good salaried ARM agents. Maybe he's clean. Maybe he's been tipped somehow."

"Then why not stop watching him?"

Bera looked disgusted. "Because we've only been watching for three weeks. How many donors do you think he needs a year? Two. Read the reports. Gross profit on a single donor is over a million UN marks. Graham can afford to be careful who he picks."

"Yah."

"At that, he wasn't careful enough. At least two of his customers disappeared last year. Customers with families. That's what put us on him."

"So you could watch him for the next six months without a guarantee. He could be just waiting for the right guy to walk in."

"Sure. He has to write up a report on every customer. That gives him the right to ask personal questions. If the guy has relatives, Graham lets him walk out. Most people do have relatives, you know. Then again," Bera said disconsolately, "he could be clean. Sometimes a current addict disappears without help."

"How come I didn't see any holos of Graham at home? You can't be watching just his shop."

Jackson Bera scratched at his hair. Hair like black steel wool, worn long like a bushman's mop. "Sure we're watching his place, but we can't get a spy beam in there. It's an inside apartment. No windows. You know anything about spy beams?"

"Not much. I know they've been around awhile."

"They're as old as lasers. Oldest trick in the book is to put a mirror in the room you want to bug. Then you run a laser beam through a window, or even through heavy drapes, and bounce it off the mirror. When you pick it up it's been distorted by the vibrations in the glass. That gives you a perfect recording of anything that's been said in that room.

But for pictures you need something a little more sophisticated."

"How sophisticated can we get?"

"We can put a spy beam in any room with a window. We can send one through some kinds of wall. Give us an optically flat surface and we can send one around corners."

"But you need an outside wall."

"Yup."

"What's Graham doing now?"

"Just a sec." Bera disappeared from view. "Someone just came in. Graham's talking to him. Want the picture?"

"Sure. Leave it on. I'll turn it off from here when I'm through with it."

The picture of Bera went dark. A moment later I was looking into a doctor's office. If I'd seen it cold I'd have thought it was run by a podiatrist. There was the comfortable tilt-back chair with the headrest and the footrest; the cabinet next to it with instruments lying on top, on a clean white cloth; the desk over in one corner. Kenneth Graham was talking to a homely, washed-out-looking girl.

I listened to Graham's would-be-fatherly reassurances and his glowing description of the magic of current addiction. When I couldn't take it any longer I turned the sound down. The girl took her place in the chair, and Graham placed something over her head.

The girl's homely face turned suddenly beautiful.

Happiness is beautiful, all by itself. A happy person is beautiful, per se. Suddenly and totally, the girl was full of joy and I realized that I hadn't known everything about droud sales. Apparently Graham had an inductor to put the current where he wanted it, without wires. He *could* show a customer what current addiction felt like, without first implanting the wires.

What a powerful argument that was!

Graham turned off the machine. It was as if he'd turned off the girl. She sat stunned for a moment, then reached frantically for her purse and started scrabbling inside.

I couldn't take anymore. I turned it off.

Small wonder if Graham had turned organlegger. He had to be totally without empathy just to sell his merchandise.

Even there, I thought, he'd had a head start.

So he was a little more callous than the rest of the world's billions. But not much. Every voter had a bit of the organlegger in him. In voting the death penalty for so many crimes, the law makers had only bent to pressure from the voters. There was a spreading lack of respect for life, the evil side of transplant technology. The good side was a longer life for everyone. One condemned criminal could save a dozen deserving lives. Who could complain about that?

We hadn't thought that way in the Belt. In the Belt survival was a virtue in itself, and life was a precious thing, spread so thin among the sterile rocks, hurtling in single units through all that killing emptiness between the worlds.

So I'd had to come to Earth for my transplant.

My request had been accepted two months after I landed. So quickly? Later I'd learned that the banks always have a surplus of certain items. Few people lose their arms these days. I had also learned, a year after the transplant had taken, that I was using an arm taken from a captured organlegger's storage bank.

That had been a shock. I'd hoped my arm had come from a depraved murderer, someone who'd shot fourteen nurses from a rooftop. Not at all. Some faceless, nameless victim had had the bad luck to encounter a ghoul, and I had benefited thereby.

Did I turn in my new arm in a fit of revulsion? No, surprising to say, I did not. But I had joined the ARMs, once the Amalgamation of Regional Militia, now the United Nations Police. Though I had stolen a dead man's arm, I would hunt the kin of those who had killed him.

The noble urgency of that resolve had been drowned in paperwork these last few years. Perhaps I was becoming callous, like the flatlanders—the *other* flatlanders around me, voting new death penalties year after year. *Income-tax evasion. Operating a flying vehicle on manual controls, over a city.*

Was Kenneth Graham so much worse than they?

Sure he was. The bastard had put a wire in Owen Jennison's head.

I waited twenty minutes for Julie to come out. I could have sent her a memorandum, but there was plenty of time before noon, and too little time to get anything accomplished, and . . . I wanted to talk to her.

"Hi," she said. "Thanks," taking the coffee. "How went the ceremonial drunk? Oh, I *see*. Mmmmm. Very good. Almost poetic." Conversation with Julie has a way of taking short-cuts.

Poetic, right. I remembered how inspiration had struck like lightning through a mild high glow. Owen's floating cigarette lure. What better way to honor his memory than to use it to pick up a girl?

"Right," Julie agreed. "But there's something you may have missed. What's Taffy's last name?"

"I can't remember. She wrote it down on—"

"What does she do for a living?"

"How should I know?"

"What religion is she? Is she a pro or an anti? Where did she grow up?"

"Dammit—"

"Half an hour ago you were very complacently musing on how depersonalized all us flatlanders are except you. What's Taffy, a person or a foldout?" Julie stood with her hands on her hips, looking up at me like a short schoolteacher.

How many people is Julie? Some of us have never seen this Guardian aspect. She's frightening, the Guardian. If it ever appeared on a date, the man she was with would be struck impotent forever.

It never does. When a reprimand is deserved, Julie delivers it in broad daylight. This serves to separate her functions, but it doesn't make it easier to take.

No use pretending it wasn't her business, either.

I'd come here to ask for Julie's protection. Let me turn unlovable to Julie, even a little bit unlovable, and as far as Julie was concerned I would have an unreadable mind. How, then, would she know when I was in trouble? How could she send help to rescue me from whatever? My private life *was* her business, her single, vastly important job.

"I *like* Taffy," I protested. "I didn't care who she was when we met. Now I like her, and I think she likes me. What do you want from a first date?"

"You know better. You can remember other dates when two of you talked all night on a couch, just from the joy of learning about each other." She mentioned three names, and I flushed. Julie knows the words that will turn you inside out in an instant. "Taffy is a person, not an episode, not a symbol of anything, not just a pleasant night. What's your judgment of her?"

I thought about it, standing there in the corridor. Funny: I've faced the Guardian Julie on other occasions, and it has never occurred to me to just walk out of the unpleasant situation. Later I think of that. At the time I just stand there, facing the Guardian/Judge/Teacher. I thought about Taffy . . .

"She's nice," I said. *"Not* depersonalized. Squeamish, even. She wouldn't make a good nurse. She'd want to help too much, and it would tear her apart when she couldn't. I'd say she was one of the vulnerable ones."

"Go on."

"I want to see her again, but I won't dare talk shop with her. In fact . . . I'd better not see her till this business of Owen is over. Loren might take an interest in her. Or . . . she might take an interest in me, and I might get hurt . . . have I missed anything?"

"I think so. You owe her a phone call. If you won't be dating her for a few days, call her and tell her so."

"Check." I spun on my heel, spun back. "Finagle's Jest! I almost forgot. The reason I came here—"

"I know, you want a time slot. Suppose I check on you at oh nine forty-five every morning?"

"That's a little early. When I get in deadly danger it's usually at night."

"I'm off at night. Oh nine-forty-five is all I've got. I'm sorry, Gil, but it is. Shall I monitor you or not?"

"Sold. Nine forty-five."

"Good. Let me know if you get real proof Owen was murdered. I'll give you two slots. You'll be in a little more concrete danger then."

"Good."

"I love you. Yeep, I'm late." And she dodged back into her office, while I went to call Taffy.

Taffy wasn't home, of course, and I didn't know where she worked, or even what she did. Her phone offered to take a message. I gave my name and said I'd call back.

And then I sat there sweating for five minutes.

It was half an hour to noon. Here I was at my desk phone. I couldn't decently see any way to argue myself out of sending a message to Homer Chandrasekhar.

I didn't want to talk to him, then or ever. He'd chewed me out but good, last time I'd seen him. My free arm had cost me my Belter life, and it had cost me Homer's respect. I didn't want to talk to him, even on a one-way message, and I most particularly didn't want to have to tell him Owen was dead.

But someone had to tell him.

And maybe he could find out something.

And I'd put it off nearly a full day.

For five minutes I sweated, and then I called long distance and recorded a message and sent it off to Ceres. More accurately, I recorded six messages before I was satisfied. I don't want to talk about it.

I tried Taffy again; she might come home for lunch. Wrong.

I hung up wondering if Julie had been fair. What had we bargained for, Taffy and I, beyond a pleasant night? And we'd had that, and would have others, with luck.

But Julie would find it hard not to be fair. If she thought Taffy was the vulnerable type, she'd taken her information from my own mind.

Mixed feelings. You're a kid, and your mother has just laid down the law. But it *is* a law, something you can count on ... and she *is* paying attention to you ... and she *does* care ... when, for so many of those outside, nobody cares at all.

Naturally I thought of murder," said Ordaz. "I always consider murder. When my sainted mother passed away after three years of the most tender care by my sister Maria Angela, I actually considered searching for evidence of needle holes about the head."

"Find any?"

Ordaz' face froze. He put down his beer and started to get up.

"Cool it," I said hurriedly. "No offense intended." He glared a moment, then sat down half mollified.

We'd picked an outdoor restaurant on the pedestrian level. On the other side of a hedge (a real live hedge, green and growing and everything) the shoppers were carried past in a steady one-way stream. Beyond them, a slidewalk carried a similar stream in the opposite direction. I had the dizzy feeling that it was we who were moving.

A waiter like a bell-bottomed chess pawn produced steaming dishes of chili size from its torso, put them precisely in front of us, and slid away on a cushion of air.

"Naturally I considered murder. Believe me, Mr. Hamilton, it does not hold up."

"I think I could make a pretty good case."

"You may try, of course. Better, I will start you on your way. First, we must assume that Kenneth Graham the happiness peddler did not sell a droud-and-plug to Owen Jennison. Rather, Owen Jennison was forced to undergo the operation. Graham's records, including the written permission to operate, were forged. All this we must assume, is it not so?"

"Right. And before you tell me Graham's escutcheon is unblemished, let me tell you that it isn't."

"Oh?"

"He's connected with an organlegging gang. That's classified information. We're watching him, and we don't want him tipped."

"That is news." Ordaz rubbed his jaw. "Organlegging. Well. What would Owen Jennison have to do with organlegging?"

"Owen's a Belter. The Belt's always drastically short of transplant materials."

"Yes, they import quantities of medical supplies from Earth. Not only organs in storage, but also drugs and prosthetics. So?"

"Owen ran a good many cargos past the goldskins in his day. He got caught a few times, but he's still way ahead of the government. He's on the records as a successful smuggler. If a big organlegger wanted to expand his market, he might very well send a feeler out to a Belter with a successful smuggling record."

"You never mentioned that Mr. Jennison was a smuggler."

"What for? All Belters are smugglers, if they think they can get away with it. To a Belter, smuggling isn't immoral. But an organlegger wouldn't know that. He'd think Owen was already a criminal."

"Do you think your friend—" Ordaz hesitated delicately.

"No, Owen wouldn't turn organlegger. But he might, he just *might* try to turn one in. The rewards for information leading to the capture and conviction of, et cetera, are substantial. If someone contracted Owen, Owen might very well have tried to trace the contact by himself.

"Now, the gang we're after covers half the west coast of this continent. That's big. It's the Loren gang, the one Graham may be working for. Suppose Owen had a chance to meet Loren himself?"

"You think he might take it, do you?"

"I think he did. I think he let his hair grow out so he'd look like an Earthman, to convince Loren he wanted to look inconspicuous. I think he collected as much information as he could, then tried to get out with a whole skin. But he didn't make it.

"Did you find his application for a nudist license?"

"No. I saw your point there," said Ordaz. He leaned back, ignoring the food in front of him. "Mr. Jennison's tan was uniform except for the characteristic darkening of the face. I presume he was a practicing nudist in the Belt."

"Yah. We don't need licenses there. He'd have been one

here, too, unless he was hiding something. Remember that scar. He never missed a chance to show it off."

"Could he really have thought to pass for a—" Ordaz hesitated—"flatlander?"

"With that Belter tan? No! He was overdoing it a little with the haircut. Maybe he thought Loren would underestimate him. But he wasn't advertising his presence, or he wouldn't have left his most personal possessions home."

"So he was dealing with organleggers, and they found him out before he could reach you. Yes, Mr. Hamilton, this is well thought out. But it won't work."

"Why not? I'm not trying to prove it's murder. Not yet. I'm just trying to show you that murder is at least as likely as suicide."

"But it's not, Mr. Hamilton."

I looked the question.

"Consider the details of the hypothetical murder. Owen Jennison is drugged, no doubt, and taken to the office of Kenneth Graham. There, an ecstasy plug is attached. A standard droud is fitted, and is then amateurishly altered with soldering tools. Already we see, on the part of the killer, a minute attention to details. We see it again in Kenneth Graham's forged papers of permission to operate. They were impeccable.

"Owen Jennison is then taken back to his apartment. It would be his own, would it not? There would be little point in moving him to another. The cord from his droud is shortened, again in amateurish fashion. Mr. Jennison is tied up—"

"I wondered if you'd see that."

"But why should he not be tied up? He is tied up, and allowed to waken. Perhaps the arrangement is explained to him, perhaps not. That would be up to the killer. The killer then plugs Mr. Jennison into a wall. A current trickles through his brain, and Owen Jennsion knows pure pleasure for the first time in his life.

"He is left tied up for, let us say, three hours. In the first few minutes he would be a hopeless addict, I think—"

"You must have known more current addicts than I have."

"Even I would not want to be pinned down. Your normal current addict is an addict after a few minutes. But then, your normal current addict asked to be made an addict, knowing what it would do to his life. Current addiction is symptomatic of despair. Your friend might have been able to fight free of a few minutes' exposure."

"So they kept him tied up for three hours. Then they cut the ropes." I felt sickened. Ordaz' ugly, ugly pictures matched mine in every detail.

"No more than three hours, by our hypothesis. They would not dare stay longer than a few hours. They would cut the ropes and leave Owen Jennison to starve to death. In the space of a month the evidence of his drugging would vanish, as would any abrasions left by ropes, lumps on his head, mercy needle punctures, and the like. A carefully detailed, well-thought-out plan, don't you agree?"

I told myself that Ordaz was not being ghoulish. He was just doing his job. Still, it was difficult to answer objectively.

"It fits our picture of Loren. He's been very careful with us. He'd love carefully detailed, well-thought-out plans."

Ordaz leaned forward. "But don't you see? A carefully detailed plan is all wrong. There is a crucial flaw in it. Suppose Mr. Jennison pulls out the droud?"

"Could he do that? Would he?"

"Could he? Certainly. A simple tug of the fingers. The current wouldn't interfere with motor coordination. Would he?" Ordaz pulled meditatively at his beer. "I know a good deal about current addiction, but I don't know what it *feels* like, Mr. Hamilton. Your normal addict pulls his droud out as often as he inserts it, but your friend was getting ten times normal current. He might have pulled the droud out a dozen times, and instantly plugged it back each time. Yet Belters are supposed to be strong-willed men, very individualistic. Who knows whether, even after a week of addiction, your friend might not have pulled the droud loose, coiled the cord, slipped it in his pocket, and walked away scot free?

"There is the additional risk that someone might walk in on him—an automachinery serviceman, for instance. Or someone might notice that he had not bought any food in a month. A suicide would take that risk. Suicides routinely leave themselves a chance to change their minds. But a murderer?

"No. Even if the chance were one in a thousand, the man who created such a detailed plan would never have taken such a chance."

The sun burned hotly down on our shoulders. Ordaz suddenly remembered his lunch and began to eat.

I watched the world ride by beyond the hedge. Pedestrians stood in little conversational bunches; others peered into shop windows on the pedestrian strip, or glanced over the hedge to watch us eat. There were the few who pushed through the crowd with set expressions, impatient with the ten-mile-per-hour speed of the slidewalk.

"Maybe they *were* watching him. Maybe the room was bugged."

"We searched the room thoroughly," said Ordaz. "If there had been observational equipment, we would have found it."

"It could have been removed."

Ordaz shrugged.

I remembered the spy-eyes in Monica Apartments. Someone would have had to physically enter the room to carry a bug out. He could ruin it with the right signal, maybe, but it would surely leave traces.

And Owen had had an inside room. No spy-eyes.

"There's one thing you've left out," I said presently.

"And what would that be?"

"My name in Owen's wallet, listed as next of kin. He was directing my attention to the thing I was working on. The Loren gang."

"That is possible."

"You can't have it both ways."

Ordaz lowered his fork. "I *can* have it both ways, Mr. Hamilton. But you won't like it."

"I'm sure I won't."

"Let us incorporate your assumption. Mr. Jennison was contacted by an agent of Loren, the organlegger, who intended to sell transplant material to Belters. He accepted. The promise of riches was too much for him.

"A month later, something made him realize what a terrible thing he had done. He decided to die. He went to an ecstasy peddler and he had a wire put in his head. Later, before he plugged in the droud, he made one attempt to atone for his crime. He listed you as his next of kin, so that you might guess why he had died, and perhaps so that you could use that knowledge against Loren."

Ordaz looked at me across the table. "I see that you will never agree. I cannot help that. I can only read the evidence."

"Me too. But I knew Owen. He'd never have worked for an organlegger, he'd never have killed himself, and if he had, he'd never have done it that way."

Ordaz didn't answer.

"What about fingerprints?"

"In the apartment? None."

"None but Owen's?"

"Even his were found only on the chairs and end tables. I curse the man who invented the cleaning robot. Every smooth surface in that apartment was cleaned exactly forty-four times during Mr. Jennison's tenancy." Ordaz went back to his chili size.

"Then try this. Assume for the moment that I'm right. Assume Owen was after Loren, and Loren got him. Owen knew he was doing something dangerous. He wouldn't have wanted me to get onto Loren before he was ready. He wanted the reward for himself. But he might have left me something, just in case.

"Something in a locker somewhere, an airport or spaceport locker. Evidence. Not under his own name, or mine either, because I'm a known ARM. But—"

"Some name you both know."

"Right. Like Homer Chandrasekhar. Or—got it. Cubes Forsythe. Owen would have thought that was apt. Cubes is dead."

"We will look. You must understand that it will not prove your case."

"Sure. Anything you find, Owen could have arranged in a

fit of conscience. Screw that. Let me know what you get," I said, and stood up and left.

I rode the slidewalk, not caring where it was taking me. It would give me a chance to cool off.

Could Ordaz be right? Could he?

But the more I dug into Owen's death, the worse it made Owen look.

Therefore Ordaz was wrong.

Owen work for an organlegger? He'd rather have been a donor.

Owen getting his kicks from a wall socket? He never even watched tridee!

Owen kill himself? No. If so, not that way.

But even if I could have swallowed all that . . .

Owen Jennison, letting me know he'd worked with organleggers? Me, Gil the Arm Hamilton? Let *me* know *that?*

The slidewalk rolled along, past restaurants and shopping centers and churches and banks. Ten stories below, the hum of cars and scooters drifted faintly up from the vehicular level. The sky was a narrow, vivid slash of blue between black shadows of skyscraper.

Let *me* know *that?* Never.

But Ordaz's strangely inconsistent murderer was no better.

I thought of something even Ordaz had missed. Why would Loren dispose of Owen so elaborately? Owen need only disappear into the organ banks, never to bother Loren again.

The shops were thinning out now, and so were the crowds. The slidewalk narrowed, entered a residential area, and not a very good one. I'd let it carry me a long way. I looked around, trying to decide where I was.

And I was four blocks from Graham's place.

My subconscious had done me a dirty. I wanted a look at Kenneth Graham, face to face. The temptation to go on was nearly irresistible, but I fought it off and changed direction at the next disk.

A slidewalk intersection is a rotating disk, its rim tangent to four slidewalks and moving with the same speed. From the center you ride up an escalator and over the slidewalks to reach stationary walks along the buildings. I could have caught a cab at the center of the disk, but I still wanted to think, so I just rode halfway around the rim.

I could have walked into Graham's shop and gotten away with it. Maybe. I'd have looked hopeless and bored and hesitant, told Graham I wanted an ecstasy plug, worried loudly about what my wife and friends would say, then changed my mind at the last moment. He'd have let me walk out, knowing I'd be missed. Maybe.

But Loren had to know more about the ARMs than we knew about him. Some time or other, had Graham been shown a holo of yours truly? Let a known ARM walk into his shop, and Graham would panic. It wasn't worth the risk.

Then, dammit, what *could* I do?

Ordaz' inconsistent killer. If we assumed Owen was murdered, we couldn't get away from the other assumptions. The care, the nitpicking detail—and then Owen left alone to pull out the plug and walk away, or to be discovered by a persistent salesman or a burglar, or—

No. Ordaz's hypothetical killer, and mine, would have watched Owen like a hawk. For a month.

That did it. I stepped off at the next disk and got a taxi.

The taxi dropped me on the roof of Monica Apartments. I took an elevator to the lobby.

If the manager was surprised to see me, he didn't show it as he gestured me into his office. The office seemed much roomier than the lobby had, possibly because there were things to break the anonymous-modern decor: paintings on the wall, a small black worm track in the rug that must have been caused by a visitor's cigarette, a holo of Miller and his wife on the wide, nearly empty desk. He waited until I was settled, then leaned forward expectantly.

"I'm here on ARMs business," I said, and passed him my ident.

He passed it back without checking it. "I presume it's the same business," he said without cordiality.

"Yah. I'm convinced Owen Jennsion must have had visitors while he was here."

The manager smiled. "That's ridic—impossible."

"Nope, it's not. Your holo cameras take pictures of visitors, but they don't snap the tenants, do they?"

"Of course not."

"Then Owen could have been visited by any tenant in the building."

The manager looked shocked. "No, certainly not. Really, I don't see why you pursue this, Mr. Hamilton. If Mr. Jennison had been found in such a condition, it would have been reported!"

"I don't think so. Could he have been visited by any tenant in the building?"

"No. No. The cameras would have taken a picture of anyone from another floor."

"How about someone from the same floor?"

Reluctantly the manager bobbed his head. "Ye-es. As far as the holo cameras are concerned, that's possible. But—"

"Then I'd like to ask for pictures of any tenant who lived on the eighteenth floor during the last six weeks. Send them to the ARMs Building, Central LA. Can do?"

"Of course. You'll have them within an hour."

"Good. Now, something else occurred to me. Suppose a man got out on the nineteenth floor and walked down to the eighteenth. He'd be holoed on the nineteenth, but not on the eighteenth, right?"

The manager smiled indulgently. "Mr. Hamilton, there are no stairs in this building."

"Just the elevators? Isn't that dangerous?"

"Not at all. There is a separate self-contained emergency power source for each of the elevators. It's common practice. After all, who would want to walk up eighty stories if the elevator failed?"

"Okay, fine. One last point. Could someone tamper with the computer? Could someone make it decide not to take a certain picture, for instance?"

"I . . . am not an expert on how to tamper with computers, Mr. Hamilton. Why don't you go straight to the company? Caulfield Brains, Inc."

"Okay. What's your model?"

"Just a moment." He got up and leafed through a drawer in a filing cabinet. "EQ 144."

"Okay."

That was all I could do here, and I knew it . . . and still I didn't have the will to get up. There ought to be *something* . . .

Finally Miller cleared his throat. "Will that be all, sir?"

"Yes," I said. "No. Can I get into 1809?"

"I'll see if we've rented it yet."

"The police are through with it?"

"Certainly." He went back to the filing cabinet. "No, it's still available. I'll take you up. How long will you be?"

"I don't know. No more than half an hour. No need to come up."

"Very well." He handed me the key and waited for me to leave. I did.

The merest flicker of blue light caught my eye as I left the elevator. I would have thought it was in my optic nerve, not in the real world, if I hadn't known about the holo cameras. Maybe it was. You don't need laser light to make a holograph, but it does get you clearer pictures.

Owen's room was a box. Everything was retracted. There was nothing but the bare walls. I had never seen anything so desolate, unless it was some asteroidal rock, too poor to mine, too badly placed to be worth a base.

The control panel was just beside the door. I turned on the lights, then touched the master button. Lines appeared, outlined in red and green and blue. A great square on one wall for the bed, most of another wall for the kitchen, various outlines across the floor. Very handy. You wouldn't want a guest to be standing on the table when you expanded it.

I'd come here to get the feel of the place, to encourage a hunch, to see if I'd missed anything. Translation: I was playing. Playing, I reached through the control panel to find the circuits. The printed circuitry was too small and too detailed to tell me anything, but I ran imaginary fingertips along a few wires and found that they looped straight to their action points, no detours. No sensors to the outside. You'd have to be in the room to know what was expanded, what retracted.

So a supposedly occupied room had had its bed retracted for six weeks. But you'd have to be in the room to know it.

I pushed buttons to expand the kitchen nook and the reading chair. The wall slid out eight feet; the floor humped itself and took form. I sat down in the chair, and the kitchen nook blocked my view of the door.

Nobody could have seen Owen from the hall.

If only someone had noticed that Owen wasn't ordering food. That might have saved him.

I thought of something else, and it made me look around for the air conditioner. There was a grill at floor level. I felt behind it with my imaginary hand. Some of these apartment air-conditioning units go on when the CO_2 level hits half a percent. This one was geared to temperature and manual control.

With the other kind, our careful killer could have tapped the air-conditioner current to find out if Owen was still alive and present. As it was, 1809 had behaved like an empty room for six weeks.

I flopped back in the reading chair.

If my hypothetical killer had watched Owen, he'd done it with a bug. Unless he'd actually lived on this floor for the four or five weeks it took Owen to die, there was no other way.

Okay, think about a bug. Make it small enough and nobody would find it except the cleaning robot, who would send it straight to the incinerator. You'd have to make it big, so the robot wouldn't get it. No worry about Owen finding it! And then, when you knew Owen was dead, you'd use the self-destruct.

But if you burned it to slag, you'd leave a burn hole somewhere. Ordaz would have found it. So. An asbestos pad? You'd want the self-destruct to leave something that the cleaning robot would sweep up.

And if you'll believe that you'll believe anything. It was too chancy. *Nobody* knows what a cleaning robot will decide is garbage. They're made stupid because it's cheaper. So they're programed to leave large objects alone.

There had to be someone on this floor, either to watch Owen himself or to pick up the bug that did the watching. I was betting everything I had on a human watcher.

I'd come here mainly to give my intuition a chance. It wasn't working. Owen had spent six weeks in this chair, and for at least the last week he'd been dead. Yet I couldn't feel it with him. It was just a chair with two end tables. He had left nothing in the room, not even a restless ghost.

The call caught me halfway back to Headquarters.

"You were right," Ordaz told me over the wristphone. "We have found a locker at Death Valley Port registered to Cubes Forsythe. I am on my way there now. Will you join me?"

"I'll meet you there."

"Good. I am as eager as you to see what Owen Jennison left us."

I doubted that.

The Port was something more than 230 miles away, an hour at taxi speeds. It would be a big fare. I typed out a new address on the destination board, then called in at Headquarters. An ARM agent is fairly free; he doesn't have to justify every little move. There was no question of getting permission to go. At worst they might disallow the fare on my expense account.

"Oh, and there'll be a set of holos coming in from Monica Apartments," I told the man. "Have the computer check them against known organleggers and associates of Loren."

The taxi rose smoothly into the sky and headed east. I watched tridee and drank coffee until I ran out of coins for the dispenser.

If you go between November and May, when the climate is ideal, Death Valley can be a tourist's paradise. There is the Devil's Golf Course, with its fantastic ridges and pinnacles of salt; Zabriskie Point and its weird badlands topography; the old borax mining sites; and all kinds of strange, rare plants, adapted to the heat and the death-dry climate. Yes, Death Valley has many points of interest, and someday I was

going to go see them. So far all I'd seen was the spaceport.
But the Port was impressive in its own way.

The landing field used to be part of a sizable inland sea. It
is now a sea of salt. Alternating red and blue concentric
circles mark the field for ships dropping from space, and a
century's developments in chemical, fission, and fusion reaction motors have left blast pits striped like rainbows by
esoteric, often radio active salts. But mostly the field retains
its ancient glare white.

And out across the salt are ships of many sizes and many
shapes. Vehicles and machinery dance attendance, and, if
you're willing to wait, you may see a ship land. It's worth the
wait.

The Port building, at the edge of the major salt flat, is a
pastel green tower set in a wide patch of fluorescent orange
concrete. No ship has ever landed on it—yet. The taxi
dropped me at the entrance and moved away to join others
of its kind. And I stood inhaling the dry, balmy air.

Four months of the year, Death Valley's climate is ideal.
One August the Furnace Creek Ranch recorded 134°
Fahrenheit shade temperature.

A man behind a desk told me that Ordaz had arrived
before me. I found him and another officer in a labyrinth of
pay lockers, each big enough to hold two or three suitcases.
The locker Ordaz had opened held only a lightweight plastic
briefcase.

"He may have taken other lockers," he said.

"Probably not. Belters travel light. Have you tried to open
it?"

"Not yet. It is a combination lock. I thought perhaps . . ."

"Maybe." I squatted to look at it.

Funny: I felt no surprise at all. It was as if I'd known all
along that Owen's suitcase would be here. And why not? He
was bound to try to protect himself somehow. Through me,
because I was already involved in the UN side of organlegging. By leaving something in a spaceport locker, because
Loren couldn't find the right locker or get into it if he did,
and because I would naturally connect Owen with
spaceports. Under Cubes' name, because I'd be looking for

that, and Loren wouldn't.

Hindsight is wonderful.

The lock had five digits. "He must have meant me to open it. Let's see ..." and I moved the tumblers to 42217. April 22, 2117, the day Cubes died, stapled suddenly to a plastic partition.

The lock clicked open.

Ordaz went instantly for the manila folder. More slowly, I picked up two glass phials. One was tightly sealed against Earth's air, and half full of an incredibly fine dust. So fine was it that it slid about like oil inside the glass. The other phial held a blackened grain of nickel-iron, barely big enough to see.

Other things were in that case, but the prize was that folder. The story was in there ... at least up to a point. Owen must have planned to add to it.

A message had been waiting for him in the Ceres mail dump when he returned from his last trip out. Owen must have laughed over parts of that message. Loren had taken the trouble to assemble a complete dossier of Owen's smuggling activities over the past eight years. Did he think he could ensure Owen's silence by threatening to turn the dossier over to the goldskins?

Maybe the dossier had given Owen the wrong idea. In any case, he'd decided to contact Loren and see what developed. Ordinarily he'd have sent me the entire message and let me try to track it down. I was the expert, after all. But Owen's last trip out had been a disaster.

His fusion drive had blown somewhere beyond Jupiter's orbit. No explanation. The safeties had blown his lifesystem capsule free of the explosion, barely. A rescue ship had returned him to Ceres. The fee had nearly broken him. He needed money. Loren may have known that, and counted on it.

The reward for information leading to Loren's capture would have bought him a new ship.

He'd landed at Outback Field, following Loren's instructions. From there, Loren's men had moved him about a good deal: to London, to Bombay, to Amberg, Germany. Owen's personal, written story ended in Amberg. How had he reached California? He had not had a chance to say.

But in between, he had learned a good deal. There were snatches of detail on Loren's organization. There was Loren's full plan for shipping illicit transplant materials to the Belt, and for finding and contacting customers. Owen had made suggestions there. Most of them sounded reasonable and would be unworkable in practice. Typically Owen. I could find no sign that he'd overplayed his hand.

But of course he hadn't known it when he did.

And there were holos, twenty-three of them, each a member of Loren's gang. Some of the pictures had markings on the back; others were blank. Owen had been unable to find out where each of them stood in the organization.

I leafed through them twice, wondering if one of them could be Loren himself. Owen had never known.

"It would seem you were right," said Ordaz. "He could not have collected such detail by accident. He must have planned from the beginning to betray the Loren gang."

"Just as I told you. And he was murdered for it."

"It seems he must have been. What motive could he have had for suicide?" Ordaz's round, calm face was doing its best to show anger. "I find I cannot believe in our inconsistent murderer either. You have ruined my digestion, Mr. Hamilton."

I told him my idea about other tenants on Owen's floor. He smiled and nodded. "Possibly, possibly. This is your department now. Organlegging is the business of the ARMs."

"Right." I closed the briefcase and hefted it. "Let's see what the computer can do with these. I'll send you photocopies of everything in here."

"You'll let me know about the other tenants?"

"Of course."

I walked into ARM Headquarters swinging that precious briefcase, feeling on top of the world. Owen had been murdered. He had died with honor, if not—oh, definitely not—with dignity. Even Ordaz knew it now.

Then Jackson Bera, snarling and panting, went by at a dead run.

"What's up?" I called after him. Maybe I wanted a chance to brag. I had twenty-three faces, twenty-three organleggers, in my briefcase.

Bera slid to a stop beside me. "Where *you* been?"

"Working. Honest. What's the hurry?"

"Remember that pleasure peddler we were watching?"

"Graham? Kenneth Graham?"

"That's the one. He's dead. We blew it." And Bera took off.

He'd reached the lab by the time I caught up with him.

Kenneth Graham's corpse was face up on the operating table. His long, lantern-jawed face was pale and slack, without expression; empty. Machinery was in place above and below his head.

"How you doing?" Bera demanded.

"Not good," the doctor answered. "Not your fault. You got him into the deepfreeze fast enough. It's just that the current—" he shrugged.

I shook Bera's shoulder. "What happened?"

Bera was panting a little from his run. "Something must have leaked. Graham tried to make a run for it. We got him at the airport."

"You could have waited. Put someone on the plane with him. Flooded the plane with TY-4."

"Remember the stink the last time we used TY-4 on civilians? Damn newscasters." Bera was shivering. I didn't blame him.

ARMs and organleggers play a funny kind of game. The organleggers have to turn their donors in alive, so they're always armed with hypo guns, firing slivers of crystaline anesthetic that melt instantly in the blood. We use the same weapon, for somewhat the same reason: a criminal has to be saved for trial, and then for the government hospitals. So no ARM ever expects to kill a man.

There was a day I learned the truth. A small-time organ-legger named Raphael Haine was trying to reach a call button in his own home. If he'd reached it all kinds of hell would have broken loose, Haine's men would have hypoed me, and I would have regained consciousness a piece at a time, in Haine's organ-storage tanks. So I strangled him.

The report was in the computer, but only three human beings knew about it. One was my immediate superior, Lucas Carner. The other was Julie. So far, he was the only man I'd ever killed.

And Graham was Bera's first killing.

"We got him at the airport," said Bera. "He was wearing a hat. I wish I'd noticed that, we might have moved faster. We started to close in on him with hypo guns. He turned and saw us. He reached under his hat, and then he fell."

"Killed himself?"

"Uh huh."

"How?"

"Look at his head."

I edged closer to the table, trying to stay out of the doctor's way. The doctor was going through the routine of trying to pull information from a dead brain by induction. It wasn't going well.

There was a flat oblong box on top of Graham's head. Black plastic, about half the size of a pack of cards. I touched it and knew at once that it was attached to Graham's skull.

"A droud. Not a standard type. Too big."

"Uh huh."

Liquid helium ran up my nerves. "There's a battery in it."

"Right."

"I often wonder what the vintners buy, et cetera. A cord-less droud. Man, that's what *I* want for Christmas."

Bera twitched all over. "Don't *say* that."

"Did you know he was a current addict?"

"No. We were afraid to bug his home. He might have found it and be tipped. Take another look at that thing."

The shape was wrong, I thought. The black plastic case had been half melted.

"Heat," I mused. "Oh!"

"Uh huh. He blew the whole battery at once. Sent the whole killing charge right through his brain, right through the pleasure center of his brain. And, Jesus, Gil, the thing I keep wondering is, what did it feel like? Gil, what could it possibly have *felt* like?"

I thumped him across the shoulders in lieu of giving him an intelligent answer. He'd be a long time wondering. And so would I.

Here was the man who had put the wire in Owen's head. Had his death been momentary Hell, or all the delights of paradise in one singing jolt? Hell, I hoped, but I didn't believe it.

At least Kenneth Graham wasn't somewhere else in the world, getting a new face and new retinas and new fingertips from Loren's illicit organ banks.

"Nothing," said the doctor. "His brain's too badly burned. There's just nothing there that isn't too scrambled to make sense."

"Keep trying," said Bera.

I left quietly. Maybe later I'd buy Bera a drink. He seemed to need it. Bera was one of those with empathy. I knew that he could almost feel that awful surge of ecstasy and defeat as Kenneth Graham left the world behind.

The holos from Monica Apartments had arrived hours ago. Miller had picked not only the tenants who had occupied the eighteenth floor during the past six weeks, but tenants from the nineteenth and seventeenth floors too. It seemed an embarrassment of riches. I toyed with the idea of someone from the nineteenth floor dropping over his balcony to the eighteenth, every day for five weeks. But 1809 hadn't had an outside wall, let alone a window, not to mention a balcony.

Had Miller played with the same idea? Nonsense. He didn't even know the problem. He'd just overkilled with the holos to show how cooperative he was.

None of the tenants during the period in question matched known or suspected Loren men.

I said a few appropriate words and went for coffee. Then I remembered the twenty-three possible Loren men in Owen's briefcase. I'd left them with a programer, since I wasn't quite sure how to get them into the computer myself. He ought to be finished by now.

I called down. He was.

I persuaded the computer to compare them with the holos from Monica Apartments.

Nothing. Nobody matched anybody.

I spent the next two hours writing up the Owen Jennison case. A programer would have to translate it for the machine. I wasn't that good yet.

We were back with Ordaz' inconsistent killer.

That, and a tangle of dead ends. Owen's death had bought us a handful of new pictures, pictures which might even be obsolete by now. Organleggers changed their faces at the drop of a hat. I finished the case outline, sent it down to a programer, and called Julie. I wouldn't need her protection now.

Julie had left for home.

I started to call Taffy, stopped with her number half dialed. There are times not to make a phone call. I needed to sulk; I needed a cave to be alone in. My expression would probably have broken a phone screen. Why inflict it on an innocent girl?

I left for home.

It was dark when I reached the street. I rode the pedestrian bridge across the slidewalks, waited for a taxi at the intersection disk. Presently one dropped, the white FREE sign blinking on its belly. I stepped in and deposited my credit card.

Owen had collected his holos from all over the Eurasian continent. Most of them, if not all, had been Loren's foreign agents. Why had I expected to find them in Los Angeles?

The taxi rose into the white night sky. City lights turned the cloud cover into a flat white dome. We penetrated the clouds, and stayed there. The taxi autopilot didn't care if I had a view or not.

... So what did I have now? Someone among dozens of tenants was a Loren man. That, or Ordaz's inconsistent killer, the careful one, had left Owen to die for five weeks, alone and unsupervised.

... Was the inconsistent killer so unbelievable?

He was, after all, my own hypothetical Loren. And Loren had committed murder, the ultimate crime. He'd murdered routinely, over and over, with fabulous profits. The ARMs hadn't been able to touch him. Wasn't it about time he started getting careless?

Like Graham. How long had Graham been selecting donors among his customers, choosing a few nonentities a year? And then, twice within a few months, he took clients who were missed. Careless.

Most criminals are not too bright. Loren had brains enough; but the men on his payroll would be about average. Loren would deal with the stupid ones, the ones who turned to crime because they didn't have enough sense to make it in real life.

If a man like Loren got careless, this was how it would happen. Unconsciously he would judge ARM intelligence by his own men. Seduced by an ingenious plan for murder, he might ignore the single loophole and go through with it. With Graham to advise him, he knew more about current addiction than we did; perhaps enough to trust the effects of current addiction on Owen.

Then Owen's killers had delivered him to his apartment and never seen him again. It was a small gamble Loren had taken, and it had paid off, this time.

Next time he'd grow more careless. One day we'd get him. But not today.

The taxi settled out of the traffic pattern, touched down on the roof of my apartment building in the Hollywood Hills. I got out and moved toward the elevators.

An elevator opened. Someone stepped out.

Something warned me, something about the way he moved. I turned, quick-drawing from the shoulder. The taxi might have made good cover—if it hadn't been already rising. Other figures had stepped from the shadows.

I think I got a couple before something stung my cheek. Mercy-bullets, slivers of crystaline anesthetic melting in my bloodstream. My head spun, and the roof spun, and the centrifugal force dropped me limply to the roof. Shadows loomed above me, then receded to infinity.

Fingers on my scalp shocked me awake.

I woke standing upright, bound like a mummy in soft, swaddling bandages. I couldn't so much as twitch a muscle below my neck. By the time I knew that much it was too late. The man behind me had finished removing electrodes from my head and stepped into view, out of reach of my imaginary arm.

There was something of the bird about him. He was tall and slender, small-boned, and his triangular face reached a point at the chin. His wild, silken blond hair had withdrawn from his temples, leaving a sharp widow's peak. He wore impeccably tailored wool street shorts in orange and brown stripes. Smiling brightly, with his arms folded and his head cocked to one side, he stood waiting for me to speak.

And I recognized him. Owen had taken a holo of him, somewhere.

"Where am I?" I groaned, trying to sound groggy. "What time is it?"

"Time? It's already morning," said my captor. "As for where you are, I'll let you wonder."

Something about his manner ... I took a guess and said, "Loren?"

Loren bowed, not overdoing it. "And you are Gilbert Hamilton of the United Nations Police. Gil the Arm."

Had he said Arm or ARM? I let it pass. "I seem to have slipped."

"You underestimated the reach of my own arm. You also underestimated my interest."

I had. It isn't much harder to capture an ARM than any other citizen, if you catch him off guard, and if you're willing to risk the men. In this case his risk had cost him nothing.

Cops use hypo guns for the same reason organleggers do. The men I'd shot, if I'd hit anyone in those few seconds of battle, would have come around long ago. Loren must have set me up in these bandages, then left me under "russian sleep" until he was ready to talk to me.

The electrodes were the "russian sleep." One goes on each eyelid, one on the nape of the neck. A small current goes through the brain, putting you right to sleep. You get a full night's sleep in an hour. If it's not turned off you can sleep forever.

So this was Loren.

He stood watching me with his head cocked to one side, birdlike, with his arms folded. One hand held a hypo gun, rather negligently, I thought.

What time was it? I didn't dare ask again, because Loren might guess something. But if I could stall him until 0945, Julie could send help ...

She could send help where?

Finagle in hysterics! Where was I? If I didn't know that, Julie wouldn't know either!

And Loren intended me for the organ banks. One crystal-line sliver would knock me out without harming any of the delicate, infinitely various parts that made me Gil Hamilton. Then Loren's doctors would take me apart.

In government operating rooms they flash-burn the crimi-nals brain for later urn burial. God knows what Loren would do with my own brain. But the rest of me was young and healthy. Even considering Loren's overhead, I was worth more than a million UN marks on the hoof.

"Why me?" I asked. "It was me you wanted, not just any ARM. Why the interest in me?"

"It was you who were investigating the case of Owen Jennison. *Much* too thoroughly."

"Not thoroughly enough, dammit!"

Loren looked puzzled. "You really don't understand?"

"I really don't."

"I find that highly interesting," Loren mused. "Highly."

"All right, why am I still alive?"

"I was curious, Mr. Hamilton. I hoped you'd tell me about your imaginary arm."

So he'd said Arm, not ARM. I bluffed anyway. "My *what?*"

"No need for games, Mr. Hamilton. If I think I'm losing I'll use this." He wiggled the hypo gun. "You'll never wake up."

Damn! He knew. The only things I could move were my ears and my imaginary arm, and Loren knew all about it! I'd never be able to lure him into reach.

Provided he knew *all* about it.

I had to draw him out.

"Okay," I said, "but I'd like to know how you found out about it. A plant in the ARMs?"

Loren chuckled. "I wish it were so. No. We captured one of your men some months ago, quite by accident. When I realized what he was, I induced him to talk shop with me. He was able to tell me something about your remarkable arm. I hope you'll tell me more."

"Who was it?"

"Really, Mr. Hamil—"

"Who was it?"

"Do you really expect me to remember the name of every donor?"

Who had gone into Loren's organ banks? Stranger, acquaintance, friend? Does the manager of a slaughterhouse remember every slaughtered steer?

"So-called psychic powers interest me," said Loren. "I remembered you. And then, when I was on the verge of concluding an agreement with your Belter friend Jennison, I remembered something unusual about a crewman he had shipped with. They called you Gil the Arm, didn't they? Prophetic. In port your drinks came free if you could use your imaginary arm to drink them."

"Then damn you. You thought Owen was a plant, did you? Because of me! Me!"

"Breast beating will earn you nothing, Mr. Hamilton." Loren put steel in his voice. "Entertain me, Mr. Hamilton."

I'd been feeling around for anything that might release me

from my upright prison. No such luck. I was wrapped like a mummy in bandages too strong to break. All I could feel with my imaginary hand were cloth bandages up to my neck, and a bracing rod along my back to hold me upright. Beneath the swathing I was naked.

"I'll show you my eldritch powers," I told Loren, "if you'll loan me a cigarette." Maybe that would draw him close enough . . .

He knew something about my arm. He knew its reach. He put one single cigarette on the edge of a small table-on-wheels and slid it up to me. I picked it up and stuck it in my mouth and waited hopefully for him to come light it. "My mistake," he murmured; and he pulled the table back and repeated the whole thing with a lighted cigarette.

No luck. At least I'd gotten my smoke. I pitched the dead one as far as it would go: about two feet. I have to move slowly with my imaginary hand. Otherwise what I'm holding simply slips through my fingers.

Loren watched in fascination. A floating, disembodied cigarette, obeying my will! His eyes held traces of awe and horror. That was bad. Maybe the cigarette had been a mistake.

Some people see psi powers as akin to witchcraft, and psychic people as servants of Satan. If Loren feared me, then I was dead.

"Interesting," said Loren. "How far will it reach?"

He knew that. "As far as my real arm, of course."

"But why? Others can reach much further. Why not you?"

He was clear across the room, a good ten yards away, sprawled in an armchair. One hand held a drink, the other held the hypo gun. He was superbly relaxed. I wondered if I'd ever see him move from that comfortable chair, much less come within reach.

The room was small and bare, with the look of a basement. Loren's chair and a small portable bar were the only furnishings, unless there were others behind me.

A basement could be anywhere. Anywhere in Los Angeles, or out of it. If it was really morning, I could be anywhere on Earth by now.

"Sure," I said, "others can reach further than me. But they don't have my strength. It's an imaginary arm, sure enough, and my imagination won't make it ten feet long. Maybe someone could convince me it was, if he tried hard enough. But maybe he'd ruin what belief I have. Then I'd have two arms, just like everyone else. I'm better off . . ." I let it trail away, because Loren was going to take all my damn arms anyway.

My cigarette was finished. I pitched it away.

"Want a drink?"

"Sure, if you've got a jigger glass. Otherwise I can't lift it."

He found me a shot glass and sent it to me on the edge of the rolling table. I was barely strong enough to pick it up. Loren's eyes never left me as I sipped and put it down.

The old cigarette lure. Last night I'd used it to pick up a girl. Now it was keeping me alive.

Did I really want to leave the world with something gripped tightly in my imaginary fist? Entertaining Loren. Holding his interest until—

Where was I? Where?

And suddenly I knew. "We're at Monica Apartments," I said. "Nowhere else."

"I knew you'd guess that eventually." Loren smiled. "But it's too late. I got to you in time."

"Don't be so damn complacent. It was my stupidity, not your luck. I should have *smelled* it. Owen would never have come here of his own choice. You ordered him here."

"And so I did. By then I already knew he was a traitor."

"So you sent him here to die. Who was it that checked on him every day to see he'd stayed put? Was it Miller, the manager? He has to be working for you. He's the one who took the holographs of you and your men out of the computer."

"He was the one," said Loren. "But it wasn't every day. I had a man watching Jennison every second, through a portable camera. We took it out after he was dead."

"And then waited a week. Nice touch." The wonder was that it had taken me so long. The atmosphere of the place . . . what kind of people would live in Monica Apartments?

The faceless ones, the ones with no identity, the ones who would surely be missed by nobody. They would stay put in their apartments while Loren checked on them, to see that they really did have nobody to miss them. Those who qualified would disappear, and their papers and possessions with them, and their holos would vanish from the computer.

Loren said, "I tried to sell organs to the Belters, through your friend Jennison. I know he betrayed me, Hamilton. I want to know how badly."

"Badly enough." He'd guess that. "We've got detailed plans for setting up an organ-bank dispensary in the Belt. It wouldn't have worked anyway, Loren. Belters don't think that way."

"No pictures."

"No." I didn't want him changing his face.

"I was sure he'd left something," said Loren. "Otherwise we'd have made him a donor. Much simpler. More profitable, too. I needed the money, Hamilton. Do you know what it costs the organization to let a donor go?"

"A million or so. Why'd you do it?"

"He'd left something. There was no way to get at it. All we could do was try to keep the ARMs from looking for it."

"Ah." I had it then. "When anyone disappears without a trace, the first thing any idiot thinks of is organleggers."

"Naturally. So he couldn't just disappear, could he? The police would go to the ARMs, the file would go to you, and you'd start looking."

"For a spaceport locker."

"Oh?"

"Under the name of Cubes Forsythe."

"I knew that name," Loren said between his teeth. "I should have tried that. You know, after we had him hooked on current, we tried pulling the plug on him to get him to talk. It didn't work. He couldn't concentrate on anything but getting the droud back in his head. We looked high and low—"

"I'm going to kill you," I said, and meant every word.

Loren cocked his head, frowning. "On the contrary, Mr. Hamilton. Another cigarette?"

"Yah."

He sent it to me, lighted, on the rolling table. I picked it up, holding it a trifle ostentatiously. Maybe I could focus his attention on it—on his only way to find my imaginary hand.

Because if he kept his eyes on the cigarette, and I put it in my mouth at a crucial moment—I'd leave my hand free without his noticing.

What crucial moment? He was still in the armchair. I had to fight the urge to coax him closer. Any move in that direction would make him suspicious.

What time was it? And what was Julie doing? I thought of a night two weeks past. Remembered dinner on the balcony of the highest restaurant in Los Angeles, just a fraction less than a mile up. A carpet of neon that spread below us to touch the horizon in all directions. Maybe she'd pick it up . . .

She'd be checking on me at 0945.

"You must have made a remarkable spaceman," said Loren. "Think of being the only man in the solar system who can adjust a hull antenna without leaving the cabin."

"Antennas take a little more muscle than I've got." So he knew I could reach through things. If he'd seen that far—"I should have stayed," I told Loren. "I wish I were on a mining ship, right this minute. All I wanted at the time was two good arms."

"Pity. Now you have three. Did it occur to you that using psi powers against men was a form of cheating?"

"What?"

"Remember Raphael Haine?" Loren's voice had become uneven. He was angry, and holding it down with difficulty.

"Sure. Small-time organlegger in Australia."

"Raphael Haine was a friend of mine. I know he had you tied up at one point. Tell me, Mr. Hamilton: if your imaginary hand is as weak as you say, how did you untie the ropes?"

"I didn't. I couldn't have. Haine used handcuffs. I picked his pocket for the key . . . with my imaginary hand, of course."

"You used psi powers against him. You had no right!"

Magic. Anyone who's not psychic himself feels the same

way, just a little. A touch of dread, a touch of envy. Loren thought he could handle ARMs; he'd killed at least one of us. But to send warlocks against him was grossly unfair.

That was why he'd let me wake up. Loren wanted to gloat. How many men have captured a warlock?

"Don't be an idiot," I said. "I didn't volunteer to play your silly game, or Haine's either. *My* rules make you a wholesale murderer."

Loren got to his feet (what time was it?) and I suddenly realized my time was up. He was in a white rage. His silky blond hair seemed to stand on end.

I looked into the tiny needle hole in the hypo gun. There was nothing I could do. The reach of my TK was the reach of my fingers. I felt all the things I would never feel: the quart of Trastine in my blood to keep the water from freezing in my cells, the cold bath of half-frozen alcohol, the scalpels and the tiny, accurate surgical lasers. Most of all, the scalpels.

And my knowledge would die when they threw away my brain. I knew what Loren looked like. I knew about Monica Apartments, and who knew how many others of the same kind? I knew where to go to find all the loveliness in Death Valley, and someday I was going to go. What time was it? What time?

Loren had raised the hypo gun and was sighting down the stiff length of his arm. Obviously he thought he was at target practice. "It really is a pity," he said, and there was only the slightest tremor in his voice. "You should have stayed a spaceman."

What was he waiting for? "I can't cringe unless you loosen these bandages," I snapped, and I jabbed what was left of my cigarette at him for emphasis. It jerked out of my grip, and I reached and caught it and—

And stuck it in my left eye.

At another time I'd have examined the idea a little more closely. But I'd still have done it. Loren already thought of me as his property. As live skin and healthy kidneys and lengths of artery, as parts in Loren's organ banks, I was property worth a million UN marks. And I was destroying my eye! Organleggers are always hurting for eyes; anyone who wears glasses could use a new pair, and the organleggers themselves are constantly wanting to change retina prints.

What I hadn't anticipated was the pain. I'd read somewhere that there are no sensory nerves in the eyeball. Then it was my lids that hurt. Terribly!

But I only had to hold on for a moment.

Loren swore and came for me at a dead run. He knew how terribly weak was my imaginary arm. What could I do with it? He didn't know; he'd never known, though it stared him in the face. He ran at me and slapped at the cigarette, a full swing that half knocked my head off my neck and sent the now dead butt ricocheting off a wall. Panting, snarling, speechless with rage, he stood—within reach.

My eye closed like a small tormented fist.

I reached past Loren's gun, through his chest wall, and found his heart. And squeezed.

His eyes became very round, his mouth gaped wide, his larynx bobbed convulsively. There was time to fire the gun. Instead he clawed at his chest with a half-paralyzed arm. Twice he raked his fingernails across his chest, gaping upward for air that wouldn't come. He thought he was having a heart attack. Then his rolling eyes found my face.

My face. I was a one-eyed carnivore, snarling with the will to murder. I would have his life if I had to tear the heart out of his chest! How could he help but know?

He knew!

He fired at the floor, and fell.

I was sweating and shaking with reaction and disgust. The scars! He was all scars; I'd felt them going in. His heart was a transplant. And the rest of him—he'd looked about thirty from a distance, but this close it was impossible to tell. Parts were younger, parts older. How much of Loren was Loren? What parts had he taken from others? And none of the parts quite matched.

He must have been chronically ill, I thought. And the Board wouldn't give him the transplants he needed. And one day he'd seen the answer to all his problems . . .

Loren wasn't moving. He wasn't breathing. I remembered

the way his heart had jumped and wriggled in my imaginary hand, and then suddenly given up.

He was lying on his left arm, hiding his watch. I was all alone in an empty room, and I still didn't know what time it was.

I never found out. It was hours before Miller finally dared to interrupt his boss. He stuck his round, blank face around the door jamb, saw Loren sprawled at my feet, and darted back with a squeak. A minute later a hypo gun came around the jamb, followed by a watery blue eye. I felt the sting in my cheek.

"I checked you early," said Julie. She settled herself uncomfortably at the foot of the hospital bed. "Rather, you called me. When I came to work you weren't there, and I wondered why, and *wham*. It was bad, wasn't it?"

"Pretty bad," I said.

"I've never sensed anyone so scared."

"Well, don't tell anyone about it." I hit the switch to raise the bed to sitting position. "I've got an image to maintain."

My eye and the socket around it were bandaged and numb. There was no pain, but the numbness was obtrusive, a reminder of two dead men who had become part of me. One arm, one eye.

If Julie was feeling that with me, then small wonder if she was nervous. She was. She kept shifting and twisting on the bed.

"I kept wondering what time it was. What time was it?"

"About nine-ten." Julie shivered. "I thought I'd faint when that—that vague little man pointed his hypo gun around the corner. Oh, don't! Don't, Gil. It's *over.*"

That close? Was it *that* close? "Look," I said, "you go back to work. I appreciate the sick call, but this isn't doing either of us any good. If we keep it up we'll both wind up in a state of permanent terror."

She nodded jerkily and got up.

"Thanks for coming. Thanks for saving my life too."

Julie smiled from the doorway. "Thanks for the orchids."

I hadn't ordered them yet. I flagged down a nurse and got

her to tell me that I could leave tonight, after dinner, provided I went straight home to bed. She brought me a phone, and I used it to order the orchids.

Afterward I dropped the bed back and lay there awhile. It was nice being alive. I began to remember promises I had made, promises I might never have kept. Perhaps it was time to keep a few.

I called down to Surveillance and got Jackson Bera. After letting him drag from me the story of my heroism, I invited him up to the infirmary for a drink. His bottle, but I'd pay. He didn't like that part, but I bullied him into it.

I had dialed half of Taffy's number before, as I had last night, I changed my mind. My wristphone was on the bedside table. No pictures.

" 'Lo."

"Taffy? This is Gil. Can you get a weekend free?"

"Sure. Starting Friday?"

"Good."

"Come for me at ten. Did you ever find out about your friend?"

"Yah. I was right. Organleggers killed him. It's over now, we got the guy in charge." I didn't mention the eye. By Friday the bandages would be off. "About that weekend. How would you like to see Death Valley?"

"You're kidding, right?"

"I'm kidding, wrong. Listen—"

"But it's hot! It's dry! It's a dead as the Moon! You did say Death Valley, didn't you?"

"It's not hot this month. Listen . . ." And she did listen. She listened long enough to be convinced.

"I've been thinking," she said then. "If we're going to see a lot of each other, we'd better make a—a bargain. No shop talk. All right?"

"A good idea."

"The point is, I work in a hospital," said Taffy. "Surgery. To me, organic transplant material is just the tools of my trade, tools to use in healing. It took me a long time to get that way. I don't want to know where the stuff comes from, and I don't want to know anything about organleggers."

"Okay, we've got a covenant. See you at ten hundred Friday."

A doctor, I thought afterward. Well. The weekend was going to be a good one. Surprising people are always the ones most worth knowing.

Bera came in with a pint of J&B. "My treat," he said. "No use arguing, 'cause you can't reach your wallet anyway." And the fight was on.

EXCITING SCIENCE FICTION FROM
THE BALLANTINE LIST

SEEDS OF DESTRUCTION	Dan Thomas	75¢
DRAGONFLIGHT	Anne McCaffrey	75¢
THE MASKS OF TIME	Robert Silverberg	75¢
NEUTRON STAR	Larry Niven	75¢
THE SEVEN SEXES	William Tenn	75¢
THE WOODEN STAR	William Tenn	75¢
THE SQUARE ROOT OF MAN	William Tenn	75¢
OF MEN AND MONSTERS	William Tenn	75¢
DAUGHTERS OF THE DOLPHIN	Roy Meyers	75¢
MORE THAN HUMAN	Theodore Sturgeon	75¢
OMNIVORE	Piers Anthony	75¢
PRIEST-KINGS OF GOR	John Norman	75¢
DOUBLE, DOUBLE	John Brunner	75¢
BROTHER ASSASSIN	Fred Saberhagen	75¢
THE CAVES OF KARST	Lee Hoffman	75¢
THE ALIENS AMONG US	James White	75¢
XENOGENESIS	Miriam Allen deFord	75¢

Uniformly priced at 75¢ each
(Plus 5¢ per book mailing charge)

To order by mail, list the titles you want, add your address with zip code, and enclose 80¢ per title. Send to: Dept. CS, Ballantine Books, 36 West 20th Street, New York, New York 10003.

**In Science Fiction
Ballantine Books Brings You
the Best of the Established Authors
and the Most Exciting New Writers**

WORLD OF PTAVVS	Larry Niven	60¢
NEUTRON STAR	Larry Niven	75¢
TARNSMAN OF GOR	John Norman	75¢
OUTLAW OF GOR	John Norman	75¢
PRIEST-KINGS OF GOR	John Norman	75¢
TO OPEN THE SKY	Robert Silverberg	75¢
THORNS	Robert Silverberg	75¢
THE MASKS OF TIME	Robert Silverberg	75¢
CHOCKY	John Wyndham	75¢
RESTOREE	Anne McCaffrey	75¢
DRAGONFLIGHT	Anne McCaffrey	75¢
CHTHON	Piers Anthony	75¢
THE WORM OUROBOROS	E. R. Eddison	95¢
MISTRESS OF MISTRESSES	E. R. Eddison	95¢
A FISH DINNER IN MEMISON	E. R. Eddison	95¢
TITUS GROAN ⎤	Mervyn Peake	95¢
GORMENGHAST ⎬ Trilogy	Mervyn Peake	95¢
TITUS ALONE ⎦	Mervyn Peake	95¢
DOLPHIN BOY	Roy Meyers	75¢
DAUGHTERS OF THE DOLPHIN	Roy Meyers	75¢

Send price of book plus 5¢ a copy for postage to
Dept. CS, BALLANTINE BOOKS, INC., 36 W.
20th St., New York, New York 10003, with your
name, address and ZIP CODE NUMBER.

The great masterpieces of fantasy by
J. R. R. TOLKIEN

The Hobbit

and

The Lord of the Rings

Part I—THE FELLOWSHIP OF THE RING

Part II—THE TWO TOWERS

Part III—THE RETURN OF THE KING

plus
The Tolkien Reader

Smith of Wootton Major and Farmer Giles of Ham

The Road Goes Ever On: A Song Cycle
(music by Donald Swann)

Note: These are the complete and authorized paperbound editions, published only by Ballantine Books.

To order by mail, send $1.00 for each book (except for *The Road Goes Ever On* which requires $3.00) to Dept. CS, Ballantine Books, 36 W. 20th St., New York, N.Y. 10003.

GREAT MASTERPIECES OF ADULT FANTASY

AVAILABLE IN BALLANTINE BOOKS EDITION

A VOYAGE TO ARCTURUS	David Lindsay
TITUS GROAN—Volume I	Mervyn Peake
GORMENGHAST—Volume II	Mervyn Peake
TITUS ALONE—Volume III	Mervyn Peake
THE WORM OUROBOROS	E. R. Eddison
MISTRESS OF MISTRESSES	E. R. Eddison
A FISH DINNER IN MEMISON	E. R. Eddison
THE MEZENTIAN GATE	E. R. Eddison

and watch for:

THE KING OF ELFLAND'S DAUGHTER	Lord Dunsany
THE WOOD BEYOND THE WORLD	William Morris
THE SILVER STALLION	James Branch Cabell
LILITH	George Macdonald

Uniformly priced at 95¢ each
(Plus 5¢ per book mailing charge)

To order by mail, list the titles you want, add your address with zip code, and enclose $1.00 per title: send to: Dept. CS, Ballantine Books, 36 West 20th Street, New York, New York 10003